House
of Bones

Annie Hauxwell abandoned the law to work as an investigator, after stints as a psychiatric nurse, cleaner, sociologist and taxi driver. She divides her time between London, where she was born, and a country town in Australia. In addition to the Catherine Berlin series, she has written for the screen and stage.

ALSO BY ANNIE HAUXWELL

In Her Blood
A Bitter Taste
A Morbid Habit

ANNIE HAUXWELL

House of Bones

arrow books

1 3 5 7 9 10 8 6 4 2

Arrow Books
20 Vauxhall Bridge Road
London SW1V 2SA

Arrow Books is part of the Penguin Random House group of companies whose
addresses can be found at global.penguinrandomhouse.com

Penguin
Random House
UK

First published by Arrow Books in 2016

www.penguin.co.uk

A CIP catalogue record for this book is available from the British Library

ISBN 9780099590972

Typeset in Adobe Garamond 12.5/16 pt in India by Thomson Digital Pvt Ltd,
Noida Delhi
Printed and bound in Great Britain by Clays Ltd, St Ives Plc

MIX
Paper from
responsible sources
FSC® C018179

Penguin Random House is committed to a sustainable future
for our business, our readers and our planet. This book is
made from Forest Stewardship Council® certified paper.

For Helen

The tradition of all dead generations weighs like a nightmare on the brains of the living.

Karl Marx

Hong Kong, 1961

The door flew open. The two naked boys sprang apart and stumbled to their feet, slick with sweat but suddenly chilled by the stare of the 7th Earl Haileybury.

The monsoonal rain beat at the rattan screen. The Wilton, the chiffonier, the oil painting of a three-masted clipper on a stormy sea, all bore a dull patina of mildew.

Jack, fourteen, gathered himself and returned his grandfather's gaze, defiant. He fumbled for his lover's hand, but the boy at his side, head bowed, his soft caramel skin a mass of goose pimples, shrank away. He was also fourteen, but Philip, as they called him, was Chinese.

A shadow fell across the rattan. Someone was watching.

'This is all very well,' sneered Haileybury. 'But what are you going to do about an heir?'

Jack was familiar with the strange, remote look in his grandfather's bloodshot eyes.

'You forget, Jack,' said the earl, 'these people serve at your pleasure. He'll turn on you when he becomes a man.'

'We're going to be together forever,' said Jack.

'No,' said the earl. 'You're not.'

He raised his walking stick and brought it down on Philip's head.

Jack felt the warm spatter on his cheek, then fainted.

The Gate of a Hundred

Sorrows

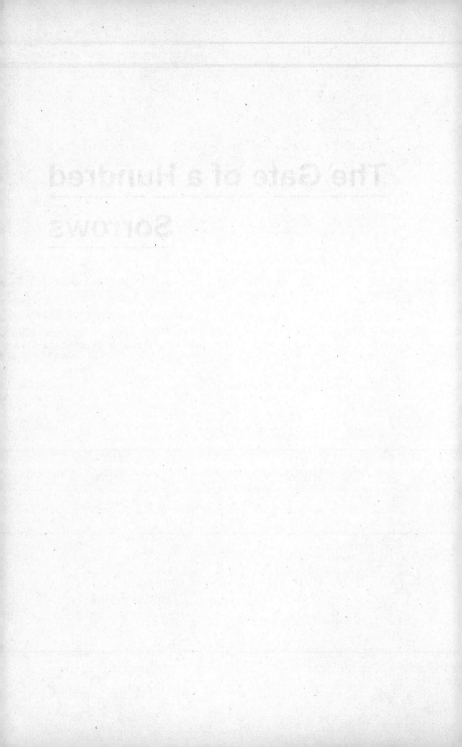

Spring. The blanket of fog shrouding London was a perversion of the season. It drifted in dense clouds across the capital as Catherine Berlin followed a hearse through the grand arch of the City of London Cemetery and Crematorium. She wondered how long it would be before she passed under it feet first.

The slow, steady crunch of tyres on gravel echoed in the still air. The hearse crept towards a mound of fresh soil and the wounded earth beside it.

The grave was not quite empty.

A million people were said to be interred on the two-hundred-acre site, the more recently deceased weighing down ancient bones excavated from medieval parish graveyards. Berlin imagined the original occupants groaning beneath the tier of coffins above.

The phone in her pocket vibrated. Ignoring the frowns of the other mourners, she fished it out, checked the caller ID, and answered.

'I've got a job for you,' said Del.

Delroy Jacobs was her closest friend. Although he didn't have a lot of competition in that department.

A Plaistow boy, what Del lacked in Oxbridge degrees and old school ties he made up for with charm, loyalty and street smarts, which he rarely used, now confined to a safe management role by the needs of his growing family: Molly, eighteen months, and twins on the way.

Del worked for Burghley LLP, a boutique outfit established by former spooks and Whitehall types. They offered discreet investigative and intelligence services. Deep pocket essential. Burghley were well connected at the highest levels.

If they were offering her a job, it was an assignment nobody else wanted. It was dirty.

'What is it?' said Berlin.

'Misper,' said Del.

A missing person. Berlin glanced at the coffin suspended above the yawning pit. Resisting the urge to run, she pushed through the throng, averted her eyes from the sea of startled faces around her, and walked away.

The heart of the city was beating weakly. At half past nine on a Monday morning, traffic was at a standstill and the skies were silent because the airports were closed. The slap of the river against granite, punctuated by mournful sirens, resounded in the unnatural peace.

The blood on the cobblestones of Wapping High Street was dry. Berlin, under the reproving gaze of Detective Constable Terence Bryant, made a show of inspecting it. He was a compact man in his late forties with skin so white that his five o'clock shadow appeared to have been drawn on. It gave him a cartoonish look. But there was nothing funny about his demeanour.

'What's this all about then?' he said. 'We have the miscreant in custody.'

Miscreant.

'There's a witness. Lives in one of those posh conversions. She saw it from her window and called it in with a good description of the assailant. We nicked him at Wapping station. And we'll get the council's CCTV, of course.'

'Open and shut,' said Berlin.

'Schoolboy,' said Bryant. 'Palmerston Hall, if you don't mind.'

Palmerston Hall. Ancient and prestigious, famous for educating prime ministers, captains of industry and generations of British aristocracy.

Bryant brought a packet of Fisherman's Friend out of his pocket and slipped one in his mouth, pointedly not offering her one.

'So, Miss Berlin,' he said. 'Who's paying you a fat fee to interfere with a police matter?'

He sucked noisily on his sweet.

'A client,' said Berlin. 'And just Berlin will do, Bryant.'

Bryant snorted. 'Why is he or she so interested?' he said.

'No idea,' said Berlin. 'I haven't been briefed yet. I came straight from a funeral.'

'Oh, I see,' said Bryant. He looked her up and down, apparently taking this as an explanation for her long black coat and black boots. 'No one close, I hope.'

'Why would the victim leave the scene?' said Berlin. 'He must have been hurt.'

'Dunno,' said Bryant. 'They sent an ambulance, but he'd gone. Probably up to no good himself,' he added.

So the victim was also a *miscreant* in Bryant's eyes.

'It's a bit odd, isn't it?' she said. 'A public schoolboy assaulting someone first thing in the morning in this neck of the woods.'

Wapping, once a dark warren of warehouses and cheap housing for dock workers, was now thoroughly gentrified.

Bryant made a small, unhappy noise. He had agreed to meet her at the scene after a terse exchange on the phone, but it was obvious he wasn't thrilled by the prospect of a civilian investigator stomping around on his patch.

'I've been ordered to cooperate with you,' he'd said, before hanging up. Which meant her client had clout.

The case, such as it was, was only a few hours old, and as far as Bryant was concerned, it was already closed.

'I won't get in your way,' said Berlin.

'You certainly won't,' said Bryant. His Adam's apple bobbed above a tight half-Windsor.

But then again, I might, thought Berlin.

She gazed up and down Wapping High Street. They were near Pier Head, an oasis of charming gardens bordered by rows of elegant Georgian town houses. The street bisected the gardens, which had once been a lock, the Wapping entrance.

It had led from the river to twenty acres of the London Docks, built to receive tobacco, rice, wine and brandy. The huge cellars beneath the warehouses had been compared to the burial chambers of the Pyramids.

Similar demonstrations of wealth and power now appeared in the form of expensive warehouse conversions looming over the narrow thoroughfare, some linked four floors above the street by cast-iron catwalks. Once hogsheads of wine and tobacco rolled across them. Now they bore pots of geraniums.

Buildings on the river commanded astronomical prices and had security to match; CCTV sprouted weed-like from beneath eaves and at the top of lamp posts.

Bryant looked pointedly at his watch.

'Anything else?' he asked.

Berlin smiled.

'I'd like to talk to the miscreant,' she said.

The front desk of Limehouse police station was protected by a floor-to-ceiling bulletproof glass partition; only two people at a time were admitted to the presence of the officers behind it.

Bryant left Berlin in the waiting room, where the public queued for admission to the inner sanctum, while he went around to the cells. This was his idea of cooperation. The station stank of sweat, disinfectant, cold burgers and fried onions. She folded her arms and affected patience. It would do no good to antagonise Bryant any further.

Eventually he appeared behind the partition and beckoned her. The door buzzed open and Berlin was admitted, to a chorus of tutting and swearing from those who'd been there first. She followed Bryant down a series of corridors and through keypad-controlled doors, until finally he showed her into a small room.

'Sit there,' he said, pointing at a wooden chair positioned in front of a monitor, which displayed an image of a youth and a woman at a table in a small interview room. The technology was new and the vision sharp. The young man's head was bowed, his face obscured by a hank of black hair.

Berlin sat down and adjusted the angle of the monitor.

The next moment Bryant walked into the frame and sat down. A uniformed officer brought a spare chair. The sound of it being dragged across the room put her teeth on edge. Good speakers, too.

Bryant switched on the recording device.

'For the sake of the tape, those present are myself, Detective Constable Terence Bryant . . .'

'Constable Tolliver,' said the uniformed officer.

'Sylvie Laurent of Godson, Bell and Rushmore,' said the woman. 'Mr Chen's solicitor.'

Berlin was surprised by the accent. She was French, in her forties perhaps, with a strong, battle-hardened face. Her mane of hair was loosely pinned in a classic chignon. The suit was expensive, but well worn. She wasn't a legal aid lawyer.

Laurent touched the arm of the youth beside her.

'Philip Chen,' he said. He didn't raise his head.

'I remind you, Mr Chen, you do not have to say anything. But it may harm your defence if you do not mention when questioned something which you later rely on in court. Anything you do say may be given in evidence. Do you understand?'

'Yes,' said Philip.

'Detective Bryant,' said Laurent. 'Mr Chen will not be making a statement at this time.'

'Is that right, Mr Chen?' said Bryant.

Philip finally looked up. His fine features, luminous skin and cascade of straight black hair held the gaze.

'I'm sorry,' he said.

Berlin noticed a slight tightening around the lawyer's mouth. Irritation. Apology wasn't in the legal playbook. She reached into her pocket and brought out a gold cigarette lighter. Her fingers played with it in an absent-minded fashion as she watched her client.

'So what happened?' said Bryant.

Philip looked at Laurent. She shook her head.

'No comment,' said Philip.

Bryant frowned.

Philip might look Chinese, but he spoke with the well-modulated upper-class accent that went with his education. Berlin bent closer to the monitor. There was sweat on his brow.

'You're not going to offer any explanation for this vicious attack, Mr Chen?' said Bryant.

'That's a very inflammatory description, Detective Bryant,' said Laurent.

'We'll decide that when we see the CCTV footage,' said Bryant. 'That's the way the witness described it.'

'My client will make no further comment,' said Laurent.

'Then I'll be detaining Mr Chen on suspicion of assault occasioning grievous bodily harm, pending further enquiries. He'll appear before the youth court in the morning.'

'He can't stay here,' said Laurent.

'It's a serious offence, madam,' said Bryant. 'His victim could be bleeding to death under a bush somewhere, or floating down the river. I can keep your client for twenty-four hours without charge. He can stay here or at the local authority secure unit. It's up to you.'

Madame Laurent was unlikely to be capable of making an informed choice.

'Take the cells,' murmured Berlin. They might be cold and smelly, but the boy would be safer there than in a juvenile facility, where his accent would guarantee a swift and merciless fate.

Laurent put her hand on Chen's shoulder. He started, as if he suddenly realised they were talking about him.

'What about school?' he said.

Bryant stood. 'Come along, lad,' he said.

For a moment Berlin saw fear in Chen's eyes.

Bryant saw it too. He was gruff, but not cruel.

'I'll take you down myself,' he said. 'The custody sergeant will keep an eye on you.'

He meant well.

2

The warehouse, huddled between two modern apartment developments, was an unreconstructed remnant. Rising damp stained the foundations, strings of green slime hung from crannies left by crumbling mortar, and paint flaked from the iron window frames and down pipes.

Ziggurats of pigeon droppings decorated the sills. The guttering hung at an angle, and beneath it a constant drip stained the brickwork. The whole place sneered at the niceties of conversion. Berlin approved.

Iron railings enclosed a narrow strip of flagstones set lower than the pavement. Berlin pushed open the rusty gates, which hung askew, stepped down, crossed to the portico and picked up the entry phone. In stark contrast to the general dilapidation, a biometric pad glowed blue, waiting for a fingerprint.

She was aware of the soft whir of a camera as it focused and scanned. The warehouse might be a ruin, but the security was state-of-the-art.

Where she was standing was only a hundred yards from the bloody cobblestones. The heavy oak door swung open silently on its refurbished hinges. Berlin hung up the entry phone – she was obviously expected – and stepped inside.

The door closed behind her, and for a moment she was held in a gloomy limbo. Then the lights came on.

A man was standing on a ribbed steel platform, equipped on three sides with safety bars, the kind of hoist they had in public venues to provide wheelchair access.

'Lord Haileybury,' said Berlin.

'Just Haileybury, please,' he said.

This was Burghley's client, and, as the subcontractor, now hers. She approached him and extended her hand.

'Berlin,' she said.

The earl supported himself on two sticks. When he hooked one over his arm to take her hand, his own was almost a claw, typical of rheumatoid arthritis. He did his best to shake hands, smiling all the while, despite the pain it must have cost him. Berlin could see it in his eyes.

Haileybury's considerable height was somewhat diminished by a curvature of the spine, but his broad, open face had an attractive quality. A wave of tousled silver-grey hair rippled over his collar. He was ever so slightly dishevelled, with an air of distraction.

'Sorry about all the security nonsense. Insurance insists on it,' he said. 'I have one or two pieces.'

He gestured, and she stepped on to the platform. Haileybury prodded a large red button with the rubber ferrule of his stick, a motor hummed and they rose in a stately fashion.

Gliding past three floors in shadow, Berlin had an impression of pulleys, geared wheels, levers and cables. It was an ascent through the *Carceri*, Piranesi's imaginary prisons. But when they came to a gentle halt on the fourth floor, the scale was overwhelming for a different reason.

A pair of stone guardian lions reared above her as she stepped from the platform into a gallery crammed with treasures: jade and bronze sculptures, ivory and sandalwood carvings, bronze fountainheads, cloisonné enamel, red lacquer boxes. Silks adorned the walls.

Immense cast-iron stanchions supported a soaring roof; the furthest wall was glass, allowing light to flood in and illuminate a phalanx of carved dragons set on granite plinths. Ornately carved tables, chairs and cabinets occupied every inch of floor space.

The 'one or two pieces' were the famous Haileybury Bequest, artefacts taken from the Old Summer Palace in Beijing, and the subject of a well-publicised stand-off between the earl and the Chinese government.

Haileybury lifted his stick and described a quick arc through the air.

'They want it all back, you know,' he said. 'All of it, including the stuff that's on loan to museums for the public good. Cheek. They're supposed to be communists. They've offered me squillions.'

She remembered something about the Prime Minister getting involved too; one of his gaffes at a Chinese state banquet.

'The government is backing me, of course,' said Haileybury. 'Precedent. Elgin Marbles and all that. Ironic, really. It was Elgin's son, an eighth earl himself, matter of fact, who ordered the destruction of the Summer Palace. You know about the Marbles.'

'We pinched them from the Greeks,' said Berlin.

'Except the Turks were running Greece at the time,' said Haileybury. 'The sultan was sweet on Lady Elgin, so he let the earl crate up the Marbles and ship them home. Massive job. Cost a fortune. It broke him. In the end he was forced to sell 'em to the British government at a loss. Never trust a politician.'

He twisted to face her.

'The Chinese say this is their history, that my forebears were looters,' he said. 'What do you say?'

He didn't wait for an answer.

'But isn't it my history – *our* history – too?'

Berlin had never thought of herself as a beneficiary of British imperialism, but he had a point.

Haileybury negotiated a path between the furniture with practised ease, making his way to two armchairs, worn wingbacks, beside a large walnut table that was littered with the mundane: newspapers, cups and saucers, an electric kettle, bottles of Scotch, reading glasses and a computer.

The chairs were arranged to take in the breathtaking view of the river through an enormous pair of double-glazed floor-to-ceiling doors, which opened on to a terrace.

Berlin followed him to this niche without comment; words couldn't do the place justice. It was like opening the door of an old shed and finding the British Museum inside.

'Of course, the government's not interested in history, it just wants another weapon in its diplomatic stoushes over trade,' grumbled Haileybury. 'It's all about politics.'

He dropped into one of the wingbacks with obvious relief. 'I'm sorry,' he said. 'You're not here for a history lesson. I'm afraid I'm a little discombobulated this morning.'

He gestured to a bottle of Ardbeg ten-year-old.

'Would you mind terribly?' he said. 'I could do with a drink. Would you care to join me?'

It was important to keep the client happy, and anyway, it would be impolite to refuse. Berlin nodded.

Haileybury poured two generous measures and handed her one.

'I just got off the phone with the lawyer,' he said. 'I'm not sure how well Philip will cope with incarceration.'

'He might have to get used to it,' said Berlin. 'Apparently there's a witness. This area's bristling with CCTV. The police don't necessarily need the victim for a conviction.'

Haileybury grimaced.

Berlin sipped her single malt and gazed at the muted outlines of Tower Bridge, the Shard and the grey, mist-laden ribbon of the river.

'Did you engage the lawyer, too?' she said.

'I felt I had to do something,' said Haileybury. 'The school called and said Philip had been in a scrap, that he would need a lawyer and so forth.'

In her book, the bloody cobblestones put the assault somewhat higher than a 'scrap', but as she was the *so forth*, it was not her place to say so. Hopefully the reason she was there would soon become clear.

Haileybury shifted uneasily in his chair, apparently unable to sit in one position for too long.

'In a manner of speaking, I'm *in loco parentis*,' he said.

'Oh?' said Berlin.

His discomfort had preceded this admission. She waited.

'I'm a trustee of a scholarship programme for talented Chinese orphans,' said Haileybury. 'The Anglo-Chinese Friendship Society. We pay their fees as boarders at my old school. Philip is one of them.'

Berlin watched him.

'Do you know what precipitated the incident?' she said.

'No idea,' said Haileybury.

'It was early,' said Berlin. 'On a Monday morning.'

It was a speculative gambit. Clients often needed some encouragement to come clean. This was no straightforward missing person case.

'Over the years I've made it a habit to offer the scholarship boys some hospitality,' said Haileybury. 'It can be rather lonely for them in this country at times.'

He stared out of the window for a moment, and then turned to look her in the eye. A challenge.

'Philip had been here for the weekend,' he said.

Now it made sense. She had been surprised when Del said Lord Haileybury would brief her personally. Someone of his standing would usually deal with the organ grinder, not the monkey. The august firm of Burghley LLP would want to keep this sort of thing at arm's length. It was a bit tacky for their tastes.

'I understand you want the victim found,' said Berlin. 'Why is that?'

Haileybury ran his stiff, crumpled hand through his hair. 'This is going to get out, isn't it?' he said.

18

'More than likely,' said Berlin. 'There's invariably someone in every police station – a cleaner, a clerk, a copper – who tips off the press. Palmerston Hall is newsworthy. Although they can't name a juvenile offender.'

She didn't add that if they put it all together, which they would, they could name Haileybury. The victim was going to turn up looking for compensation when he learnt who was involved. The earl would want him found and paid off before he took his long, sad story of being bashed by a public schoolboy *friend* of Lord Haileybury to the press.

She wanted to hear him say it.

'How many trustees are there?' she asked.

'Three, including myself,' said Haileybury. 'You needn't concern yourself with the others. They're very discreet.'

'Has Philip ever done anything like this before?' said Berlin.

'No, never,' said Haileybury.

'I'd hoped to talk to him this morning,' said Berlin. 'But it will have to be tomorrow, after he's bailed. He may be able to provide the sort of detail I'll need if I'm to have any chance of locating this person. When Philip left here, was he angry or upset?'

'No,' said Haileybury. 'Not at all.'

She pressed a little harder.

'If I can find this person – and it's a big if – then what?' she said.

Haileybury eased himself out of his chair and stood with his back to the terrace doors, facing her. He seemed to be bracing himself for something.

'I believe this incident is part of a campaign of harassment. It's a warning, a signal that they have leverage and can use it against me.'

This was unexpected. Speedy recalibration was required, but the Ardbeg had taken the edge off.

'Leverage?' said Berlin. 'You mean blackmail?'

The diffuse light behind Haileybury was a ghostly aura.

'I am rather fond of the boy,' he said. 'Of which they are no doubt aware.'

'Who are "they"?' said Berlin.

Haileybury looked at her as if she hadn't been paying attention.

'The Chinese, of course,' he said. 'If we can show this is the work of their dirty tricks brigade, it will cause them a great deal of embarrassment. Possible expulsions, all sorts. They watch me all the time. The PRC – the People's Republic of China – are ruthless, you know.'

She'd been completely wrong about Burghley. It wasn't the more salacious aspects of this job that had put them off; it was the possibility of being dragged into a diplomatic incident involving an unpredictable foreign power and a paranoid aristocrat.

She proffered her glass for a refill.

'Perhaps you could run that past me again,' she said.

3

Bryant stood beneath a gnarled horse chestnut tree in St John's churchyard, sucking on a Fisherman's Friend. He could watch discreetly from here; he knew exactly who lurked in the decrepit warehouse on the other side of the street.

Bryant was Wapping born and bred. In the eighteenth century, his great-great-grandfather had owned a pub in the High Street, the Waterman's Arms, long gone. A good thing too, his grandmother would have said. She had been a very devout woman. Church of England, but High.

Bryant had grown up with the history of Wapping and its denizens, and a lot of what he knew wasn't to be found in books. The churchyard he was standing in was all that remained of St John's, which now boasted two-bedroom apartments *full of character with original features*.

The one hundred bodies removed from the crypt were not mentioned in the glossy brochures. They may have been Low Church corpses, but it was a godless act anyway, according to Gran.

He shuffled, his collar chafing in the humidity. It was humiliating, a serving officer reduced to this, but he needed to be sure who was sticking their nose in, which meant following this blasted woman. She had clearly been around the block a few times and didn't take much pride in her appearance.

His boss, Detective Chief Inspector Tomalin, had pointed a finger towards the ceiling when Bryant asked him where the order to cooperate with her had come from.

He'd been told to extend every courtesy to the private investigator, although Tomalin added that her role wouldn't affect the case; there would be no interference.

Bryant knew what that was worth if higher-ups were involved. They would talk to the Crown Prosecution Service over a skinny latte, and once *they* got their hands on it they would live up to the name more commonly used by coppers: 'Can't Prosecute, Sorry'.

He didn't like it. It smelt wrong. Like the mucky odour coming from the drains in this weird, clammy weather. He popped another Fisherman's Friend in his mouth and waited.

Leaving Haileybury's, Berlin was conscious that her reaction to his story might have been influenced by the single malt, the effects of which she was still enjoying. Until Bryant stepped into her path.

'Jesus Christ!' she said. 'What are you playing at?'

'I knew it. I just knew it,' he said.

He was so wound up he was practically fizzing.

'I beg your pardon?' said Berlin.

'I know who lives in there,' said Bryant.

'Bully for you,' said Berlin.

'What did he have to say?' he demanded.

'Do me a favour, Bryant,' said Berlin. 'Sod off.'

'I'm not a turnip,' said Bryant. 'The assault occurred just down the road, he's got friends in high places and you scuttled off to see him as soon as you left the station.'

'Surveillance without reasonable cause is harassment, Detective Bryant. I'll be lodging a complaint,' said Berlin.

She tried to walk away, but he grabbed her arm. A cloud of aniseed fumes engulfed her.

'Get your bloody hands off me,' she said. 'Those cough sweets have got you wired.'

'The high and mighty eighth earl wants the victim found,' said Bryant. 'What else is there for you to do? And I know why. So he can protect his catamite.'

The word exploded from his mouth in a flurry of spittle.

Berlin almost laughed.

'Catamite?' she said. 'Who do you think you're dealing with, Oscar Wilde?'

'I know what goes on in there,' said Bryant.

'Do you?' said Berlin. 'How?'

Bryant let her go. They were standing beneath an old tree. One of its thick limbs creaked in a current of tepid air. The hoary sentinel was wheezing.

'What's your problem, Bryant?' said Berlin. 'You've pretty much got the boy on the assault. What more do you want? You said yourself the victim was probably up to no good.'

'And you said the circumstances of the assault were a bit odd,' said Bryant.

He had a point.

'So why do you care if Haileybury's involved?' said Berlin. 'Chen's old enough to consent. There are a lot of dirty old men about. As you seem to be only too well aware.'

Bryant was squinting at her, apparently trying to decide if she was taking the piss, when a sudden squall threw grit and dust in their faces.

There was a sharp crack. They both looked up.

The rotten limb, splintered from the trunk, hung above their heads at a precarious angle. Berlin took a quick side-step, but Bryant just stood there, staring up at the branch, until Berlin shoved him out of harm's way.

He didn't say anything, just gave her a small, enigmatic smile before he turned and walked off.

She had the feeling he'd wanted the limb to fall.

Berlin took the bus, the D3, which would drop her close to home in Bethnal Green. Her leg was aching, thanks to an old Achilles tear repaired badly, and her feet burned, the result of nerve damage from frostbite.

She was still managing, just, not to fall back into the arms of her old flame, or even its stand-ins, methadone or buprenorphine, which she loathed for their cold, deadening effect. Prescription codeine washed down with Talisker was her fallback position for pain. Analgesia had never played any part in her addiction to heroin.

Abstinence was a relentless state and she couldn't yet put her hand on her heart and say she had fully embraced it. Age hadn't diminished her agitation; fifty-eight felt no different from eighteen when it came to anxiety.

She wasn't at all sure she wanted this job. The peer's tirade about the Chinese intelligence service didn't really fit the facts and stretched credulity. Haileybury was reaching for an excuse for his boy; how often had some psychopath's mother insisted her son wouldn't hurt a fly?

Whichever way you cut it, the earl was intent on a cover-up. Helping a privileged public schoolboy avoid the consequences of a nasty crime didn't sit well with her. A kid from one of the sink estates would still be in a cell waiting for legal aid to turn up.

On the other hand, there was something slightly off about the whole business; Haileybury's explanation could have some element of truth. But which element?

The bus was stuck in traffic halfway across Whitechapel Road. Berlin took out her phone and dialled. Del answered, panting.

'Don't tell me you're jogging at lunchtime?' said Berlin.

'Squash with the boss,' said Del. He lowered his voice. 'Sir Simon May, a senior partner putting in a rare appearance at the coalface. He's the source of your current job.'

'How are you doing?' said Berlin.

'I'm losing,' said Del.

'Very sensible,' said Berlin.

'How are things at your end?' said Del. 'Behaving yourself with the gentry?'

'They have excellent cellars,' said Berlin.

'Where you belong,' he said. 'Below stairs.'

Only Del could get away with such a comment.

'This job has all the upstairs-downstairs features the tabloids could want: a seventeen-year-old delinquent public schoolboy and an ageing aristocrat.'

In recent years, both houses of the Palace of Westminster, not to mention other bastions of British civil society, had been exposed as harbouring more than their fair share of depravity. The Great British Public would ask how long this association between the earl and the schoolboy had been going on. The question had crossed her mind, too.

'So you're okay with it, then?' said Del.

He knew her well enough to know she would have doubts.

Leaving aside the political angle, Bryant's open hostility and prejudice had made her uneasy. Philip Chen was seventeen. If he had a sexual relationship with Haileybury it was legal. Just.

That wouldn't deter a homophobic detective; Bryant would look for every opportunity to drag the peer into it. His strange behaviour in the churchyard made that a certainty.

An old man parading a young woman on his arm attracted a certain sneaking admiration. It was different when it was a young man. And Haileybury himself had said he was practically *in loco parentis*. It might be tasteless, but it was nobody's business.

'Yes,' said Berlin. 'Against my better judgement.'

'It will be a walk in the park,' said Del.

She could hear the relief in his voice. He liked to keep her busy and the partners happy.

Berlin was Molly's godmother, but she didn't see her very often. Linda, Del's wife, wasn't that comfortable with the idea of Berlin as a role model for Molly, or, for that matter, Del. Berlin liked to think that her work in

26

the field provided him with a vicarious outlet. He didn't always see it that way. Neither did Linda.

'This one's off the books,' he added. 'And whatever you need in the way of expenses.'

No contract. No paper trail. No budget. Everything done on a nod and a wink. The old-boy network.

'I have to get back to losing,' said Del. 'Sir Simon has a plane to catch.'

'What did he tell you about this job?' she said.

'Not much. Just that it needed discretion, sensitivity and an unorthodox approach.'

'That's me, is it?' said Berlin.

'Yeah,' said Del. 'Tight-lipped, touchy and unpredictable.'

Berlin chuckled. It was the first laugh she'd had in a while. She decided not to mention the Chinese angle; if Sir Simon hadn't told Del, fine. He would just worry. Her previous encounters with foreign agents hadn't always turned out well. She flexed missing toes.

The bus finally juddered and moved forward.

4

Bryant was pleased when all his so-called colleagues cleared off home and the squad room was his. He worked better alone and there would be no awkward questions about what he was doing. He bent over the computer and fiddled with the USB stick, finally getting it into the slot.

At least he'd had the satisfaction of putting that Berlin woman in her place. She'd been drinking, he'd smelt it on her breath. Probably hitting the bottle with Haileybury. Birds of a feather. She wouldn't give him any trouble.

He'd skipped lunch and spent a long afternoon at the council's CCTV control room, where he had an old mate with as much patience as him for the niceties of paperwork. They eventually found the footage involving Chen and saved it on to the stick.

He copied the video on to the hard drive. It would be logged when it suited him, if it was used in evidence. A double click brought the grainy footage to life. The images weren't great, but when he froze the video, he could see that the face of Philip Chen was contorted with fury.

He pressed play again. The boy threw a punch and the victim reeled back, hands to his face. That would be the blood on the cobblestones. Noses bled profusely. Pity.

The Berlin woman was right about one thing: it was unusual. Assaults at that time of the morning were the forte of drunken youths and junkies. A lone assailant with nothing to gain, oblivious to the CCTV, implied something else. Something more personal.

Whatever the motive, he was determined to get to the bottom of it, particularly now he knew Haileybury was involved.

'Any problems this morning, Bryant?' said Tomalin.

He started and fumbled with the mouse, blanking the screen. The bloody DCI was watching him from the doorway.

'No, sir,' he said.

'Good,' said Tomalin. 'Go home.'

Easy to say when you had a wife and three kiddies tucked away in a nice semi in Chigwell.

He switched off his computer and slipped the USB stick into his pocket.

'Yes, sir,' he said. 'Goodnight.'

Bryant left the station by way of the custody suite. The sergeant on night shift was arranging his Thermos and snacks the way he liked them, and cleaning the console and the computer keyboard with antibacterial wipes.

Bryant pointed at the cells.

'Sleeping like a baby when I came on,' said the sergeant. 'Must be guilty.'

Only the innocent paced and fretted when banged up. For the guilty, it came as a relief.

The fear Bryant had seen earlier in the boy's face wasn't about a night in the cells. Something else was on his mind. Perhaps now he felt safe.

'See you first thing,' said Bryant.

The sergeant nodded.

'I'd put money on it,' he said.

Haileybury stood on his terrace and watched the light die behind Tower Bridge. An email had confirmed the investigator was on board. She was an odd fish, but then he hardly wanted some buttoned-up by-the-book type involved in the affair.

He leant on the parapet. The terrace extended out over the river, an endless shadow that tonight appeared to absorb the city lights, not reflect them.

The river endured and accommodated all, flowing on regardless, a constant reminder of the things he held dear: continuity, loyalty and the promulgation of excellence in all its forms. He preferred to think of these as traditional, rather than old-fashioned, values, which exposed the shallow contemporary attachment to moral relativism and the cult of the amateur.

As far as he was concerned, twentieth-century Britain had created little of lasting value, references to Mary Quant, Francis Bacon and the Beatles notwithstanding. There was an adamant refusal amongst the chattering classes to acknowledge the fact that we are not all created equal.

At that moment he felt a chill, a cold presence; not a ghost, but someone lost, just the same.

'My poor boy,' he murmured.

Disoriented, he gripped the balustrade, enveloped in a memory carried on the sultry breeze. In his decline, the always tremulous border between past and present was dissolving precariously. He must hold on a little longer.

He went inside and drew the curtains.

Bryant took the long way home, via the Thames Path, ignoring the glimmering skyline in favour of the oily swathe that undulated below. The river always mesmerised him. Backwash slapped the embankment as a barge loaded with steaming refuse chugged downstream.

To his mind, there was a lot more rubbish in London that should be put out. This case might just be the opportunity he'd been waiting for.

Berlin's pace slackened as she reached the stairs that led up to her flat on the second floor of a former council block. It wasn't fatigue that slowed her footsteps, it was dread.

She'd eaten at her local, the Approach, and let the evening drift away with more Scotch. Usually more than content with her own company, tonight she was afraid to be alone with her thoughts.

She negotiated the three locks on the front door, shut it quietly behind her and went straight to the bathroom, where she grabbed a couple of codeine from the cabinet and went back to the kitchen for a glass of water.

The flat was small – a living area with a tiny kitchen, bedroom and bathroom – and it was oppressively stuffy.

She sidestepped the stack of cartons lining the wall and opened a window. The air that wafted in was warm and acrid. She shut it again, then stood there, paralysed.

A thin grey line on the horizon was rolling inexorably towards her. Grief. She swallowed the codeine and walked out again.

5

Lee Wang Yan paused beside an open window for a moment and took a deep breath. He found the humidity and fumes of the London night air comforting. It reminded him of home. Quickly he turned away from the window and continued on his way down the long passage.

It was late, but a light still burned in the upstairs kitchen. He paused outside the door and listened. The slap of cards and the chink of glasses punctuated moans and grumbles.

The moment he turned the handle, the whining ceased.

Deng, the injured party, reclined in an armchair with a half-empty bottle of cheap whisky at his elbow. He was playing poker with his pals and making the most of his sacrifice. They preferred Texas Hold 'em to the more traditional pastime. Lee tried to disguise his disdain.

'You delivered the message,' he said.

'And the boy delivered his,' said Deng, wincing to emphasise his pain.

'A tap on the nose. It's not even broken,' said Lee. 'And your ribs will heal quickly.'

A grunt was the only reply.

He left them to it and went downstairs.

The young were so soft today, so reluctant to endure even a moment's suffering. Raised by indulgent parents in a world of plenty, they possessed an exaggerated sense of entitlement.

Deng had handled the situation poorly, although Philip's outburst had been completely unexpected. The boy was capable of considerable violence when provoked, a trait that could prove useful if channelled in the right direction. Finessing his rage would be something of a challenge.

A back door that lacked an alarm gave on to a large garden. The trees rustled and shadows flickered as he lit a cigarette, but he was unconcerned. This neighbourhood was as safe as houses, as the British would say.

The gate opened without a squeak, and he strolled down the road. Its solid, elegant buildings and clean, well-maintained pavement were pleasing and irritating in equal measure; so smug. Although what the British had to be smug about these days was unfathomable. Their delusions were, however, useful, as were their weaknesses, and he was able to exploit both to great effect.

Philip Chen's belief that he was protected by power and privilege would unravel as it became apparent his membership of the elite was conditional. He could rapidly become just another unsavoury foreigner with questionable habits. He would learn the hard way. Lee's own lesson in humility had been particularly harsh.

He gobbed in the gutter. He knew how it disgusted them.

*

Lee returned to his room and locked the door. The blinding headache he endured nightly had set in. He lay down and plumped his pillows, trying to find a comfortable position. He'd been trying for more than fifty years.

From the drawer of the bedside table he withdrew a slim leather case, which he unzipped and laid flat on the bed. The old-fashioned glass barrel syringe and stainless-steel needle gleamed.

The mere sight reassured him; he tightened the rubber tube around his bicep, clenched his fist and prepared for merciful oblivion as his vision degenerated into jagged flashes. It didn't matter, he could do it in the dark.

He closed his eyes.

6

Every morning was busy at the Thames Magistrates' Court, and this Tuesday was no different. The youth court sat in the same brutalist building. Assailed by its ripe odours – sweaty adolescence, fried chicken and stale cigarette smoke – Berlin pushed her way through the crowd looking for Philip Chen and his lawyer. No one gave ground. The assembled throng spoke many languages, but all shared a common code: surly.

When she spotted Bryant on the other side of the lobby, Berlin veered in that direction, but before she got there, he saw her coming and shot into the courtroom, where Chen and Laurent were probably already waiting. It was frustrating, but they would all have to come out again eventually. The youth court was closed to the public.

In the meantime, she needed a large black coffee. Wandering London until the early hours, a response to the restlessness that often seized her at night, didn't do anything for her mood or her ability to concentrate.

It felt as if the smog blanketing London had seeped into her brain. Edginess exacerbated her lack of clarity. She had to beware of reaching for something stronger than coffee and more soothing than Scotch.

*

Bryant enjoyed the sensation of the courtroom door closing behind him as Berlin approached. Perhaps it was petty, but there were still places a sworn officer could go that a civilian investigator couldn't. It was a diminishing space, with all the outsourcing and privatisation that was going on, and he'd make the most of it.

Berlin would be after him for a copy of the CCTV footage. He could say, quite truthfully, that the proper process took time. Chen was entitled to a copy, because he was in it, but Berlin wouldn't be happy with the delay.

She couldn't know, and he wasn't going to tell her, that the video wouldn't help find the victim. He'd been wearing a baseball cap and a hoodie, which kept his face in deep shadow. It would keep her busy, and out of his hair, doing the legwork.

A quick ring-around of A&E departments had also been fruitless; plenty of bashings, but none had come in early yesterday morning. The amount of blood on the cobblestones was considerable, albeit most probably from the victim's nose.

He had to admit he owed that to Berlin. If she hadn't insisted on meeting at the scene, he wouldn't have bothered taking a look. She was an ill wind that had blown some good, as it turned out. The blood supported his argument that the victim could be badly hurt, despite leaving the scene.

He took his seat at the bar table. Chen and the lawyer were already seated. The boy didn't look too clever this morning. The magistrate cleared her throat and they all paid attention. She shuffled through some documents and spoke without looking up.

'Detective Bryant, I understand you would prefer to see this young man remanded to a local authority facility,' she said.

Bryant stood.

'That's correct, madam,' he said. 'We have a witness who saw the incident and a CCTV recording of a serious assault, but we need more time to determine the nature of the injuries suffered by the victim and thence the offence with which Mr Chen will be charged. There was a quantity of blood found at the scene. Mr Chen has considerable means and as a foreign national is a flight risk.'

He sat down.

Laurent stood up.

'Madam, my client will defend this charge,' she said.

The magistrate looked up.

'Will he?' she said. 'Mr Chen, you understand this hearing is simply about the terms of your bail?'

Philip stood up.

'Yes, madam,' he said.

The magistrate removed her reading glasses and took a good look at him.

Bryant gritted his teeth. She was showing an unhealthy interest in this public schoolboy.

'What happened, Mr Chen?' said the magistrate.

Bryant wanted to leap to his feet, but there was no point. She could do as she liked at this stage of the proceedings.

Chen glanced at Laurent, who nodded.

'The . . . er . . . gentleman I struck importuned me,' said Philip.

Bryant was gobsmacked.

The magistrate made a sympathetic noise.

'Where will you reside, Mr Chen?' she said. She slipped her reading glasses on again. 'I see that you can't return to Palmerston Hall as a boarder, given the circumstances, and you have no family in this country.'

The lawyer was on her feet immediately. She put a hand on Philip's shoulder. It was a cracking performance.

'My client has some health issues, madam,' said Laurent. 'Exacerbated by the stress of this incident. He will reside at the Abbey until the matter is resolved. The Abbey is a facility—'

'I'm familiar with the Abbey, thank you,' said the magistrate.

Laurent spoke quickly.

'In relation to the alleged flight risk, Mr Chen's passport is held by the school and they will gladly surrender it to the police, madam.'

The magistrate nodded.

'So ordered,' she said.

Bryant gathered his papers and cursed.

Berlin could tell from the look on Bryant's face that he'd been outmanoeuvred.

'Problems?' she said.

'They're sending him to the Abbey,' said Bryant.

Laurent was laying the groundwork for mitigation. A 'nervous condition', no doubt, which the highly paid shrinks at the Abbey would gladly attest to at his trial, if it got that far.

'I see,' said Berlin. 'Look, Bryant, any chance of a copy of the council's video? You know how long it will take me to get it otherwise.'

'Gladly,' said Bryant.

For a moment she thought he was taking the piss.

He fished a memory stick out of his pocket and thrust it at her.

'Here,' he said. 'Let me know if you see anything that suggests they can run the guardsman's defence.'

He stomped off before she could mumble her thanks.

Philip was going to run with gay panic, a sort of temporary madness in reaction to a homosexual advance. Laurent might be a novice when it came to crime, but she was making all the right moves: the highly strung lad with the face of an angel, target of a predatory queer.

A quiet word with Philip Chen was in order, and without his lawyer breathing down her neck. They had very different agendas: Laurent's job was to get Chen off; Berlin's job was to find his victim.

It would be prudent to keep the two things very separate to avoid any obligations of disclosure on the part of the lawyer. Don't ask, don't tell.

She would give Chen time to get settled in at the Abbey before she took a trip out there. It had been a while, but she was sure she'd still be able to find her way around.

The steps that led from the magistrates' court down to the broad pavement were still crowded. Berlin weaved her way through legions of defendants in borrowed suits, their lawyers, who were hardly any better turned out, and uniformed coppers there to give evidence.

The sharpest dressers in the pack were the detectives, both male and female distinguished by their smart leather jackets and shiny shoes. There was no sign of Bryant, who didn't fit that profile.

A group of Chinese bootleg DVD sellers milled about chatting and smoking, unperturbed by what for them would be a routine appearance before the Thames magistrates. She used to see them when she was down here with Del, applying for search warrants; in another life the two of them had worked together for the government, pursuing local loan sharks. Happy days.

The DVD sellers were a dying breed, struggling against modernity. She knew how that felt. She watched as they stubbed out their cigarettes and filed inside.

In normal circumstances she would have taken the video home to watch, but she couldn't face going back to the flat. She could do with a drink, too.

She called Haileybury.

'I've got the CCTV video of Philip's incident,' she said. 'I'd like you to take a look.'

'I'm at your disposal,' said Haileybury.

Berlin hung up. The old earl was very obliging. She wasn't buying his Chinese conspiracy, but she was warming to his excellent Scotch. She hailed a black cab.

7

Bryant was forced to clean out the pool car before he could contemplate driving it to Palmerston Hall. Empty soft drink cans, kebab wrappers and worse were knee-deep on the floor. Some officers had no self-respect.

He took advantage of the car and did a quick supermarket shop before he went to the school. The Met owed him about a hundred hours in overtime, so he felt justified. He would drop the shopping off at the flat, and change his shirt and tie while he was about it. Best foot forward for the ruling class.

The lift was working. His luck was in. It shuddered and wheezed its way to the eighteenth floor, reminding him of the way his Gran used to shuffle about in her pinny, coughing and spluttering.

Unlike the lift, once she had arrived at the top floor she only went down again once. She said there was nothing to go down for: no neighbours sitting outside their front doors for a gossip, no cheeky delivery boys to chide.

Slum clearance, they'd called it. Now, barely thirty years later, the almost empty tower block stood amidst a wasteland of concrete and rusting playground equipment, condemned in turn, ready for another bunch of greedy developers.

Bryant surveyed the streets below as he did up his tie. He could see Wapping High Street from Waterside Gardens to Pier Head.

He never walked into the flat without being ambushed by the view; people paid millions for it. London sprawled beneath them, exposed, dense and steaming; the crust of a rancid pie had been rolled back to reveal the dark meat within, a stew that would turn the stomach.

He automatically picked up the binoculars and leant against the wall; the worn patch was testimony to how much time he spent in this position. He'd even bought a pair with night vision; there was only rubbish on the telly.

It had begun as a way of passing the time with Gran; her sight was poor, so he would describe the goings-on below as the new people moved in to the luxury conversions.

'The lady with the King Charles spaniel is having a sofa hoisted in through her front window,' he'd say.

'Fancy,' Gran would retort.

It amused them to call his mate at the council, who would come racing down to check on the removalist's permits. Nine times out of ten they weren't in order and a lot of gesticulating and stomping would follow, including an occasional shove and, if they were lucky, a punch or two.

He would paint what Gran called 'a word picture' of the pantomime, and she would laugh until the tears ran down the soft pillows of her cheeks.

They both took a particular interest in the long-standing resident who was responsible for their airy exile.

'What's the gentleman up to, Terence?' Gran would say.

She never called him Terry.

They would settle down with tea and a chocolate digestive and speculate on what was in the boxes that arrived at Haileybury's from Fortnum & Mason and Waitrose.

When there were visitors, Gran would try to guess their jobs. The man with the peg on his nose was the plumber, the girl with the rippling biceps was the physio. Others Bryant recognised from the news.

The fun went out of it when Gran lost interest.

He couldn't get a laugh out of her no matter how hard he tried, even when he described the pest controller as a bloke with a lump of Cheddar and a sledgehammer.

That was when he began watching with a purpose. He didn't know *how* it would make a difference, but he was determined that one day it would. It gave him a grim satisfaction to watch Haileybury without him having a clue. It was a kind of power.

In the street below, a cab pulled up. He adjusted the focus as the passenger got out. It was Berlin. She and the earl were getting very matey.

He was about to put the binoculars down when a moped, like the ones the pizza places used, came pootling down the street. The bright stars on top of the bloke's crash helmet caught the sun as he pulled up near St John's churchyard.

Bryant shifted his focus to the pizza bloke, who had a phone in his hand. He could have been checking a map or delivery instructions, but he wasn't. It looked very much like he was taking a photo, and it wasn't a selfie.

Berlin had disappeared beneath Haileybury's portico and would still be waiting to be let in, so unless this bloke had a particular interest in the dilapidated architecture of the London Docks, she was the object of his attention.

A moment later he rode away.

Bryant checked the time and made a note in the exercise book he kept beside the binoculars on the sill. Thirteen full ones were in a pile on the shelf.

8

The video on Haileybury's laptop screen didn't make pretty viewing. The victim walked into the frame, a short, stocky figure wearing jeans and a hoodie pulled down tight over a baseball cap. He came up behind Philip. When Philip turned around, his face was clear, but the victim's was hidden.

Suddenly Philip threw a punch; the bloke staggered back and fell to the ground, clutching his nose. There was no sound on the video, but as he attempted to crawl away, Philip was clearly shouting at him, enraged.

The victim wrapped his arms around his head.

It was a good move, because Philip began to kick him. He landed two or three good ones to the body, then looked up with a startled expression and ran, probably when the witness yelled at him from her window.

The victim made his exit more slowly, staggering to his feet, then disappearing out of the frame.

Haileybury sat back in his chair, grim.

'Is anything about him familiar?' said Berlin.

Haileybury shook his head.

'Philip maintains this person *importuned* him,' said Berlin.

'Oh good Lord,' said Haileybury.

'I haven't been able to talk to Philip yet,' said Berlin. 'But I'll check with the witness if she saw or heard something that would indicate the victim's ethnicity. It's impossible to tell from the video if he's Chinese.'

Given the direction in which he'd gone, he could have stumbled down the passage that ran between Haileybury's warehouse and the building next door.

It was dark and very narrow and led to the watermen's stairs and the river. Down there he could easily have been missed by a police officer or medic who wasn't looking that hard anyway.

'When you discuss these matters with Philip, I'd be grateful if you would tread gently,' said Haileybury.

'Why's that?' said Berlin.

'The lad has one or two *issues*, as they say in modern parlance,' said Haileybury.

He hesitated.

'Do you have any family, Berlin?'

'I should go,' she said.

Haileybury wondered about Berlin's precipitous departure; she was difficult to read. Self-contained, taciturn, she had listened without comment when he spoke of the Chinese and their machinations. Professional courtesy, or because she thought he was delusional?

On the other hand, he didn't sense any disapprobation on her part. It would have been very easy for her to judge him; most people would. Perhaps she was too well aware of her own weaknesses; people in glass houses and all that.

She was the right person for the job, as Simon had said, and wouldn't allow any preconceptions to get in the way. It was a sound recommendation. Burghley wouldn't be billing him. Apparently Berlin was happy to be paid with folding money; she was an outlier, which would be useful.

He felt Philip would respond to her. Someone for him to turn to when things got rough. Which was bound to happen.

At home, Berlin took some codeine and watched the video again, this time in slow motion. Philip didn't seem to be simply shouting abuse at his victim. He was saying something, and his cheek glistened. She froze the frame. He was crying.

There was something going on here: an argument, a remonstration, an exchange indicating that either Philip was acquainted with his victim or he was reacting to something specific. It was a beginning. She'd take it up with the witness. Perhaps she'd heard something.

At Haileybury's behest, Sylvie Laurent had texted her the witness's mobile number. When m'lord said 'jump', the response was 'how high?'

But the witness, one Helena Cathcart, had yet to return Berlin's calls. Her statement had been tendered at the hearing that morning.

Ms Cathcart, an investment banker, resided in a luxury warehouse conversion in Wapping High Street. An early riser, she'd been drinking coffee and gazing out of the window when the incident occurred.

Turning up on the banker's doorstep or calling at her workplace wouldn't cut it. The diary would be full. Berlin found her on LinkedIn and sent a message asking for a brief meeting at her convenience concerning the incident in Wapping High Street.

Cathcart would assume she was either a lawyer or a police officer and wouldn't ignore the request, but she would make a fuss about the time it was all taking and how she wished she hadn't got involved. One's civic duty could be so tiresome.

It was getting on for four o'clock, six hours since the ten o'clock hearing at the youth court but still too soon to visit Philip at the Abbey. He would barely have got through the lengthy assessment and admission process.

She opened a new browser window. She needed to do some digging on Haileybury and get some background on the Chinese intelligence service, just in case they were involved. If the victim of Philip's assault really was an agent of the PRC, they would make another move. She could hardly wait.

9

Bryant was stuck in the third circle of hell, otherwise known as the M25. He had telephoned ahead to let Palmerston Hall know he was on his way, with a court order in his pocket, to pick up Chen's passport. The chap he'd spoken to was the bursar, who had told him the head would hand over the passport personally.

He was looking forward to it. He had one or two questions for the person running that august establishment; like why one of his charges, a minor, was spending unsupervised weekends in London in the company of a dissolute aristocrat.

The traffic edged forward and he imagined Gran's reaction if she knew he was on his way to give the headmaster of Palmerston Hall a bit of stick.

She would have been tickled to think he was in such a position, but not surprised that one of their pupils had gone off the rails. She knew all about the upper classes.

On a Sunday morning she would settle down with tea, biscuits and the *News of the World*, which was kept well out of his reach when he was a nipper, and mutter about the likes of Lord Lucan and other privileged reprobates.

'They get away with murder,' she would opine darkly. 'And worse.'

When she'd had her fill, she'd toss the paper into the grate, condemning those who appeared in its salacious pages to the fires of hell. If only he could make that dream come true, he'd die a happy man.

He helped himself to a lozenge and licked his lips.

It was after hours and the guardhouse was closed. A gent quick-marched to the car and asked for ID.

'Detective Constable Bryant,' said Bryant. 'Metropolitan Police.'

He flashed his warrant card.

'Mayhew,' said the gent. 'Bursar. I'll take you up, if you don't mind, sir.'

He hopped into the car.

Bryant didn't mind a bit. A show of respect for the plod was rare these days.

The long, winding drive was dark. Bryant flicked on the headlights.

'Get much of this sort of thing, do you?' he said. 'Boys going off the rails?'

'Doesn't innocent until proven guilty apply to Palmerston Hall scholars?' said Mayhew.

That was the end of that conversation.

He parked as directed by Mayhew, who then escorted him into the imposing building and along various corridors until they reached a sort of waiting room.

'Take a seat. The Head will be out in a minute,' said Mayhew, and then left him to it.

Bryant felt constrained to sit upright on the uncomfortable chair. He worked hard at being studiously unimpressed by the oil paintings of old boys hung around the room, who included prime ministers, admirals and air vice marshals. It seemed many had died serving Queen and Country. Probably of gout in an armchair at their club.

He rose when a woman appeared.

'Detective Constable Bryant?' she said.

'Yes,' said Bryant. 'I believe the headmaster's expecting me.'

'I am,' she said. She extended her hand. 'Flora Trevelyan, head of Palmerston Hall.'

Forty minutes later, Bryant drove away from Palmerston Hall with Chen's passport in his pocket and not much else to show for the trip, so disconcerted had he been by the charming, attractive woman who had urged him to take another home-made biscuit because Cook was rightly proud of them.

He banged the steering wheel. There was no fool like an old fool. Gran would have chuckled to see how easily his head could be turned; Flora Trevelyan had deflected his mumbled questions with ease.

Philip Chen was an orphan with no known family in China. According to the terms of his scholarship, the head of Palmerston Hall, whoever he or she might be at the time, was his legal guardian until he reached eighteen.

When Bryant had tried, meekly, to suggest that the boy was spending his weekends unsupervised and possibly engaged in unhealthy activities, Trevelyan had smiled and explained that at seventeen he was legally entitled to come and go as he pleased.

The only stipulation was that his housemaster should be aware of his whereabouts and he was to comply with all the usual rules and regs applying to boarders. Financially he was independent. The scholarship paid him a generous stipend.

When Bryant asked about Chen's academic performance, Trevelyan indicated it was satisfactory. Didn't the awarding of a scholarship mean the boy was clever? Trevelyan wouldn't be drawn on that, and he had been too awestruck to press her, like a tongue-tied probationer.

Still, he had the distinct impression that very little was expected of Chen, by her or the Anglo-Chinese Friendship Society. But when he observed that the trustees of the charity seemed very generous, Trevelyan had corrected him. It wasn't a charitable trust; it was a family trust.

He didn't need three guesses.

IO

At one in the morning, Berlin's agitation reached a peak. It wasn't unusual; in the small hours, no amount of Scotch could assuage the restlessness that infested her bones. She laced up her Peacekeeper boots, donned her long coat and tucked her straggly blonde hair under a black woollen watch cap.

She was unafraid on the street because she knew she looked like someone who should be given a wide berth.

It wasn't just an impression.

Her insomnia had little to do with her addiction; in fact, she struggled to remember which had come first. Her soul was nocturnal. She found peace when walking, roaming silent canal paths in the east, or prowling the secret gardens and alleys of the City of London.

Tonight, in a break from routine, she walked west. At a reasonable pace it would take her about an hour and a half to reach her destination, a leafy, fashionable corner of London where large detached mansions sat amidst grounds that had resisted subdivision.

No one knew who really owned the Abbey, although it had been in operation for decades. It was held privately, behind a series of companies registered offshore.

Discretion was still the better part of valour in the English canon. It also beat the taxman.

By the time she approached the high red-brick wall, the woollen cap was soaked with sweat. She couldn't remove it because her hair would reflect the light. This foray had to be low-key.

The Abbey had a policy that new admissions were not allowed visitors for the first seventy-two hours of their stay, when many clients were at the peak of their agitation because the medication hadn't kicked in; this was exactly the state in which she hoped she would find Philip Chen.

He would be more forthcoming when vulnerable.

All visitors had to be on a list and screened on arrival. Mobiles, electronic devices, weapons and drugs were surrendered at reception. This included nicotine. Residents weren't allowed phones or computers lest they retard the process of breaking ties with the *wrong crowd*.

The Abbey was a very plush Pentonville.

Whether or not Chen had problems other than anger management, it would be a good place to keep him under wraps. It was well appointed and the staff were circumspect. It welcomed rock stars, footballers and politicians; anyone suffering from *nervous exhaustion* who could afford the privilege of dealing with their issues in luxury.

In the eighties it had been known as the Magic Mountain. Celebrity rehab.

The security, designed principally to keep out the paparazzi, was weak at night, when the conditions for long-range photography were poor. Precautions were limited to motion-detector floodlights. These presented no challenge if you were careful, and anyway, no one took any notice when they lit up, because foxes kept triggering them.

Berlin squeezed through the grand wrought-iron gates. Avoiding the drive and the flagstone path that cut across the lawn, she circled the building and made her way to the back door. Blinds covered the windows, but light leaked out at the edges. The night staff were up and about.

A couple of overflowing skips stood on concrete pavers near a back door, the smell of warm bread drifting from a vent above it. The Abbey baked their own bread, naturally.

Berlin tiptoed across the gravel and hid between the skips. Five minutes later the door opened. A man in a uniform emerged, closed the door quietly and took something from his pocket.

Berlin stepped out.

The man started and dropped a pack of cigarettes.

'Fekkin' 'ell,' he said.

'Hello, Colin,' said Berlin. 'Old habits die hard, eh?'

Colin Shearer was the night porter, which was tantamount to putting the fox in charge of the henhouse. Berlin had never been a resident, but Colin himself had spent some time there when it was still possible to do the detox programme on the National Health Service. That was once-upon-a-time ago.

She and Colin had moved in similar circles back in the day. Neither of them could remember much about it.

Colin had never left the Abbey, graduating from client to employee. The management had recognised he was indispensable to the smooth running of the place.

Popularly known as 'Tesco' – every little helps – Colin supplied the bulimics with Dunkin' Donuts, the anorexics with laxatives, the alcoholics with vodka and the junkies with any sort of drug they cared to name.

Berlin had stayed in touch with him over the years. A surprising number of the cokehead bankers she had pursued as a financial investigator eventually wound up at the Abbey.

Colin was always ready, on a quid pro quo basis, to give her access or the intel she needed on their associates. The only substance he still struggled with was nicotine, a predilection now regarded as the most antisocial habit of them all.

Berlin sat a few feet away as he lit up.

'How did he look?' she asked.

'Pretty crap,' said Colin. 'During handover the charge nurse said he was volatile, which round here translates as "in a right state". Poor little bugger.'

Colin was a true humanitarian; he couldn't bear to see another creature suffer. He didn't make a fortune out of his retail activities, just expenses, which was why he'd never been ratted out. Life was too short, according to Colin, to deny yourself.

'Detox?' said Berlin.

'Believe it,' said Colin. 'He came back positive on every test except blood. Urine, saliva and hair.'

She should have known. It was probably ice. Dirt cheap, popular with youth and easily capable of triggering an overreaction. It would explain the assault.

'Methamphetamine?' she said.

'Opiates,' said Colin.

That was a surprise.

'The detection window for opiates in urine is two to four days, right?'

'Yeah,' said Colin.

Philip Chen had been arrested on Monday and tested by the Abbey late Tuesday morning, which meant he'd been using over the weekend, presumably while he was at Haileybury's.

'Bring him down to the laundry, will you, Colin?' said Berlin. 'I need a word.'

Colin glanced at his watch.

She handed over the usual fee.

II

The laundry was a cavernous, dimly lit basement with plenty of dark nooks and crannies in which business could be transacted, veiled by the constant rumble of washing machines and dryers. Telltale smoke was also masked by the overpowering odour of industrial disinfectant and detergent.

The door opened. A slim figure, silhouetted against the bright light of the hallway, hesitated.

'Over here,' said Berlin. 'My name's Berlin. I'm working for Lord Haileybury.'

Philip shuffled towards her. The door closed behind him.

'Jack sent you?' he said.

'Jack?' said Berlin.

'Haileybury,' said Philip.

His tone was testy, as if she was being deliberately obtuse.

'Right,' said Berlin. 'Jack sent me. Have you spoken to him?'

'The police took my phone and then they gave it to the people here.'

'I can give him a message, if you like,' said Berlin.

'What about?' he said.

It was difficult to tell if his reactions were off because of the medication or if his confusion was genuine.

'I don't know,' said Berlin. 'Thank you, or I'm fine, or sorry?'

'I'm not fine,' said Philip.

'I get that,' said Berlin.

And you're not sorry.

'Why are you here?' said Philip.

'Haileybury – Jack – wants me to make some enquiries about what happened on Monday,' said Berlin.

Philip sank to the floor and hugged his knees.

'Colin lied,' he said. 'You haven't got anything for me.'

Berlin sat down beside him.

'I need to ask you some questions about the man you had the altercation with.'

Softly, softly. I'm on your side.

'What about him?' said Philip.

'He hasn't reported the incident,' said Berlin. 'And the police can't find him, although it appears he was injured, possibly quite badly.'

'I suppose he doesn't want to report it because he's a pervert,' said Philip. 'I was defending myself against his disgusting advances.'

'Give me a fucking break,' said Berlin.

She bit her lip. Softly, softly hadn't lasted long.

'What does that mean?' said Philip. 'Whose side are you on anyway?'

'Was the man you bashed Chinese, Philip?' she said.

He stared at her, wide-eyed. 'Why would you ask that?' he said.

He immediately realised his mistake.

'No, no,' he said. 'He wasn't Chinese.'

'Come on, Philip,' said Berlin. 'You need to be straight with me. I *am* on your side, but if you lie to me it's going to cause problems.'

'I can't think straight,' he said.

He was on the verge of tears, clenching and unclenching his fists, sweating, jumping out of his skin.

It was all too familiar.

'I understand,' said Berlin.

'You can't possibly,' said Philip. 'This is hell.'

'Isn't the medication helping?' said Berlin.

'It's not the same,' said Philip.

His desperation struck home.

'Tell me about it,' she said.

Philip frowned.

She raised her empty hands in a gesture of resignation.

'Heroin,' she said. 'Twenty-five years, on and off.'

More on than off, although she'd been clean for nearly eighteen months.

'Oh God,' said Philip. 'Can this go on for a lifetime?'

She had no good news for him.

The machines either side of them thumped and whirred. A sharp tang of industrial solvents hung in the warm air.

There was nothing like addiction to bring people together. Age, gender, class; all differences dissolved in a deep empathy. Disgrace, shame, longing. Pariah status worked like magic, creating a bond.

'What was it all about, Philip?' she said. 'He was Chinese . . .'

'I never said that,' said Philip.

'I know what you said. He was Chinese. Who was he, exactly?' said Berlin. 'I've seen the CCTV. He spoke to you. What did he say?'

Philip studied her for a moment.

'Do you think you can help me out?' he said.

It was almost disingenuous. Junkies. Always had their eyes on the prize, no matter what.

Two could play at that game.

'Maybe,' said Berlin. 'Later.'

Philip glanced around the laundry, as if someone could be hiding and listening to their conversation.

'If you help me,' he said, 'I'll tell you everything.'

Colin switched off the alarm to let her out.

'Can you get hold of his mobile?' she said.

'No way,' said Colin. 'They keep them in the safe.'

'He thought I was delivering dope,' she said.

'I didn't exactly say that,' said Colin. 'But I had to say something to get him down there. He seemed scared.'

'Keep an eye on him for me, will you?' said Berlin. 'Let me know if anything unusual goes on.'

Colin laughed. 'Around here,' he said, 'we don't really do usual.'

Berlin walked home along streets that were busy with London's scurrying night denizens: rats, foxes and the homeless, all competing for a dry bed and the contents of rubbish bins.

Confessing her addiction to Philip had taken her by surprise. Sharing wasn't in her nature, even when it might prove useful. The career path facing Philip, who was using more than recreationally, wasn't a happy one.

High-functioning addicts were either rich or lucky, or both. Or they were remnants of Berlin's own era, when users had been treated in a humane way by the medical profession.

Philip's generation of users was automatically regarded as weak-willed, disease-ridden and amoral, antisocial parasites for whom prison was too good and abstinence the only option.

She had managed her own dependence so efficiently that her mother had only recently discovered she'd been using heroin most of her adult life. As a result, their always rocky relationship had taken a turn for the worse.

Drugs were something that people, particularly parents, associated with teenagers, not, as Peggy had put it, women getting on for pension age who should know better.

The row that followed had been vicious.

She quickened her pace in a bid to outrun her train of thought. But when she turned into her street, she stopped dead. Her flat was lit up like Christmas.

The front door was ajar. Berlin pushed it open gently and peered inside. There was someone shuffling around in the kitchen, but from here she couldn't see who it was; she took a deep breath, counted to three, then kicked the door wide open and stomped inside.

Del dropped the tea caddy. Earl Grey spilt everywhere. 'Shit!' he said.

'For God's sake, Del. What are you doing?' said Berlin. 'It's five in the fucking morning.'

His shock turned to anger.

She was so surprised she retreated. He never lost his temper.

'Why didn't you tell me about Peggy?' he said.

She didn't know what to say.

They were surrounded by bulging cardboard boxes stuffed with china figurines, Reader's Digest classic collections, old Constable calendars and carnival glassware.

The detritus of her mother's life.

She felt giddy, teetering at the brink of a precipice. Her knees went from under her and the light receded to a pinprick.

12

The next thing she knew, Del was handing her a mug of tea, probably made from Earl Grey scooped off the floor.

'Christ, I didn't faint, did I?' she said.

'Yeah,' said Del. 'But you don't get out of it that easily. I still want an explanation.'

'I don't want to talk about it,' said Berlin.

It sounded as weak as she felt.

'For God's sake,' muttered Del. 'When did it happen?'

'Ten days ago. The funeral was on Monday.'

'Did Bella go with you?' said Del.

'She's away,' said Berlin.

'She's very fond of you,' said Del. 'She keeps an eye out for you, you know.'

'Yeah, through the spyhole in her front door,' said Berlin.

'What's got into you?' said Del.

'Nothing,' said Berlin. She sipped her tea. 'I don't want to talk about it.'

She made an effort to lighten the tone.

'You're lucky I didn't call the constabulary when I saw the front door,' she said.

'I thought if I left it open you'd know it was me,' said Del.

'Why?' said Berlin.

'Because I'm the registered key holder, remember?'

He found a dustpan and brush in the cupboard under the sink and began to sweep up the rest of the tea leaves.

Berlin put her mug on the table and reached for the bottle of Talisker.

'Grab a couple of glasses, will you?' she said.

He did as she asked, giving them a quick wipe with a clean tea towel that happened to be peeking out of one of Peggy's boxes.

'Where have you been?' said Del. 'I've been trying to get in touch with you. Out on the prowl?'

He handed her the glasses. She poured and handed one back to him.

'I went to the Abbey to see Philip Chen,' she said. 'I thought he might know something that would help me find his victim.'

She raised her glass.

'Cheers,' she said. 'The dear departed.'

Del frowned. Either he didn't approve or he wasn't buying the act. She didn't care. The Scotch tasted the same. He sipped his. She knocked hers back and poured another.

'Don't you think it's a big investment in the future of a seventeen-year-old boy?' she said. 'Me, the lawyer, the Abbey.'

'There's a real risk to Haileybury's reputation,' said Del.

'He could use the law to protect that,' she said. 'Defamation takes a deep pocket, which is not his problem. But what he's doing could actually increase his exposure. It's overkill, unless there's more at stake here than he's letting on. Why don't you ask Sir Simon what this job is really about?'

'Be serious,' said Del. 'We're paid to do a job and keep our mouths shut.'

'We, white man?' said Berlin. 'I'm the one out there fighting the good fight.'

He gave her a wan smile. Del was the son of a Jewish dad and a Jamaican mum who held strong and opposing views about everything. He was a negotiator, not a scrapper.

'Christ, I nearly forgot,' he said. 'He's been trying to reach you. Haileybury, that is.'

Her phone had been switched to silent while she was at the Abbey. She took it out of her pocket: five calls from Del, and before that, three from Haileybury.

'When he couldn't get hold of you, he called Sir Simon, and Sir Simon called me,' said Del. 'Once I was awake, I thought I'd make an early start and pop over. Haileybury's an important client and, you know . . .'

She knew. It was nothing to do with Haileybury. When she didn't respond to his calls, Del started to worry.

With abstinence came reduced tolerance and, if you fell off the wagon, an overdose. It was one of the reasons she hadn't told him about Peggy. He would be clucking around her like a mother hen, trying to protect her from herself.

'But if you feel, you know, that you need some time . . .' said Del.

'Oh for God's sake,' said Berlin. 'This is exactly why I didn't tell you about Peggy.'

'What do you mean?' said Del.

'You want me to sit around weeping because I've just buried my mother?'

'No, I . . .'

'Actually I left before the burial part,' she said. 'So drop the care and concern and let me get on with my job. What does Haileybury want at this godforsaken hour anyway?'

'Apparently there's a body in the river,' said Del.

'So?' said Berlin.

'He's in a state about it,' said Del. 'Worried that it's your victim, I suppose.'

'Oh for fuck's sake. Bodies turn up in the river all the time,' said Berlin. 'And he's not *my* victim. Even if it is him, what am I supposed to do about it?'

She wasn't at the beck and call of some lord.

'He wants you to go over there and check it out,' said Del.

'That's ridiculous,' said Berlin.

'Remember the golden rule,' said Del.

'Yeah,' said Berlin. 'The man with the gold rules.'

She poured another Scotch. She was going to need it.

13

Lee switched on his desk lamp, lit a cigarette and opened the photos that an email informed him were waiting on the server. He preferred to think of himself as an early riser rather than a poor sleeper. Strong black coffee helped him maintain the fiction.

A series of shots taken with a telephoto lens filled his screen. The report noted that the subject had been at court, although she didn't appear to be a police officer, at least not of the regular kind, or a social worker or a lawyer. Nor did she fit the profile of a friend of the family. Women didn't play a large part in the Haileybury milieu.

It was possible she'd been assigned as personal protection for Philip; an older woman flew under the radar. She was somewhat frayed around the edges, but with a certain steely quality. She could carry an armoury under that long black garment, and the boots would be readily weaponised. The limp spoke of an ancient affray.

He picked up the phone and dialled.

When his call was answered, it was clear he'd woken the indolent brute. Good, it would keep him on his toes.

'I want you to keep a close eye on this woman. Find out who she is and what she's up to,' he said.

He heard a cigarette being lit, followed by coughing.

'For God's sake, she's just an old woman,' came the grumbled response. 'What kind of problem could she be?'

It was the sort of lazy thinking he had to contend with every day.

'Don't underestimate her,' he said. 'She could be working for our counterparts. Find out. Get on to it. Now.'

He hung up.

When you'd lived as long as he had, you learnt that the old were much more dangerous than the young; they had so little left to lose.

The dawn was murky, obliging the police launch to use its twin floodlights. They were trained on the old watermen's stairs. The beams rose and fell as the launch bobbed up and down with the current, catching the narrow passage beyond the stairs in the fluctuating light.

Now you see it, now you don't.

Berlin made a beeline not for the most senior but the most weather-beaten officer present: a constable. He was leaning over the embankment on the other side of Haileybury's place, watching his colleagues corralling a body with two long poles. Berlin joined him.

It was a delicate operation. The corpse, floating face down, kept drifting away from them. One sleeve had become entangled with the rusty rods protruding from the reinforced concrete on the watermen's stairs.

'Why is it taking so long?' said Berlin.

'If they snare it too forcefully, bits could become detached and they'll be obliged to dive for them or chase them down the river,' said the constable.

A mackintosh ballooned out around the body.

'What do you think?' she said.

The constable didn't look up.

Experts when it came to the impact of tide, current and temperature on the condition of a corpse, it was said the water police could even tell you which bridge a jumper had gone off. Pathologists deferred to them on how long a body had been in the water.

'Mmmm,' he mused. 'Difficult to say from here.' He scratched his grey stubble.

'Take a guess,' she said.

'Burberry,' he said.

'What?' said Berlin.

'The raincoat. It's a Burberry.'

He looked at her and grinned.

'Ha ha,' said Berlin. 'Very bloody funny.'

Someone shouted. They both turned.

Bryant was barrelling towards them.

'Say nothing,' he shouted. He was addressing the constable. 'Don't tell her anything.'

The constable muttered something. It could have been *oh no*.

Bryant was breathless by the time he reached them.

'She could be a suspect,' he announced, taking Berlin by the arm and leading her away from the embankment and back to the street. The constable followed.

She didn't resist because she wanted the assembled coppers to see she was cooperative, and bemused.

Rather than lift the body into the launch and take it to the police landing dock, they had manoeuvred it on to a stretcher, which was being drawn up the watermen's stairs by their colleagues.

The coroner's van was waiting.

Bryant had the tousled, wild-eyed look of someone who had woken violently.

'What's all this about, Bryant?' said the constable.

Berlin noticed he didn't address Bryant as 'Detective', a courtesy that would usually be extended in front of a civilian. The other police present were grinning. Bryant was apparently not held in high regard.

He pointed an accusing finger at Berlin.

'This person, acting on behalf of a corrupt third party, is pursuing the missing victim of a vicious assault in order to silence him.'

There was some truth in it.

The coroner's assistants were advancing towards them, wheeling the gurney on to which the police had transferred the body.

'Who's this corrupt party, then?' asked the constable.

Bryant pointed at the warehouse.

It seemed it was common knowledge who lived there.

'And when was this assault?' said the constable.

'Monday morning,' said Bryant. 'Not far from this very spot.'

'And what, she came along and pushed him in, did she?' said the constable.

There was the sound of suppressed sniggering in the background. The coroner's assistants were steering the gurney towards their van.

'Hang on a minute,' said the constable.

The assistants stopped, but the sodden body on the smooth steel surface of the gurney didn't. The bloke at the rear leaned forward to grab it, but the mackintosh, smeared with green slime from the stairs, was slippery, and the body slid off the gurney. Its head almost hit the cobblestones.

The coroner's assistant hung on to the legs as best he could.

The constable didn't seem the least bit disconcerted.

He squatted to stare at the upside-down face of the deceased, cocking his head to get a better look.

Berlin was aware of a sharp repellent odour lingering beneath the more musky smell of mould.

'Your victim was running around Monday, was he, Bryant?' said the constable. 'Today's Wednesday.'

'Yes,' said Bryant. He didn't take his eyes off Berlin.

'Well, this bloke has been in the river for at least a week,' said the sergeant. 'So I think the lady's off the hook. So to speak.'

The sniggering turned to guffaws.

Bryant flushed scarlet. He let go of Berlin, stomped over to the body, bent down and peered at it. When he straightened up, he turned on his heel and marched away.

The coroner's assistants joined in the general laughter that followed him.

He was an idiot, but Berlin felt for him. To all intents and purposes he was doing his job. The scenario was plausible; the victim could have staggered down the passage and fallen in. Plausible, but wrong.

The bit about her being a suspect was paranoid and delusional, but she had some sympathy with that, too. She'd found herself on the wilder reaches of speculation at times, later discovering that the truth was even worse than she'd imagined. Humanity was capable of such ugliness, it was easier to turn away. Most people did. Bryant didn't.

The constable watched him disappear down Wapping High Street, then turned to Berlin.

'Watch out for him,' he said. 'He's a weird one, and there's a bit of history between him and the earl.'

He walked away before she could ask him what it was.

There was no light in Haileybury's window at the top of the warehouse, but she felt sure he was watching.

14

Berlin stood at Haileybury's terrace doors and watched the sky lighten, slate to dove grey. The earl looked and smelt as if he'd been up all night drinking. He was drawn, and his hand trembled as he poured their Scotch.

'Heart-starter,' he said.

He handed her a cut-glass tumbler that winked as it caught the first rays of the sun.

'Would you mind?' he said, indicating the doors.

She slid them open and followed him out on to the terrace.

'I'm really so sorry I called you out on a wild goose chase,' he said. 'I became a little overwrought during the night, as one does when one is alone with one's thoughts.'

If it was designed to disarm her, it worked.

'There's no need to apologise,' said Berlin. 'That's what I'm paid for, to be your eyes and ears on the ground.'

'Nevertheless, my imagination rather ran riot when I saw the police launch below,' said Haileybury. 'And then there was the unfortunate intervention by the detective involved with Philip's case.'

'Look at it this way,' said Berlin. 'If that bloke had been recently deceased, Bryant would have been all over it, trying to make a connection. He's very determined to make Philip pay.'

'Why?' said Haileybury.

'It seems he has some personal issues with you,' said Berlin.

'Me?' said Haileybury.

'Detective Constable Terence Bryant,' said Berlin. 'Ring a bell?'

'No,' said Haileybury.

'But you have contacts in the Met?' said Berlin.

'Well, yes,' said Haileybury. 'But not at that level.'

The implication being that there was no one worth knowing below the rank of commissioner.

It was mild, but Haileybury shivered in the breeze from the river, so they went back inside. Once the terrace doors were closed, the warehouse felt warm and dry.

'It's always so comfortable in here,' said Berlin. 'It's impressive, given the size of the place.'

'The air conditioning is museum standard,' said Haileybury. 'A certain temperature and humidity are essential to the preservation of the collection. I think it helps to preserve me, too.'

He sat down in his wingback chair with a grimace.

'Please sit, Berlin,' he said.

She remained standing.

'Did you know Philip used drugs?' she said.

'Ah,' said Haileybury.

He fiddled with the electric kettle on the table and searched amongst the detritus.

'Where are those tea bags?' he said.

So he did know.

'The Abbey tests everyone,' said Berlin. 'He was positive for opiates.'

'Yes,' said Haileybury. 'I was aware he would need some assistance in that respect, which is why the Abbey was the best place for him.'

'Thanks for the heads-up,' she said.

'I didn't think it was material,' said Haileybury.

She took a deep breath and reminded herself he was the client.

'Philip's victim was Chinese,' she said.

Haileybury's eyes lit up.

'You see,' he said. 'I was right.'

'Perhaps,' said Berlin. 'But he was also his dealer.'

Haileybury frowned.

'It explains why he left the scene in such a hurry and why Philip is so reluctant to talk about him,' said Berlin.

'How did you come to this conclusion?' said Haileybury.

'I didn't,' said Berlin. 'Philip admitted it. He didn't go into details, but I'm guessing either he owes this person money, or he's being shaken down. Given his connection with you, that's a real possibility.'

Haileybury seemed to be miles away, as though he hadn't heard a word she said. She pressed on.

'Of course, there's no reason why a dealer couldn't also be working for the Chinese government, but it seems unlikely. The simplest explanation is usually the best.'

'That's your professional opinion?' said Haileybury.

It was an odd remark, and disconcerting given that she was trying to handle the whole thing with some sensitivity. She was tired and he was starting to get on her nerves.

'Yes,' she said. 'We need Philip to confirm the details, to drop this sexual provocation ploy and explain why he really acted as he did. Then you and the lawyer will be able to make a more informed choice about the best way to proceed.'

Haileybury sighed.

'If only it were that simple,' he said.

'What's the problem?' said Berlin.

'This fellow isn't Philip's drug dealer,' said Haileybury.

'How can you be so sure?' said Berlin.

'Because I am,' he said.

15

Bryant was summoned to Tomalin's office first thing. The inspector made no attempt to hide his contempt. Bryant met his gaze, unrepentant.

'You look like shite, Bryant,' said Tomalin.

'Thank you, sir,' said Bryant.

'What have you got to say for yourself? The water police are having a good laugh at our expense.'

'If you'll let me explain, sir. I may have been a little hasty, but I have reason to believe someone will try to get to the victim of this assault and persuade him not to testify. One way or another.'

'That's a serious accusation, Bryant. Got any evidence to back that up?'

Bryant remained silent.

'No? I thought not,' said Tomalin. 'The boy alleges some sort of indecent harassment, doesn't he? So what's your damn point?'

'We don't know the full story, sir,' said Bryant. 'For starters, what was this public schoolboy doing in Wapping at that hour on a Monday morning?'

'It doesn't matter,' said Tomalin.

'With respect, sir, we don't know the extent of the victim's injuries, and this private investigator has been hired by—'

'Stop right there,' barked Tomalin. 'I don't want to hear it. Do the paperwork and forget this case. It's a waste of bloody time. That's an order.'

Bryant clamped his mouth shut before he said something he regretted. This lot were all in it together. He turned and walked out smartly, leaving the door open behind him.

'And clean yourself up, man,' shouted Tomalin.

Bryant was surprised to find himself walking beside the river as the red mist subsided. The bloody water police. Gossiping like old fishwives. When he went in for the police, everyone expected him to join them eventually, because he lived so close to the station.

But the truth was he was frightened of the water. It was only through luck that he'd passed his swimming test when he joined the Met.

It was at the municipal baths in Mile End. He'd spent a sleepless night worrying how he was going to get through it. When he got there, bright and early, they told him the boiler had broken down.

The place was freezing and the instructor just wanted the test over and done with. He'd told Bryant to get in the water, while he sloped off to the nice warm café next door for a cup of tea.

Bryant got into the shallow end and stood there until the instructor came back. By then he was blue with cold and the instructor shouted at him to get out and go and get a hot drink. It wasn't really cheating. He'd done exactly as he'd been told.

The irony was you didn't even have to pretend to be able to swim to join the Met these days. And all shapes, sizes, colours and so-called sexual orientations were welcome.

His humiliation this morning had yielded a valuable lesson, and he wasn't going to waste it. Bugger the inspector. Haileybury was definitely in this up to his neck. He must have called Berlin to see what was going on when he saw there was a body in the river, which meant he also thought there was a possibility Chen's victim could be dead.

So far these enquiries had been conducted more or less in accordance with standard procedure, but it was time to go off piste.

He'd missed something and he was bloody sure that Berlin would know what it was; he would take a closer look at her. There had to be a reason she'd been roped in by the earl, and if he could find it, it might just point him in the right direction.

He shoved two Fisherman's Friends in his mouth, then another. He wasn't obsessed, he was just thorough.

A bloody dealer. Berlin strode along the Thames Path, oblivious to the pain in her feet. She'd tried, unsuccessfully, to slam the front door on her way out of Haileybury's, but she'd made her feelings pretty clear before she'd left.

Burghley had sold her a pup. Her discretion and sensitivity had nothing to do with this job; it was all about her addiction.

Sir Simon bloody May had bet on the fact that if she worked out what was actually going on, she would turn a blind eye. What really pissed her off was that she hadn't been told up front. Without a thorough briefing she would waste time chasing down irrelevant leads.

Lord Haileybury, purveyor of dope to the young, banging on about his collection and a Chinese conspiracy. What was the point of all that nonsense? Philip had acknowledged his victim was Chinese, but if he wasn't the boy's dealer, perhaps he was Haileybury's.

Given her history, Berlin would have a much better chance of finding him than most people. Perhaps Bryant was on the money: Haileybury wanted the victim found so he could arrange a pay-off, or worse. She was the perfect candidate for the job all right. Tight-lipped and unorthodox.

Now she would show them touchy.

She took out her mobile and made a call.

'Limehouse police station,' answered a bored voice.

'Detective Bryant, please,' said Berlin.

'Hang on,' came the response. A tinny version of Pachelbel's Canon drifted down the line.

Berlin paused and glanced around; without noticing, she'd walked all the way to the lock at Limehouse Basin.

It was a location she avoided. The turbid water was a reminder of past mistakes.

'He's not in,' said the bored voice. 'Want to leave a message?'

A rat ran along a line securing a narrow boat to a pontoon and slithered into the mucky pool. She'd seen the result of her recklessness washed up amongst its curdled scum once before.

'No,' said Berlin. She hung up.

Sir Simon was vindicated. She would turn a blind eye.

The pain in her feet was suddenly unbearable.

Philip was the real victim here. Whatever Bryant's attitude, the boy would suffer the most – he already had – and she didn't want to make it worse.

Was it a convenient rationalisation? Telling herself she was protecting the boy allowed her to assume the moral high ground. She knew in some deep recess of her heart that she had a less laudable motive.

A voice she recognised – comforting, seductive – was asking her if she was really going to walk away from this.

She turned and went back the way she'd come.

Strange Heavens and Dull Hells

16

The charge nurse at the Abbey was less than impressed by Bryant's warrant card.

'He's not allowed visitors yet. Come back tomorrow,' he said. 'Anyway, he's having a late lunch.'

'I'm not a bloody visitor, I'm a police officer,' said Bryant. 'I can get a couple of local uniforms to drop in and say hello on a regular basis, which I'm sure will be a great comfort to your clients, or you can get Chen down here and find me an empty office so we can have a quiet chat. He can have his late lunch later.'

The office was small, but the charge had been kind enough to provide a cup of tea and a plate of biscuits while he waited. When he ushered Chen in, the boy peered at Bryant as if he'd never seen him before. His lips were flecked with white at the corners and he moved slowly, as if his limbs were too heavy.

He was doped up to the eyeballs.

'I didn't realise his nerves were that bad,' said Bryant.

The charge nurse looked at Bryant as if he were thick. The penny dropped. So this was the first thing he'd missed: Chen was on drugs. They were weaning him on to legal ones.

Bryant gave the charge a nod. He got the message and left.

'Sit down, Philip, before you fall down,' said Bryant.

Philip complied.

'Do you know who I am?' said Bryant.

Philip nodded. 'Where's my lawyer?' he said.

'You don't need a lawyer today,' said Bryant. He helped himself to a shortbread. 'This is strictly informal. Off the record. You know what that means?'

Philip's head drooped. He could nod off at any moment.

'It means I can't use anything you tell me in court,' said Bryant. 'So there's nothing to worry about.'

'Okay,' said Philip.

'I understand you're an orphan, Philip,' said Bryant.

Philip nodded.

'I know what that's like,' said Bryant. 'My mum died when I was little. I was brought up by my Gran.'

'What about your father?' said Philip.

'I never knew him,' said Bryant.

They'd had a name for children like him. He'd first heard it in the playground. When he went home and asked his Gran why they were calling him a bastard, she gave him a clip round the ear.

'Do you know a woman called Berlin?' said Bryant.

'Yes,' said Philip.

'She works for your friend Lord Haileybury,' said Bryant.

'Yeah,' said Philip.

'So what's she doing for him?'

'Don't know,' said Philip.

'I suppose he thought she would be able to help you out in some way.'

'Not really,' said Philip. His lip curled.

'Oh?' said Bryant. 'Don't you like her?'

'She's a drug addict,' said Philip.

Bryant was stunned. He quickly gathered himself, careful not to overreact.

'What makes you say that?' he said.

'She told me,' said Philip. He helped himself to a biscuit. 'Why don't you arrest her?'

Bryant believed him. It wasn't the sort of thing you'd make up out of thin air.

But for some reason, watching this privileged little shit throw Berlin under a bus really stuck in his craw.

'How did you meet her?' he said.

'She came to see me,' said Philip.

'Are you a drug addict, Philip?' said Bryant.

'No,' said Philip. 'I've got a nervous disposition.'

Haileybury led the way to an arrangement of armchairs, chaise longues and side tables. Two walls were taken up with floor-to-ceiling mahogany bookcases. A magnificent roll-top desk occupied one corner. Cabinets displaying muskets and other antique firearms lined another wall. Velvet upholstery was rampant. There were even velvet drapes, although the room was windowless.

'A Victorian gentleman's smoking room,' said Berlin. 'Now all we need is a gentleman.'

Haileybury chuckled. He hadn't seemed surprised to see her at the door again after her angry departure. He'd admitted her without comment, his manner circumspect and respectful. Berlin recognised it as empathy with the fallen.

They had travelled down on the steel platform, so this was either a basement or a cellar.

The tall, straight walls of the warehouse were a facade that contained a densely constructed labyrinth. She stood in front of a large oil painting of a beautiful three-mast square-rigged vessel running before a storm.

'It was my great-great-grandfather's,' said Haileybury.

'The painting?' said Berlin.

'The ship,' said Haileybury.

She should have known.

'A clipper,' said Haileybury. 'One of the fastest, at the time.'

'Tea?' said Berlin.

'In a manner of speaking,' said Haileybury. 'Opium. He shipped it from India to China, sold it and brought back tea to slake the insatiable thirst of the British public.'

So dealing was a family tradition.

'That's a lot of firepower,' said Berlin.

Both sides of the clipper were bristling with cannon.

'Pirates, hostile natives and so forth,' said Haileybury. 'It wasn't a pleasure cruise.'

By hostile natives she supposed he meant the Chinese themselves. *Plus ça change.*

A drinks tray waited on one of the side tables.

Haileybury poured two large Scotches, then, with the air of a man performing a sombre ritual, went to the desk, took a key from his pocket, unlocked a drawer and withdrew a filigreed silver box.

Returning to the side table, he opened the box and with a tiny silver spatula scooped up a smidgen of the black, tar-like substance it contained. He dropped some first in one glass, then the other, and swirled them around.

'A special blend,' he said. 'Would you care to join me?'

17

Before he left the Abbey, Bryant checked the visitors' book.

Catherine Berlin's name didn't appear.

'He's got a nervous disposition, has he?' said Bryant.

The charge nurse pulled a face.

'Haven't they all?' he said. 'The food's rubbish, the pillows are all wrong . . .'

'Who's paying the bill?' said Bryant.

The charge nurse shrugged.

'Any flowers, fruit, messages, that sort of thing?' said Bryant.

'Only from the lawyer,' said the charge nurse. 'I feel sorry for the kid in a way. No one seems to care.'

He was wrong. There was someone who did.

Before he got in the car, Bryant called Berlin, but was flicked to voicemail.

'Bryant here,' he said. 'I've just been to visit your boy at the Abbey. You'd better give me a call.'

If Chen was right and Berlin had a drug problem, it would give him some useful leverage. He might even be able to persuade her to play on his team.

She didn't strike him as a natural ally of the gentry.

*

The ease Berlin felt was beyond compare; she was sick of living with the swamp inside her, tired of constantly tiptoeing across its surface for fear of sinking into anxiety and despair.

Haileybury introduced her to the pipe, producing from the silver box a block of uncut, unadulterated opium in a quantity sufficient to buy her flat and those of her neighbours.

In the smoke, all care dissipated and all concern drifted into the distance, whence it could be viewed with detachment. Wrapped in a blanket of luxury and privilege, she was fearless. Wealth was one thing, but when coupled with power and connections, it was unassailable.

Realising she was alone, she wandered amongst the beguiling treasures; behind a beautiful four-panel black lacquered screen she found a low door. Giggling, she bent and tried the iron ring handle, but it was locked.

A mechanical noise broke the silence and Haileybury rose into the room accompanied by a draught of cold air. The Wizard of Oz. Berlin laughed. The platform shuddered to a halt. So there was another floor below this one.

Haileybury smiled, stepped off the platform and returned to his armchair. He was moving more freely. He opened the Scotch without wincing, and poured a drink using a hand that was not rigid.

When he saw she was watching, he gestured with his fingers, as if he was sprinkling fairy dust. 'It's the only time I'm pain-free,' he said.

Berlin realised that her legs and feet weren't aching.

There were four portraits hanging on one wall. 'Who are they?' she said.

Haileybury came and stood beside her, pointing at each one in turn. 'That's my great-great-grandfather, the fifth earl, of whom you've already heard. This fellow is the sixth, my great-grandfather, a wonderful inventor. And this one is my grandfather, the seventh Earl Haileybury, who was a complete and utter bastard.'

'But you're the eighth,' said Berlin.

'Yes,' said Haileybury. 'Regretfully, my father died before his father, so he never came into the title. I was more or less brought up by my grandfather.'

He turned his back on the portrait.

Berlin saw a painting of Peggy hanging amongst the others. She smiled at the elegant Leyton house-wife, captured in dark oils. Detached, serene, she was able to look her mother in the eye and view her with equanimity.

The moment passed, but the warm glow stayed with her.

Food appeared, and more Scotch, which tasted exquisite.

Minutes later, or hours, she was learning to play mah-jong. The clacking of the yellow bone and bamboo tiles was musical. The delicately painted symbols danced: winds, dragons, flowers, seasons.

Sleep, on a soft pile of Turkish pillows, was a revelation.

'One is bound to surrender to the dream. To resist is to deny nature,' said Haileybury.

His words floated above her.

'What do you dream about?' said Berlin.

'The same as you, my dear,' said Haileybury.

18

Berlin stumbled out of the cab at Pellicci's feeling as if she'd returned from another planet. Everything looked washed out, grubby and unappealing. She needed strong coffee and fried food. It was Thursday afternoon. She'd disappeared down the rabbit hole at Haileybury's some-time Wednesday.

Paying off the cabbie, she noticed a Chinese bloke on the other side of the road with an armful of DVDs. He wasn't harassing pedestrians in the usual fashion. He was watching her.

The café was relatively quiet. She took a window seat and looked back across the road. The Chinese bloke had gone. She was jumpy, her head full of Haileybury's stories of sinister oriental agents. He had passed on his paranoia. Eggs, beans, sausage and chips would sort her out.

But when the DVD seller walked in, she lost her appetite.

There are two kinds of surveillance: the kind you don't notice, and the kind you do because you are meant to. In either case, confronting your tail would be met with the same blank stare, denial and possibly amusement.

She left Pellicci's without ordering, strolled down the high road, took the first right and waited.

Mr DVD appeared around the corner.

Berlin stepped out, into his path. He pulled up short.

'Can I help you?' she said.

He looked confused. He was carrying a greasy paper bag that gave off the distinct whiff of a bacon sarnie.

'Sorry,' he said. His accent was thick. 'No understand.'

He tried to walk around her, but she grabbed him.

'Don't give me that no-speaka-da-English crap,' she said. 'Let's see some ID.'

He tried to pull away, but she gripped his wrist and hung on. He began to talk very fast in Chinese. She was having none of it.

'I've got the message,' she said.

He shoved her, but she turned the momentum to advantage and twisted his arm up behind his back. He cried out and dropped his sarnie, then turned to deliver a swift and vicious head butt. He took off, leaving the sandwich on the ground.

What a waste.

She rubbed her forehead. A lump was already forming.

She sat on a low wall nearby and tried to take stock.

They watch me all the time. Haileybury hadn't been histrionic about it; it was a statement of fact as far as he was concerned. If it was true, she had appeared on their radar and now they were checking her out.

Intelligence services ran highly developed surveillance operations. Mr Bacon Sarnie hadn't struck her as very sophisticated, but it might have been intended. A warning.

Haileybury was hard to get a handle on; he was strong on Anglo-Chinese history and Qing dynasty treasures, but vague on a lot of other things. Like where he got his opium.

She took the stairs to her flat slowly, and had barely closed the front door behind her when someone knocked. She was wasted, nauseous, had come off worse in a tussle, and was certainly not in the mood for someone who had to have been watching and waiting for her to come home.

It couldn't be Bella; she would still be drying out.

She peered through the spyhole. Jesus Christ. That was all she needed. She opened the door again.

'What the hell do you want?' she said.

Bryant nudged his way inside; she didn't have the strength to stop him.

'You didn't return my calls or respond to my texts,' he said. 'I've tried I don't know how many times.'

'You've been staking out my flat,' she said. 'I warned you about unauthorised surveillance.'

'You look like shite, if I may so,' said Bryant. 'Been on a bender?'

He kicked a couple of the cartons.

'Planning a midnight flit?'

'My mother died,' said Berlin. 'I'm sorting out her stuff.'

'Oh,' stammered Bryant. 'I'm sorry for your loss.'

He shifted from foot to foot, and backed off a little, apparently discomfited.

Serve him right.

'Perhaps we should do this another time,' he said.

'No,' said Berlin. 'Now you're here, what do you want?'

'There have been some developments in the case,' he said.

'Such as?' said Berlin.

'Helena Cathcart has suddenly remembered she wasn't wearing her glasses,' said Bryant.

'The witness?' said Berlin.

'That's her,' said Bryant. 'Chen's going to walk.'

'What about the CCTV?' said Berlin.

'The council deleted it,' said Bryant.

He needed her copy.

'I wondered if . . .' said Bryant.

It was painful to watch.

'Oh for God's sake,' she said.

He hadn't been obliged to give it to her in the first place. Now he would owe her one. She retrieved the laptop from the sofa and sat down at the table. Bryant stood behind her. His USB stick was still in the port. She woke the computer up and double-clicked the USB drive.

Nothing happened.

She tried again. There was nothing on the stick. She scanned the directory and recent deletions. Nothing.

'What the fuck?' she said.

'Who's had access to your computer?' said Bryant.

'No one,' said Berlin.

'Well, another *no one* got to the server at the station where I backed it up,' said Bryant. 'I've put in for a forensic audit, but they've got a backlog.'

'It doesn't make sense,' said Berlin.

There was no sign of a break-in.

Bryant circled the table and stood on the other side of it. He folded his arms.

'Are you trying to pull a fast one on me, Berlin?' he said.

So much for sensitivity.

'No, I'm bloody not,' said Berlin. 'It's not on the stick and I haven't got a copy. I wouldn't have gone through this pantomime if I had it, I'd have just thrown you out.'

'I've seen Chen, you know, at the Abbey,' said Bryant. His self-satisfied tone grated.

'So?' she said.

'Did Haileybury put you up to it?' said Bryant.

'I beg your pardon?' said Berlin.

'Got something on you, has he?' said Bryant. 'Prevailed on you to interfere with evidence?'

She stood up so fast her chair clattered to the floor.

'Get out,' she said.

Bryant backed away. She followed him across the room.

'Is this all about drugs, Berlin?' he said.

A bolt of rage shot through her. She got in his face.

'Who the fuck do you think you are?' she said.

'You and the earl and his bum boy all drugged up together?' he said. 'Nice.'

The back of her hand connected with his smug mouth before she realised what she was doing.

Bryant reeled back, then came for her. She ducked out of reach, strode to the front door and flung it open.

'Touch me and it will be your last act as a police officer, I promise you,' she said.

Bryant hesitated.

'Your mother must have been very proud,' he said.

Berlin slammed the door after him, then slid to the floor, shaking. She'd lost twenty-four hours, evidence and the last remnants of her self-control.

The descent into the abyss had been quicker than she remembered.

On the way downstairs, Bryant dabbed his lip with his handkerchief. Jesus Christ, what next? The worst thing was, he couldn't do a thing about it. Tomalin would have his guts for garters if he found out he'd been there.

That woman had a lot to answer for.

Her time would come.

19

Lee adjusted the desk lamp. The fading light troubled him, although he suspected his eyes were the real problem. The headaches affected his sight, sometimes for days after the pain had receded.

He also found it a strain reading on a computer screen. He scanned the documents that required his attention: a brief biography, a medical history and transcripts of recent telephone conversations.

Lee liked to have the measure of the enemy, and Catherine Berlin was an intriguing subject. Born in Bethnal Green, where she still lived in a flat she owned; state education followed by a mediocre degree. No family, so no vulnerability on that score.

A long, inglorious career as an investigator in both the public and private sectors, now working for Haileybury, which meant she and the People's Republic were at odds. But not necessarily enemies.

The logs revealed she had spent more than twenty-four hours at the earl's Wapping residence. Their relationship appeared to be evolving; he suspected he knew why, given the information contained in the medical records.

If this aggressive woman's relationship with Haileybury could change, so could his.

Human beings were driven by impulses they barely recognised, let alone understood or were able to control. His job was to harness the base urges of others and steer them in a direction that served a larger cause. He was good at it, because he'd mastered his own. Up to a point.

No man could yoke his heart.

The Berlin documents would soon grow in volume and number. He stubbed out his cigarette and took two tablets from his pocket, which he swallowed without water.

It was difficult to assess whether Berlin was a risk to Philip. The boy was the future, so if she was a threat, she would have to be eliminated, one way or another.

Philip must be protected and guided towards his true purpose. The challenge was dealing with his weaknesses. Lee rubbed his temples. Thinking about this conundrum didn't help his headache.

The corruption that ensnared Philip wouldn't be easy to overcome. The private investigator appeared to be a tough customer, but she had succumbed quickly.

He was not the most serious threat she faced.

The mobile in his suit pocket vibrated and he put his hand over his heart, as if to still it. The pulse was insistent. He slipped it out of his pocket and accepted the call, but didn't speak. He was expected to listen, and as he did, the vice around his skull tightened.

Finally a response was required.

'May I ask if that is strictly necessary?' he said.

The reply was curt.

'I understand,' he said.

He put the mobile back in his pocket and picked up the internal phone.

'Bring the car to the back,' he said. 'I'm going out. No driver.'

Some tasks required solitude.

20

After Bryant had gone, Berlin collapsed on to the sofa and tried to make sense of his revelations. She wasn't at her sharpest.

The business with the missing video was disturbing; someone with professional skills had broken into her flat and hacked the password on her computer.

The witness had recanted, the video had gone; someone was doing Haileybury's dirty work. It also implied she was window dressing, useful for liaison with the police, the school and the Abbey. She had to admit she was hurt.

On the other hand, the opium implied criminal connections. She hadn't asked Haileybury about its source, which would have been an egregious breach of user protocol, but if he had access to a supply of such an unusual commodity, it meant he had powerful friends in strange places.

Triads were a possibility, given his family's long history with China. She could be walking blind into a turf war.

According to her research, the Haileyburys had been a presence in Hong Kong from the late eighteenth century, when they began trading with the Middle Kingdom, so-called because the Chinese believed they were at the centre of the earth, surrounded by barbarians.

No doubt this impression was confirmed when the Haileyburys arrived.

She had never encountered Triad enforcers, only their middle management, during a loan shark investigation when they kept the muscle well hidden. She had found them polite, disciplined and ruthless, running a military-style operation. She and Del had spent long nights trying in vain to map their network.

Organised crime was so called for a reason; the boundary between those who were law-abiding and those who were lawless was ephemeral, and as she'd often found to her cost, the law-abiding did not always occupy the moral high ground.

She picked up her phone and called Haileybury.

He answered promptly.

'The case against Philip has fallen apart,' she said. 'There are problems with the evidence.'

'So I understand,' said Haileybury. 'I had an email from Sylvie Laurent with the same rather pleasing news. Police incompetence.'

Of course he was pleased, although for some reason she couldn't bring herself to share his delight. In fact, she wasn't just irritated, she was angry. She couldn't get past the feeling that he was responsible.

'The copy of the CCTV video on my computer has been deleted,' she said. 'Someone must have broken into my flat and hacked my password.'

'Are you sure?' said Haileybury. 'You might have deleted it by accident.'

'I don't make mistakes like that,' said Berlin.

'You're only human, Berlin,' said Haileybury. 'And you have been rather, shall we say, distracted recently.'

She wanted to say *which is all your fucking fault*, but managed to restrain herself.

'Distracted by what?' she said.

Let him put a name to it.

'Your recent bereavement, for one thing,' said Haileybury.

'Who told you about that?' said Berlin.

'You did,' he said.

She thought she might throw up.

'Sometimes, after indulging,' said Haileybury, 'one can suffer certain lapses in time and memory.'

He sounded concerned. She couldn't stand it.

'Do you want me to keep looking for the victim?' she said. Her voice was weak.

'Yes,' said Haileybury. 'He must be found. The Chinese must be held to account for this provocation.'

Berlin was rattled by the suggestion that she'd been distracted and deleted the file herself. It could have been done remotely, when she was online, but that skill came at a high price.

The earl could afford it, and he had plenty to offer. Perhaps there was someone like her out there, hankering for another taste of the sublime Haileybury vintage.

Normally she would walk away from a client if she suspected them of a breach of trust on this scale. All clients lied, but this intrusion was of a different order.

The problem was, Haileybury had got under her skin, in more ways than one. Everything was uncertain, including her own take on events, but she absolutely had to know what was going on; if she succumbed to that sort of self-doubt, it was a long road back.

Then there was Philip.

Using drugs to undermine her was one thing.

Using drugs to manipulate a seventeen-year-old boy was something else.

The best source of information about the predator was the prey, in this case, Philip. He wasn't forthcoming, so her next best bet was friends and associates. She was already familiar with his habits.

She called a cab.

Haileybury swirled the Scotch in his glass and watched the black smudge dissolve into smoky tails, streaks of promise suspended in the amber. There had been a querulous note in Berlin's voice. Simon had picked her for toughness of mind, amongst other qualities, but he was probably unaware her mother had died so recently.

It introduced a certain unpredictability into the situation; bereavement could affect one profoundly, as he knew only too well.

Recognition of one's foibles didn't give you mastery over them. Berlin knew that. She was proud, and given a job to do, she would see it through.

After that, she wouldn't be his problem.

21

The taxi pulled up and Philip Chen's domain came into view. Berlin caught her breath. The Victorian Gothic towers of Palmerston Hall, wreathed in mist, rose in manorial splendour from rolling green swards. The peaked roof and spires of the chapel, which was much older than the towers, was a defiant silhouette against the leaden late-afternoon sky.

The border-style barrier and guard at the gatehouse suggested that whatever the school's august history, these days it was a favourite of wealthy oligarchs and potentates.

Taxis were not allowed beyond the barrier; eschewing the golf buggy shuttle that was offered by the guard, whose name tag identified him as Butterworth, Berlin elected to walk to the main building, a good half-mile. Butterworth frowned, but didn't try and stop her. She had phoned ahead; her name was on the list.

A canopy of ancient evergreens lined the drive. The silence beneath them was oppressive and the air was chilly. The blank windows did nothing to warm her; their light was cold, an institutional fluorescence, and the figures flitting across them almost spectral.

When at last she reached the steps that led up to the imposing portico, a stern older man with a pencil moustache and buzz cut was waiting to greet her. He was tall and lean, with square shoulders and pale blue eyes.

Butterworth must have warned them she was coming on foot.

'Mayhew,' the man said. 'Bursar.'

Berlin followed Mayhew down the endless parquetry corridors fragrant with lavender polish. Finally they reached a door leading into a vestibule that served as an office.

He unhooked a two-way radio from his belt, put it on the small desk, knocked softly at a set of double doors, then opened one and stepped aside to allow Berlin to enter. She walked in and the door closed behind her.

The wood-panelled drawing room was immense; the fireplace alone was as big as Berlin's flat. Even more surprising was the woman who emerged from behind the massive desk to greet her.

'Flora Trevelyan,' she said. 'Very pleased to meet you.'

Trevelyan was thin to the point of emaciation, exquisitely groomed and with a bright white expensive smile of welcome. Her glossy dark bob fell back into place after each toss of her head. She was as far from Berlin's idea of a headmistress as you could get.

Berlin took the manicured hand Trevelyan proffered. It was very cold.

'We rarely receive a visit from a private investigator,' cooed the headmistress. 'This is very exciting. Tea, or something stronger?'

Berlin bit her lip. 'Tea would be fine,' she said.

It went against the grain. She couldn't afford to lose focus. Again.

Trevelyan pressed a button on an intercom.

'Mayhew, would you bring us some tea?' she said.

The voice was all cut glass, but there was a hint of flatness in the vowels. Flora Trevelyan was not to the manor born. Berlin sat in the chair she indicated.

'Thank you for seeing me,' she said.

'Not at all,' said Trevelyan. 'We rely on the continuing support of our successful alumni.'

'Their contributions to the chapel roof restoration fund, that sort of thing,' said Berlin.

Trevelyan's laugh was a brittle tinkle.

A knock at the door heralded Mayhew bearing a tray of tea things and biscuits. He placed it on the occasional table between them. Berlin half expected him to bow and shuffle out backwards, but he just turned and left.

'I'm not sure how we can help you,' said Trevelyan as she poured their tea. 'Given Philip's absence.' She handed Berlin a cup and saucer and picked up her own.

'Do you anticipate he'll be able to return to school?' said Berlin.

'If he makes a full recovery, and there is a positive outcome with respect to his legal proceedings,' said Trevelyan.

Berlin selected a biscuit. It was nearly six and she hadn't eaten.

'Does Philip have a best friend, or someone he knocks around with at school?'

'I'm not aware of a particular friend,' said Trevelyan.

'What about any hobbies? Chess club? Astronomy society? Football team?'

'I don't believe Philip is very sports-oriented,' said Trevelyan.

Berlin's cup and saucer rattled as she put them down.

'Ms Trevelyan,' she said. 'We're on the same side here. You want to protect your school's reputation and . . .'

'I can assure you our only concern is Philip's welfare,' snapped Trevelyan.

'. . . and I want to protect my client's interests,' said Berlin. 'The two things are much the same, given the relationship between Lord Haileybury and Palmerston Hall. Not to speak of Lord Haileybury's relationship with Philip Chen.'

She emphasised *relationship*.

Trevelyan flushed.

Bingo.

Philip's room was preternaturally pristine for a seventeen-year-old. But then what did Berlin know about teenage boys? Anyway, it was unlikely that Palmerston Hall boarders would be expected to clean up after themselves; there would be a battalion of housekeepers to take care of all that.

They had not encountered any pupils on their way to Philip's house, nor teachers or his housemaster for that matter. They'd cleared the decks. Trevelyan said the boys had been told their schoolmate was ill and in hospital, no visitors allowed.

'May I?' said Berlin. She didn't wait for an answer as she approached the fitted wardrobe.

'I really don't see how this will help you,' said Trevelyan.
Berlin didn't feel the need to explain.

When she slid open the wardrobe door, she was surprised to find it empty. So were all the drawers.

'Philip's things are in storage,' said Trevelyan. 'For safe keeping.'

Out of sight, out of mind. They didn't expect him back.

They had missed a pair of high-end headphones hanging on the bedpost. She bent to look under the desk. The six sockets of the power board were empty.

When she stood up, Trevelyan was glowering at her.

'Were there any personal items amongst his things?' said Berlin. 'Photos, mementos from Hong Kong?'

'No,' said Trevelyan. 'And I'm sure you understand I can't allow you to inspect his property. Now, unless there's anything else?'

'No, that's all,' said Berlin. 'For now.'

22

Bryant was making a cup of tea when he heard a shout go out on his local police scanner: uniforms to attend a report of a body. He was out the door as soon as the dispatcher finished giving the details.

Bryant ducked under the crime scene tape draped across the churchyard and wound through mildewed tombstones leaning drunkenly over sunken graves.

He displayed his ID to the constable on the door, who entered his name and number on a clipboard and waved him down some stone steps inside the church. They were steep, uneven and treacherous, but Bryant took them two at a time.

When he reached the bottom, an officer in a mask, white overalls and blue booties raised her hand. When she slipped off her mask, his heart sank. It was Detective Inspector Langfield. Not one of his fans.

'That's far enough,' she said.

Portable floodlights illuminated a body lying in the middle of the low-ceilinged crypt. Bryant did as he was told and stood still, taking in the gloomy space. It gave him the heebie-jeebies.

A narrow passage crammed with ancient tombstones ran down one side and disappeared into darkness. Glass panels lined two walls. Behind the panels were mounds of bleached bones. As the officers moved around the body, their shadows flickered across the jumbled skeletons, which seemed to jump about.

Bryant averted his eyes from the unnerving spectacle and craned to take in the corpse lying on the smooth, undulating flagstones. The pathologist was crouched over the figure, a man in jeans, trainers and a hoodie. He was about the right size and his clothes were consistent with the CCTV footage.

'What are you doing here, Bryant?' said Langfield.

'This could be my victim,' said Bryant.

'What, another one?' said Langfield.

The other officers had a good giggle.

'You know what I mean,' blustered Bryant.

'Yeah, I know what you mean,' said Langfield. 'All right, suit up, but stay out of the way.'

Berlin's taxi crept along, thwarted by the sluggish London traffic. Her search for Philip's victim had also been stymied.

Finding the victim was now Bryant's only hope of a successful prosecution, which had to be another factor motivating Haileybury to continue the hunt, apart from his plan to discredit the PRC.

Bryant had manpower and resources on his side, but she had a rich, powerful client. She also had twenty years of experience as an investigator and was free of the prejudices that could blind the likes of the policeman. He wanted a result. She wanted more than that.

The state of Philip's room at the school bothered her. Someone had cleaned it out. A boy his age would own at least one computer, as well as a smartphone and probably a tablet. She'd get Colin to check if they were at the Abbey.

Whoever had dealt with Philip's stuff had missed the headphones. It was a giveaway. Likewise Trevelyan's instant response to her question about personal items; a blanket denial didn't ring true. It was unlikely the head of Palmerston Hall had packed up the boy's things herself.

Philip had started at Palmerston Hall when he was six. He must have brought something with him: a photo of the orphanage, or a postcard of the province, or a teddy bear or something. Did they have teddy bears in China?

Perhaps she was just being sentimental.

Bryant managed to contain his impatience and keep clear of the experts, but the wait for the SOCOs and the pathologist to finish seemed interminable. It was well past dinner time when finally they began to pack up their kit.

Langfield and her offsiders waylaid the irritable pathologist for a conflab. Bryant contrived to hover nearby.

'. . . and there's evidence of drug use,' concluded the pathologist. 'That's all I'm prepared to say for now.'

'Recent?' said Langfield. 'Do you think he OD'd?'

'He's got a number of minor injuries, including at least one broken rib. Time and cause of death will have to wait.' He glanced at his watch, snorted and strode off.

Bryant wasn't sure if this was a result or not; the evidence of drug use could be a good thing, implicating Chen in a deal gone wrong, or a bad thing if the bloke had actually died of an overdose rather than Chen's assault. Whichever way you cut it, drugs were involved in this business.

He turned his attention to a SOCO who was bagging up the man's belongings, which appeared to consist of an Oyster card, some change and a bunch of DVDs with photocopied covers. The SOCO glanced up.

'Interested in *Nuns in Heat*?' he said.

Bryant frowned.

'That's one less knock-off DVD seller down the market,' said the SOCO. 'He'll be a bastard to identify, probably arrived in a container.'

'He's Chinese?' said Bryant.'

'They all are,' said the SOCO.

Bryant felt the hairs on the back of his neck stand up. This was the man. He knew it. It couldn't possibly be a coincidence that both Chen and his victim were Chinese.

'All right to take a closer look, boss?' he called.

Langfield glanced up and nodded.

His booties slid across the flagstones and he crouched down at the head of the corpse, which lay at a gentle angle, eyes wide open.

No one was paying him any mind. Positioning himself to hide what he was doing – he didn't want to be thought ghoulish – he used his phone to take a photo. It wasn't what you'd call a happy snap.

Quickly retreating to a corner, he struggled out of the blue booties with one hand and made a call with the other. It was answered with a curt '*Oui?*'

'Mrs Laurent,' said Bryant. 'This is what we English refer to as a courtesy call. Later this evening I'll be attending the Abbey to arrest your client on suspicion of murder. You may wish to be present, given his status as a juvenile.'

He hung up. Ringing the lawyer wasn't strictly necessary, but he wanted to rub it in. Word would pass up and down the line; Laurent would call Palmerston Hall, Trevelyan would call Haileybury, Haileybury would call Berlin, and Berlin would call him.

He could hardly wait.

23

The cab had just turned into Bethnal Green Road when Berlin's phone rang. She answered the call. It was Colin.

'I thought you said Chen was an orphan,' he said.

'That's what I was told,' said Berlin.

'Well, there's a bloke here says he's his father.'

'Philip's father?' said Berlin.

'Yeah,' said Colin.

'Chinese?' said Berlin.

'Yeah,' said Colin. 'Very polite, but insists he wants to see his son. Came a long way and all that. The charge nurse is tearing his hair out.'

Her heart beat a little faster. She could hear the wind whistling around Colin. He was outside, smoking.

'What does Philip say?' she said.

'That's the thing,' said Colin. 'They can't find him. He can't have gone far because he's in his pyjamas. Look, I have to go. You wanted a heads-up. You got it.'

'Stall him until I get there,' said Berlin.

'Stall who?' said Colin. 'The father? You're joking. I'm the night porter.'

'Do something,' said Berlin. 'Anything. Double bung.'

'For Christ's sake,' said Colin.

'I'm on my way,' said Berlin.

She hung up.

'The Abbey, as fast as you can,' she said.

The cabbie looked at her in the rear-view mirror. He made no move other than to raise an eyebrow.

'Double the fare,' she said.

Haileybury put the phone down, poured another Scotch and knocked it back. Laurent had suggested he engage experienced criminal counsel immediately. He grasped the phone again, fumbling to dial correctly.

Every joint in his body throbbed with tension. When he moved, a sharp jolt of pain shot around his wrist and up his arm, settling in his shoulder. The grinding ache in his knees and hips made his eyes water. He wouldn't cry.

'Simon,' he said, when his call was answered. 'They're going to arrest Philip on suspicion of murder. For God's sake, what am I going to do?'

Berlin texted Colin to meet her at the skips. It was twilight. The motion-activated security lights hadn't kicked in, but if anyone was looking out of the window, they couldn't miss her.

She stood in the shadows and waited. Finally the back door opened and Colin beckoned her inside.

'What's going on?' she said.

'Fuck knows,' said Colin. 'They still haven't found Philip.'

'Is the Chinese bloke still here?' said Berlin.

'Yeah,' said Colin. 'He won't be going anywhere soon. He's got a flat tyre.' He grinned.

Berlin wondered how much this was going to cost her.

'Where is he?' she said.

'In reception,' said Colin. 'The charge nurse has been trying to get on to someone at the school to find out what to do. He's shitting himself because the kid's gone.'

'When did he go missing?' said Berlin.

'Dunno,' said Colin.

'Was it before he was told about his visitor, or after?' said Berlin.

Colin blinked. 'Yeah, now you put it like that, he might not even know his father's here.'

Philip had been a guest at the Abbey for four days. He would know the routine by now, and the impact of the first whack of medication would be diminishing.

He wouldn't go far. His bail conditions obliged the Abbey to notify the police if he went missing. If it was her, she would put on her PJs, say a loud goodnight to all, shut her bedroom door, and wait for things to quieten down before taking some time out. No one would notice.

'All right, Colin,' she said. 'Thanks. I'll take it from here.'

He looked expectant.

'The cabbie cleaned me out,' she said. 'You know I'm good for it.'

Colin retreated inside, scowling. She made a mental note to pay him sooner rather than later; she couldn't afford to lose his goodwill.

The father was a problem. She wanted to see him, but she didn't want him to see her. What were the chances that Philip had a father who, hearing of his son's dilemma, had tracked him down to the Abbey? Friend of the family? What family? Emissary from Haileybury? That was her role.

This daddy was more likely to be a Chinese agent or a gangster; she had no ambitions to tangle with either. She retreated to the gates, which were closed, to wait.

Philip was wearing gym pants and a sweatshirt when he squeezed back through the gates. It was a bit after eleven. The only pub in walking distance would have just called time.

He jumped when she stepped out.

'Shit,' he said. 'You frightened me.'

'I suppose you've got your pyjamas on underneath,' said Berlin.

He smelt like a brewery.

'You've had a skinful,' she said.

'I needed something,' he said. 'You know.'

She knew.

'Alcohol and medication is a pretty toxic brew,' said Berlin.

'Good,' he said.

Wilful, surly, self-destructive. All too familiar.

'What are you doing lurking about here, anyway?' he said.

'Waiting for you,' said Berlin. 'So is your father.'

'What?' he said.

He was drunk, but his confusion wasn't just a function of the alcohol.

She gestured in the direction of the clinic.

'There's a bloke up there waiting for you, says he's your father. They've been looking for you.'

At the sound of a vehicle, they both turned. A car was creeping down the drive, its headlights on full beam. Instinctively they stepped back into the shadows, hugging the high brick wall and retreating further along it.

The car, a dark SUV, rolled closer to the gates and stopped. The driver's door opened and the interior light went on.

Berlin heard Philip's sharp intake of breath.

A man got out, shut the door, lit a cigarette then strolled in their direction.

Philip's hand closed around Berlin's. He tugged gently, signalling that they should make a run for it.

Before they could move, a car pulled up on the other side of the gates. The man stepped smartly out of the glare of its headlights. There was a clunk, followed by a pulsing blue light, a portable beacon. It was an unmarked police car. It sounded its horn.

The man raised a hand in acknowledgement, dragged open the gates and quickly got back into his car. The police car flashed its headlight in thanks, and the two vehicles passed each other as they sped in different directions.

Philip was crouching down beside the wall, his thick fringe covering his eyes. If I can't see you, you can't see me.

She knelt beside him.

'Philip,' she said. 'He's gone.'

She tried to ease her hand out of his, but he hung on. When he looked up at her, it was the most beautiful, scared face she'd ever seen.

'Who is he?' she said.

'Mr Lee,' he whispered. 'He's not my father.'

His vulnerability touched a place in her she didn't know existed. She put her arm around him.

'It's okay,' she said. 'You're safe.'

It was reassurance you might offer a frightened child, and in this instance totally unjustified. She couldn't believe she'd made such a foolish statement. She tried to backtrack.

'I'll take you up to the clinic and explain you were with me,' she said. 'They would have called the police when they couldn't find you.'

Philip sprang to his feet.

'I can't go back now,' he said. 'They know where I am.'

Whoever 'they' were, it was telling that the man who claimed to be Philip's father hadn't hung around to discuss his missing son with the police.

Philip backed away.

'Calm down,' she said. 'I can't make you go back if you don't want to. We'll walk up to the high road and get a cab. Let me make a call first.'

The simplest thing to do was to go to Haileybury's and sort it out there. But when she took her phone out of her pocket, a text message from the earl was waiting. *Body found. Arrest imminent.*

The police weren't at the Abbey because Philip had breached his bail conditions. Their mission was more urgent than that. Bryant would be eager for his moment of triumph.

Haileybury's would be the first place the zealous detective would look after a fruitless search of the clinic and the immediate area. They had to get away from there, fast.

'Let's go,' she said. She set off at a brisk pace, Philip trotting along beside her. 'Stay close to the wall until we get to the high road,' she said.

'Where are we going?' said Philip.

'Somewhere safe,' she said.

Wherever that was.

24

Bryant was apoplectic. Chen had been missing for hours, but the Abbey hadn't bothered to notify the police. It was lucky he'd turned up to arrest the little blighter, or God knows how long it would have been before he found out the boy had done a bunk.

The charge nurse, a different one from the other day, seemed flustered.

'A man was here asking for Philip,' he said. 'But we couldn't find him. He left just before you arrived.'

'What man?' said Bryant.

'He said he was his father,' said the charge. 'But we had nothing in our file about a father, and he wasn't on the list, so I—'

'What was he driving?' said Bryant.

'How would I know?' said the charge. 'He had a flat tyre. He fixed it and said he was going to look for Philip, so maybe he found him and . . .'

Bryant didn't stay to hear the rest of his self-serving rubbish.

On the way out, he called in a BOLO on Chen, with a special alert for ports and airports, adding that he could be travelling with an older man, also Chinese. He got in the car and put his foot down.

Halfway down the drive, he passed a Mercedes coming the other way. It was the French lawyer. Good luck to her.

He drove through the gates and wondered about the chances of clocking the black Lexus he'd seen leaving. The denizens of this neck of the woods loved 'em.

When his mobile rang, he glanced at the caller ID and answered. Word had got around, just as he knew it would.

'I hear you've found a body,' said Berlin.

'Yes, if it's any business of yours,' said Bryant.

'Have you arrested Chen yet?' she said.

Bryant hesitated. 'Not yet,' he said.

It had perhaps been a mistake to announce the arrest. He hadn't expected it to all go pear-shaped.

'Care to share any details about the deceased?' said Berlin.

'I've got to go,' said Bryant.

'Who found the body?' said Berlin.

He was about to tell her to get stuffed, but then again, in some circumstances she could go where he could not. She was in and out of Haileybury's like Flynn.

Keep your friends close, and your enemies closer.

'A clergyman,' said Bryant.

'Are you serious?' said Berlin.

'Perfectly,' said Bryant.

'Where?' said Berlin.

'At St Bride's,' said Bryant. 'In the crypt.'

'When will you get the results of the post-mortem?' said Berlin.

'I'm not working for you, Berlin,' said Bryant. 'But don't worry. It's him.'

'Your say-so won't cut it on its own,' said Berlin. 'What makes you so confident?'

He hung up. He'd show her.

Berlin swore. He was too cocky by half. Her phone pinged. He'd sent a photo. The sightless eyes gave away the man's status, but what really held her attention was the faint purple bruise on his forehead.

He wouldn't be eating any more bacon sarnies.

This was the man Bryant believed was Philip's victim. For a moment the world tilted. She swallowed hard.

They were on a night bus. Philip was digging into a packet of chips, oblivious. He had wanted to sit upstairs like a kid, wide-eyed and enjoying the sights. She watched him, the playful child still lurking inside the barely adult body. His character was similarly half formed.

She put the phone back in her pocket and cleared her throat, lest her voice came out a squeak.

'Bryant will have issued a BOLO,' she said.

'What's that?' said Philip.

'Be on the lookout,' she said.

'Because of the bail thing?' said Philip.

She hadn't shared the news that he was wanted for murder. Bryant could be getting way ahead of himself. What could he have so far? The victim was Chinese. It could be a coincidence, but Bryant probably didn't believe in them. She didn't either, which meant her instincts were correct and the DVD seller had been following her.

By the time they'd reached their stop and walked the half-mile to the house, Philip was flagging. It was clear he had no idea where he was; this corner of London might just as well have been Outer Mongolia.

Pound shops, betting shops, serried ranks of sooty terraced houses, rusty car bodies in weed-strewn front gardens, concrete forecourts fronted with blackboard signs announcing 'Beer Garden'.

The aromas of diesel, fried chicken and greasy kebabs.

Leyton.

Berlin unlocked the front door. The brass knocker was already dull; she breathed on it and gave it a rub with her sleeve. Philip followed her into the narrow hallway.

'Is this your place?' he asked.

'It is now,' said Berlin.

The telephone had been disconnected, but the gas and electricity were still on. The house was deathly quiet.

A lot of the smaller bits and pieces, memorabilia, had been carted down to her flat, but the furniture was still here. It was worth almost nothing to a second-hand dealer; there was no place for these solid last-a-lifetime pieces in the bright disposable lexicon of contemporary interiors.

Using lavender polish and a soft cloth, Peggy had lovingly preserved the dark wood; the drop-side table with barley-twist legs, the oak sideboard and the occasional tables. Few occasions ever arose. Peggy didn't entertain.

Berlin didn't like any of it, but she couldn't face dumping her mother's commitment to elbow grease in a skip.

'Put the kettle on,' she said.

Philip stared at her as if she'd asked him to scale Mount Everest.

She went upstairs, locked herself in the toilet and cried.

When she came down, two cups of tea – Peggy couldn't abide mugs – were waiting on the kitchen table. Philip was peering into the fridge.

'There's no milk,' he said. 'It will have to be black, but there are no lemons.'

'We'll have to rough it,' she said. 'Sit.'

He sat. She put her phone on the table in front of him, displaying the image of the dead man.

'That's the man you assaulted, isn't it?' she said.

'He looks . . .' said Philip.

'Dead,' said Berlin. 'Yes. He is.'

'He can't be,' said Philip. 'I mean, I only punched him on the nose.'

'Then you put the boot in,' said Berlin.

'Once or twice, that's all,' said Philip. 'It couldn't have killed him.'

'A punctured lung, a ruptured spleen, internal bleeding. Who knows?' said Berlin. 'You can die from one punch, and sometimes slowly.'

'Oh God,' said Philip. He buried his face in his hands.

'Who is he?' said Berlin.

'I told you,' he said. He mumbled through his fingers. 'My dealer.'

'Bullshit,' said Berlin. 'I know exactly where you get your dope.'

He looked up, his expression wary.

'What do you mean?' he said.

'Haileybury told me,' she said. 'We shared a pipe.'

More than one. The memory of that perfect serenity stirred something inside her; she felt it nibble, and knew it would soon gnaw.

'Have you . . . have you some, by any chance?' said Philip.

It stirred in him, too.

'No, I bloody haven't,' she said.

He rose, listless, and tipped his tea down the sink.

'That was disgusting,' he said.

She'd just told him a man he'd assaulted had died, and he was complaining about the tea.

'I'm sorry we don't meet your standards,' she said. 'But given that you're wanted for murder, you'd better get used to it. Unless you've got somewhere better to go.'

'I'm perfectly capable of looking after myself,' he announced, nostrils flaring, all haughty defiance and pomposity.

'I've noticed,' said Berlin. 'Let me lend you the taxi fare to . . . where?'

He slumped back into his chair.

'What do you want from me?' he said.

'I was hired to find the man you attacked,' said Berlin. 'He's found. Now I want to know who he is and why you attacked him.'

'I didn't kill him,' said Philip.

'Maybe, maybe not,' said Berlin. 'That's up to the pathologist. Who is – was – he?'

'I can't think straight,' said Philip. 'I'm so tired. Can we do this in the morning?'

It was another attempt to stall her, but he did look thoroughly defeated.

He wasn't going anywhere, because he didn't have anywhere to go.

25

Haileybury stood on the terrace in the foggy Friday dawn. Philip was out there somewhere in God only knew what state, and here he was unable to do a damn thing about it.

If only he could take some action himself, instead of having to rely on others all the time.

He peered into the yellow mist as it drifted up the river, rendering familiar sights sinister. The shape of things was shifting. He was losing control.

The Abbey had undertaken to contact Sylvie Laurent, and not the police, if Philip returned. Haileybury prayed the boy got in touch with someone on his side before the law caught up with him. That was the role he'd hoped Berlin would play, but she wasn't responding to his calls or texts.

People were so damn unreliable.

More disturbing was the news that some chap had turned up at the Abbey claiming to be Philip's father. His flesh crawled; the breeze felt as if it were scouring his skin. He needed something stronger than aspirin to get through this.

He grabbed his sticks and hobbled indoors.

*

Berlin's first thought as she opened her eyes was that Peggy would die if she knew she'd slept on the sofa in the front room. It mattered not that it was faded and lumpy; it was still 'for best'.

Peggy hadn't been able to enjoy anything; the good china, the good glasses, the good tablecloth, it all came out at Christmas and was then whisked away again. The event was always marred by anxiety, lest someone break a glass or spill sherry on the bloody tablecloth.

Her father and grandfather were the exact opposite; they knew how to have a good time. She had inherited those genes. In spades.

She felt rough. There was no codeine, no liquor, no decent coffee, not even bloody cough medicine in the house. Peggy had been a strong believer in toughing it out.

Her back creaked nearly as much as the springs as she eased herself off the sofa and went upstairs.

The banisters shimmered as she floated up, the solidity of things dissolving as she touched them. She needed a drink, or something.

When she peeked around the door of her old bedroom, Philip was still sound asleep in the narrow bed. Above him hung a faded poster of the greatest fucking rock band in the universe. He'd probably never heard of Led Zeppelin.

She paid a quick trip to the bathroom and splashed cold water on her face, then went back downstairs and left a note on the kitchen table. *Gone to Matins.*

*

134

A scrap of crime-scene tape fluttered in the breeze. Alone in the churchyard, Berlin tried to imagine how the man Philip had attacked on Monday morning, and whom she had confronted on Tuesday, had ended up dead in St Bride's crypt by Thursday.

'Can I help you?'

The offer of assistance had come from a tall man in a shabby suit and a dog collar. He was unlocking the church doors.

'I was hoping to visit the crypt,' she said.

'I'm afraid it's not open at the moment,' said the clergyman.

'Oh,' said Berlin. 'That's disappointing. This is my last day in London.'

The struggle between the obliging, helpful Christian and the one who followed the rules was palpable. Helpful won.

'Five minutes, then,' he said.

Berlin found the crypt oppressive. It extended into darkness, the length and breadth of the church above. The ceiling was low, and despite the modern infrastructure, there was no disguising the purpose of the place. To accommodate the dead.

'Do you get many rough sleepers down here?' she said.

The clergyman looked surprised.

'No,' he said. 'The church is locked at night. We do occasionally get people in the garden, but . . .'

'So it's only open during the day?' said Berlin.

'Yes,' said the clergyman.

'Do you have an alarm system?' she said.

'We do, but it's quite old. Recently we've had workmen down here and they're not always as security conscious as . . . I thought you wanted to see the ossuary?'

'CCTV?' she said.

'Er, no,' he said.

'Was it you who found the body?' she said.

She watched as the helpful Christian berated himself for being such a soft touch.

'I'll have to ask you to leave now,' he said.

The clergyman escorted her up the ancient stone steps, locked the crypt door and hurried off. A few devout parishioners were arriving for the early service, so she followed them inside.

Berlin didn't have a religious bone in her body, but the elegant neoclassical interior was so beautiful, and the organ music so soothing, that she sat down in a pew at the back to admire the elegant arches and tall windows.

The black and white tiled floor shone. She wanted to lie down, rest her forehead on those cool, gleaming tiles and sleep for a week. She closed her eyes.

A thunderous chord from the organ made her jump.

She must have dozed off, because for a moment she thought she was in the chapel at the cemetery again, unable to look at Peggy's coffin. The blast was a wake-up call. She'd been sleepwalking through this case.

Once outside in the churchyard, she recovered herself and stood for a moment.

Whether he had been killed in the crypt or somewhere else, then dumped, the gesture wouldn't be lost on the deceased's associates. It sent a message.

In spite of what she'd said to Philip, it was unlikely the man had died as a result of the assault. Even less likely was the proposition that he dragged himself to the crypt to die sometime after he'd fled from her in Bow. He was fit enough then.

On her way out, she noticed a wooden noticeboard in the garden. It listed the names of churchwardens past and present. One name caught her eye.

The message got louder.

Bryant looked up from his desk to see Tomalin standing in the doorway of the squad room gazing at him with utter distaste.

'My office,' said Tomalin.

Bryant followed him down the hall.

'Shut the door,' said Tomalin.

Bryant did as he was told.

'Your suspect has done a runner, has he, Bryant?' said Tomalin. 'Of course, you haven't got a shred of evidence to connect this deceased illegal alien with Chen.'

'With respect, sir,' said Bryant, 'he hasn't been identified yet. He might not be illegal.'

'What difference does it make?' said Tomalin. 'There's no connection that would satisfy the CPS.'

'We're still waiting on forensics,' said Bryant.

'We?' said Tomalin. 'This is Langfield's case and she doesn't think it's got anything to do with your assault.

But what I want to know is why Chen bolted from the Abbey.'

'I couldn't say, sir,' said Bryant.

'Did you give anyone a heads-up about arresting him?' said Tomalin.

Bryant's hand strayed to his pocket for a comforting Fisherman's Friend, but he managed to restrain himself.

'Just as I thought,' said Tomalin. 'Did it ever occur to you that this information might reach Chen? That he could take fright and scarper?'

'Take fright, sir?' Bryant failed to keep the sneer out of his voice. 'More like a guilty conscience, I'd say.'

Tomalin glowered.

'Listen to me, Bryant,' he said. 'This is now a missing person inquiry. Chen is not to be treated as a fugitive, do you understand?'

Bryant was gobsmacked.

'A misper?' he said. 'For a start, he's breached his bail conditions for the assault.'

'You've got no evidence of that, either,' said Tomalin.

It was the way he said it. Tomalin was aware of his application for a computer audit. He knew the video had gone.

'I've got a witness,' said Bryant.

Tomalin couldn't know the witness had recanted.

It didn't help. Tomalin started to shout.

'If anything happens to that boy, or you step out of line one more time, you'll rue the day you were born, Bryant.'

'Will that be all, sir?' said Bryant.

'Yes,' said Tomalin. 'Get out of my sight.'

Bryant strode out of Tomalin's office, closing the door behind him with a soft click.

He and Gran had been pushed around by higher-ups their whole lives. This time the establishment had picked the wrong bloke to ride roughshod over.

He would go down fighting.

26

Philip was at the kitchen table when Berlin got back to Leyton.

'There's nothing to eat,' he said.

'Good morning to you too,' she said. She dropped a supermarket bag on the table. 'Here.'

He retrieved the eggs, bacon and bread from the bag and looked expectant.

'There's a frying pan on that shelf,' she said. 'It's the flat round thing with the long handle.'

After they'd eaten – he didn't do a bad job – they drank more builder's tea, listened to Radio Four and pretended it was a normal morning.

'Have you ever been to St Bride's in Fleet Street?' she said.

'Once, I think,' said Philip. 'Jack took me to a carol service there at Christmas. Why?'

'That's where they found him,' she said. 'Your victim. In the crypt.'

'I wish you'd stop saying that,' said Philip. 'He's not the bloody victim, I am.'

'How's that?' said Berlin.

'His name's Deng. They sent him to threaten me,' said Philip.

'Who sent him?' said Berlin.

'Lee,' said Philip.

She would have to get the rubber hose out in a minute.

'Come on, Philip,' she said. 'What did this Deng say that upset you enough to stick the boot in?'

Philip pushed his bacon rind around his plate with his fork.

'Jack's paying you,' he said.

'I haven't seen a penny yet,' said Berlin.

'Does it mean you have to tell him everything?' said Philip.

'I was retained to find the man you assaulted,' said Berlin. 'He's been found, although only you and I know for sure it's him. Haileybury has a theory about the incident, and in order to confirm it, I need some details about this bloke. Understand?'

'I'm not an idiot,' said Philip. 'So you're just doing this for the money?'

He knew that Haileybury could offer other incentives she might find attractive.

'I'm not expecting to be paid in kind, if that's what you mean,' she said. 'I'm an investigator. It's what I do to pay the bills.'

'I'm sick of all these questions,' said Philip.

She was getting sick of *him*.

'My job is to find things out,' she said. 'If I can't, it pisses me off. I get irritable and grass up murderers.'

'Okay,' said Philip. 'I get it. Now *you're* threatening me.'

Berlin thumped the table. He jumped.

'Listen to me,' she said. 'The Metropolitan Police want you, Haileybury wants you, and the People's Republic of China wants you. If I get in their way, they won't hesitate to make me suffer. Why should I bother?'

He poured a mound of salt on to the table and began to make swirls in it with his finger.

'What's Jack's theory?' he said.

'That Deng worked for the Chinese government and they want to use you to force him to return the collection.'

He focused on the salt.

'He's right,' he said.

Progress.

'Be specific,' said Berlin.

'You have to promise not to tell Jack,' he said.

'How are they going to use you, Philip?' said Berlin.

It was either sex or drugs; his relationship with Haileybury or opium. Or both.

There was a long silence. She could hear the neighbour's radio, the traffic, a dog's monotonous, plaintive bark: let me out.

'It's about my mother,' said Philip.

This didn't quite fit with her tabloid scenario.

'I thought you were an orphan,' she said.

'So did I,' said Philip. 'But I'm not. I was stolen.' He burst into tears.

Berlin's heart lurched. She got up, walked around the table, and patted his shoulder.

'It's okay, Philip,' she said. 'It's okay.'

'It's not fucking okay,' he said. 'Lee's got her, and if I don't cooperate, something will happen to her. Something very, very bad.'

He clung to her and sobbed.

'Jesus,' muttered Berlin.

Blackmail was ugly, but this was rock bottom.

27

Lee stood on a busy corner in the Square Mile, scrutinising an office building, his mobile pressed to his ear. Bankers, hedge fund managers and harried clerks surged around him, intent on lunch. He was just another Asian businessman looking for property, a safe haven for his cash outside the PRC.

His number was blocked. The call was picked up on the sixth ring, indicating some prevarication about answering.

'*Madame*,' he said. '*Pardonnez-moi. Mon Français n'est pas bien.*'

'Who is this?' said Laurent. 'How did you get my mobile number?'

'Please go to the window,' said Lee. 'I would like to meet with you.'

'Make an appointment,' she said.

'*S'il vous plaît*,' he said quietly. 'Go to the window.'

'Who are you and what do you want?' said Laurent.

'*Madame*, I'm going to send you a photograph,' said Lee.

He sent the image and waited.

A moment later Laurent appeared at the window.

Lee nodded and smiled at her.

*

Lee led Laurent to a small café in St Botolph's Alley.

'The patisserie is average, but the coffee is very reliable,' he said.

Laurent appeared to be composed – she was a lawyer, after all – but when they sat down at an outside table and she lit a cigarette, he was gratified to see her hands shaking.

'My name is Lee,' he said. 'I represent certain interests. The picture is very . . . touching?'

'It means nothing,' she said.

'Please, *madame*,' said Lee. 'Let's not insult each other's intelligence.'

'Monsieur Lee,' said Laurent, 'I am a commercial law-yer. My job is to construct trusts, havens, shall we say, for assets, cash, property . . .'

'And sometimes people,' said Lee.

'In ways that are perfectly legal,' said Laurent.

'And utterly impenetrable,' said Lee. 'So why were you chosen to represent Philip Chen?'

Laurent played with her lighter, stroking its fine rose-gold ribs.

'That is a very handsome lighter,' said Lee.

'It was a present from my husband,' she said.

Her sigh was tantamount to an admission.

'You and I are both outsiders, *madame*,' said Lee. 'You are dealing with a club you can never join. Why do you think your partners chose you for this task?'

She stirred her coffee.

It was because she knew no one and no one knew her. No one who counted.

'I ask again,' said Laurent. 'What do you want?'

He held up his phone and displayed the image he had sent her. It was an old black and white photo in a silver frame, what the English used to call a 'snap'.

'What do we see?' said Lee.

Laurent glared at him, but remained tight-lipped.

'Very well then,' said Lee. 'We see a tall, smiling man in a Barbour jacket and houndstooth check shirt, his arm around the shoulders of a Chinese boy in Palmerston Hall uniform. A boy still in short trousers.'

'Innocent enough,' said Laurent.

Lee raised an eyebrow.

'You are aware, of course,' he said, 'that Philip Chen is a citizen of the People's Republic of China.'

'Meaning?' said Laurent.

Lee held her gaze.

'This business could turn into a diplomatic incident,' he said.

Laurent stubbed out her cigarette and immediately lit another.

'You have me at a complete disadvantage,' she said. 'I hear only innuendo and gossip. Your threats are meaningless.'

Lee winced. 'That's not a very lawyerly response, if I may say so,' he said. 'You insult me. Threats? In your profession perhaps you are more comfortable with the term *leverage*.'

She swatted at the blue cloud of smoke drifting above her.

'Your English is perfect,' she said. 'I assume you have held many, shall we say, consular posts.'

'We understand each other, *madame*,' said Lee. 'I have this photograph and other documents of interest. I also have the boy.'

'Do you mean you know where Philip is?' she said.

'I mean I have him in my pocket, as the British so quaintly put it,' said Lee.

'If you have any influence over the boy, please ask him to contact me immediately,' said Laurent.

'I will do no such thing until your client agrees to negotiate,' said Lee. 'Why should I use my relationship with the boy to Haileybury's advantage?'

He rose and gave her a small bow. French women of her age expected that sort of thing.

'You have my number,' he said.

'How did you acquire this influence over Philip?' said Laurent.

Lee smiled.

'You know us Orientals,' he said. 'Very sneaky.'

28

Berlin unlocked the cabinet in the front room where Peggy kept the good glasses. She'd have gladly drunk from the bottle, but she had to get out of the kitchen, take a deep breath and process Philip's revelations.

She was struggling to keep up. What had begun as a punch-up in Wapping on Monday morning had turned into a political conspiracy by Friday afternoon.

What really unnerved her was her own turmoil. It was this fucking house. Locked in with these maternal spectres. Except his mother was real. Probably. She had to try and keep a modicum of objectivity, for both their sakes.

At the table, Philip was still intent on his mountain of salt. She poured generous measures of Scotch into the sparkling crystal tumblers. It was sacrilege just having them in the kitchen.

Philip sipped his whisky. She gulped hers.

'So who told you all this?' said Berlin.

'Lee,' said Philip.

'The bloke at the Abbey who said he was your father?' said Berlin.

'Yes,' said Philip.

'You said he wasn't your father,' said Berlin. 'So we know he lies.'

She breathed again.

'Where did you meet Lee?' she said.

'At a function for Chinese students at the embassy,' said Philip. 'I got an invitation in the mail at school.'

That knocked the Triads out of contention.

'What was his job at the embassy?' she said.

'He said he looked after the welfare of high-achieving scholars abroad.'

'What was his pitch?' said Berlin.

'He said the Chinese government was concerned that young men like me weren't aware of the opportunities that might be available when they returned home. I'd never thought of China as home, so it was a shock to think I might have to go back there.'

'No one ever discussed that with you?' said Berlin.

'No,' he said. 'All they told me was that I was born in Hong Kong, my parents both died and I'd been selected for a scholarship. That was all.'

'They didn't tell you how they died?' said Berlin. 'Or if you had other family?'

'No,' said Philip.

'Didn't Haileybury know?' said Berlin.

'Why would he know?' said Philip.

It was a good question. How much interest would a trustee take in a boy's background? There were two others, who according to Haileybury were both discreet. The earl had suggested she needn't concern herself with them; this sort of suggestion more often

149

than not was a clear signal that she should look in that direction.

The trustees would owe a legal duty of care to any recipient of a scholarship, and would also have access to the paper trail. Discreet or not, they would bear a closer look.

'Do you remember anything about Hong Kong?' said Berlin.

'Not really,' said Philip. 'Sometimes I'm not sure if what I remember actually happened, or if I imagined it.'

'Do you remember anything at all about your mother?' she said.

'No,' said Philip.

'How often did you see Lee?' said Berlin.

'I met him for lunch a few times in Soho, and we had tea at the embassy once. He asked me not to mention it to anyone. He said their interest would be misinterpreted.'

That was an understatement, given Haileybury's dispute with the Chinese government, of which Philip was well aware.

He would have been flattered by the attention and the subterfuge; everyone enjoyed having a secret.

Philip had been groomed.

'What did you talk about?' said Berlin.

'My heritage, the Opium Wars, stuff like that,' he said. 'The suffering caused by the British and their trade. The millions of addicts.'

This wasn't just history for him. The tales of addiction would have struck home. She could see where this was going.

'What else?' she said.

'He told me how the Haileyburys acquired the collection,' said Philip.

She was pretty sure Lee wouldn't have used the word *acquired*.

'But you're not a kid,' she said. 'Surely Haileybury had explained all this.'

'Not in those terms,' said Philip.

Lee had used classic techniques on the boy, the sort of approach that would be used to turn someone into an asset.

'And then Lee introduced the idea that you were loot, too?' said Berlin.

'He said I was taken from my mother.'

'Who by?' said Berlin.

Philip focused again on his salt mountain, unwilling to engage any further. She couldn't let him avoid this.

'Who by?' she said.

'The Anglo-Chinese Friendship Society, I suppose,' he said.

His voice had gone up an octave. His body was rigid.

'You suppose?' said Berlin. 'Human traffickers don't spend a fortune educating you. They buy cheap and sell dear.'

The dog down the road started barking again.

'So maybe they bought me,' said Philip.

The swirls in the salt were becoming more chaotic.

'When Lee told you this story, why didn't you simply ask Haileybury for the truth?' said Berlin.

'It's not a story,' said Philip. 'You don't understand. Jack is very touchy about the Chinese government. I didn't tell him because I knew he wouldn't like it. He wouldn't even like me talking to these people. I didn't want to upset him.'

Never get on the wrong side of your dealer.

'The Chinese have got it in for him,' she said. 'This could all be designed to alienate you from him. You have to tell him.'

'How can I?' he said. 'Deng said if I didn't cooperate, my mother was at risk.'

'Cooperate with what?' said Berlin.

'Betraying Jack,' he said.

'How?' said Berlin.

His head dropped and his fringe fell across his face.

'Philip,' said Berlin. 'I need you to be straight with me.'

'No,' he shouted.

He swept his arm across the table. Salt and Scotch flew everywhere.

The barking dog began to howl.

29

The last place Haileybury wanted to be was at the House. He had been forced to share his office with two life peers. One of them ran in now, shuffled through the mountain of paper on his desk and ran out again, without so much as a by-your-leave.

'We've been inundated with these clowns since 1999,' said Haileybury. 'There are only ninety hereditary chaps left, for God's sake.'

From the brusque nod she gave him, it was evident Sylvie Laurent could not have cared less.

He pushed the phone back across the desk at her.

'It proves nothing,' he said. 'A trustee with one of the scholarship boys.'

'With respect, Lord Haileybury, Monsieur Lee suggests it implies more than that,' said Laurent. 'The photo is quite old. The question is when was it taken and who is the boy?'

'Madame Laurent, an older man who enjoys the company of fit young men may be pathetic, but as far as I'm aware, that's not a criminal offence.'

'Lee suggested he had other material,' said Laurent.

'Then let him produce it,' said Haileybury.

'He threatens a diplomatic incident and says he has a great deal of influence over Philip,' said Laurent.

'Poppycock,' said Haileybury. 'Did this fellow Lee show you any identification?'

Laurent shook her head.

'There you are,' said Haileybury. 'He's bluffing. Have you mentioned this to anyone else?'

'No,' said Laurent.

'And the photo?' said Haileybury.

'No, no,' said Laurent. 'No one.'

'So ignore him,' said Haileybury. 'This campaign they are waging against me is getting quite out of hand. I'll speak to my contacts in Whitehall.'

'Then what are your instructions, Lord Haileybury?' said Laurent, taking out her pen and notebook.

Typical. Covering her own arse.

'If Lee approaches you again, you may tell him to shove his negotiations where the sun doesn't shine,' said Haileybury. 'However that translates in legalese.'

When Laurent had gone, Haileybury grabbed his sticks, hobbled to the door and locked it. He needed a few moments to himself.

The bloody legal profession was constitutionally two-faced; lawyers always acted in their own interests if they perceived a threat, citing professional ethics or an obligation to the court or some such rubbish. Loyalty meant nothing to them. It wasn't mentioned in the statute books and was unknown in common law.

First, kill all the lawyers.

His mobile chimed 'Oranges and Lemons'. It was his habit to assign ringtones to his contacts. He snatched it up.

'Any news?' he said.

He listened for a moment.

'I'm at the House,' he said. 'I'm coming straight home. I'll meet you there.'

30

Berlin felt uneasy in the churchyard. The branch Bryant had stood under so resolutely had not yet fallen. The detective had been quiet, which was a worry. He wasn't a man to give up easily.

Some coppers put things in the too-hard basket and kept their heads down until pension time. She admired tenacity, but it was a pain in an opponent.

A car from a local minicab firm pulled up outside Haileybury's and the driver scooted out to assist the earl. Haileybury would have an account, but she'd bet he was a good tipper.

When the car had gone and Haileybury was at his front door, she crossed the road.

He jumped when he saw her, and grabbed her arm.

'Where have you been?' he said. 'I've been out of my mind with worry.'

She had promised Philip she wouldn't tell Haileybury about Lee, but it was a self-serving pledge; she was going to get information, not give it.

Then there was the small matter of Deng.

Sir Simon May was a warden at St Bride's. His name on the board in the churchyard had spoken volumes. He wasn't just a senior partner at Burghley; he was also the former chairman of the Joint Intelligence Organisation.

If Deng had been murdered, either side could have done it and deposited the body in a location associated with the well-known senior spook, the message being *we are in the game.*

The British or the Chinese could have persuaded the witness to recant, too, and had the video deleted.

Haileybury ushered her to one of the matching wing-backs at the massive table, crowded with all the things he liked to keep within reach. Philip had been one of them.

A chess set, backgammon and board games were piled in one corner, and she imagined the pair playing as they watched the traffic on the river below, passing a pleasant afternoon with crumpets and tea. An English idyll.

'Philip is fine,' she said.

'Where is he?' said Haileybury.

'Somewhere safe,' said Berlin.

'Is there any chance of us getting together?' said Haileybury. 'I would very much like to see him, or even speak with him, simply to reassure him he has my complete support, you understand. And to ease my mind. It doesn't have to be a very long conversation.'

'Would that be wise, given Chinese surveillance?' said Berlin. 'Any contact with you carries a risk of exposure. Then there's the police interest.'

She caught a glint of irritation in his eye.

'I suppose you're right,' he said. 'In any event, he's safe. You're worth your weight in gold, Berlin.'

'Let's clear up a couple of things before you start handing out the accolades,' she said. 'Did you persuade the witness not to testify? Did you destroy the CCTV evidence?'

Haileybury raised his twisted hands in shock.

'Good Lord,' he said. 'How do you think I could accomplish that? I can't even open a jam jar.'

'Burghley might assist,' she said.

'Look, Berlin,' said Haileybury. 'I don't deny that I'm often *assisted*, as you put it, by parties sympathetic to my cause. You seem to forget this isn't just about Philip and me; the national interest is at stake here.'

'Because the Chinese government is orchestrating events?' said Berlin.

'That's what you're supposed to be finding out, isn't it?' said Haileybury. 'Nothing happens in China without a nod from the government. Individuals might act on their own initiative, but it's always with tacit support.'

'And we respond in kind?' said Berlin.

'Let's say Whitehall won't interfere if someone close to them takes measures to counter a foreign power,' said Haileybury.

'Including murder?' said Berlin.

'Us or them?' said Haileybury.

He wasn't the least bit perturbed by the question, as if assassination was standard operating procedure in the intelligence playbook.

'You must remember how important this matter is to the Chinese,' he said. 'They refer to the looting as a wound that doesn't heal.'

'Is Philip an orphan?' said Berlin.

It was the last question he was expecting. Caught completely off guard, he mumbled and stumbled.

'Well . . . what?' he said. 'What's that got to do with it? Of course he is, he has to be, to be eligible for a scholarship.'

He studied her for a moment, then groaned.

'Oh Lord,' he said. 'It's not this thing about his mother, is it?'

'What makes you say that?' said Berlin.

Now it was her turn to be wrong-footed.

'It is,' said Haileybury. 'Christ.'

He slumped back in his chair.

Berlin felt the ground shifting under her once again.

Everything in this case was ambiguous; there wasn't one single, certain, undeniable fact on which she could base her next move. She had failed to apply the ABC of investigation – assume nothing, believe no one, check everything – and now she was paying the price.

She sighed. 'Perhaps we could have a drink?'

31

Haileybury had broken out a rare single malt and, as always, was being very free with it. It was more than a seduction. The wingback chair seemed to wrap itself around her. She longed for him to produce the filigreed silver box.

'We've had this business about his mother on and off for years,' said Haileybury. 'He believes she's alive in Hong Kong somewhere, and if he could just find out where, they would be reunited.'

'How does he rationalise being at Palmerston Hall?' said Berlin.

'He simply ignores anything that doesn't fit with his delusion,' said Haileybury.

Philip wasn't alone there.

'He doesn't seem to doubt he was taken from his mother, who didn't want to part with him,' said Berlin.

'*Idée fixe*,' said Haileybury.

'Are there documents, birth certificates, death certificates, that sort of thing?' she said.

'Of course,' said Haileybury. 'The trust is administered by the Friendship Society's lawyers. A trustee in Hong Kong screens the boys and assesses suitability for the programme. It's all above board.'

'Look at the British establishment,' said Berlin. 'It's pretty clear what happens when a child is shunted off to an institution at the age of six. If you don't mind my saying so.'

Haileybury didn't seem at all offended.

'Quite,' he said. 'Take the members of the Cabinet, for example.'

They both enjoyed a chuckle.

'The impact on a Chinese orphan, dispatched halfway across the world, is likely to have been just as emotionally damaging, if not worse,' said Berlin.

'I don't like to be critical,' said Haileybury, 'but Philip has always been rather highly strung.'

She could only agree. She was aware that the earl could be playing her, but they were both drunk and she could be playing him. They were in it together for now, but someone, eventually, would have to come out ahead.

'Who are the Society's lawyers?' said Berlin.

'Godson, Bell and Rushmore,' said Haileybury.

Who else?

The afternoon wore on. Berlin's interview technique was faltering; she'd put the same question to Haileybury in different forms, pressed him for details that were hard to fabricate on the fly, and drawn him out by always asking 'Anything else?' not 'Is that all?'

So far, after that initial stumble, he had passed with flying colours.

But now the probing routine was getting tired, and so was she.

'There's a very good Italian just along Wapping High Street,' he said. 'They don't deliver, but we can call ahead, if you don't mind popping down there and picking it up?'

He produced a menu from amongst the detritus on the table. So much for crumpets. She chose lasagne, then went to the bathroom, leaving Haileybury to order.

When she returned, he was standing at the window, gazing at the river.

'This is very good of you,' he said. 'Philip usually does the honours. No cash required. I've got an account. It will be ready by the time you get there.'

She put on her coat and the steel platform carried her down. As she glided past each floor, she was struck again by the extraordinary collection. The stone lions grinned at her. No wonder Haileybury wanted to hang on to them.

The imposing oak door swung open easily, thanks to its precision-engineered hinges, and swished shut behind her.

She buttoned up her coat as she crossed the portico and opened the creaking gates. Suddenly a man in a crash helmet was in front of her. The stars on his helmet glinted.

'Excuse me,' she said, and tried to walk around him, but he grabbed her and dragged her back beneath the portico.

'Christ, what's going on?' she said.

'Where's the boy?' he hissed.

He thrust his forearm against her throat.

'Fuck off,' said Berlin.

The slap caught her cheekbone and her head snapped back.

'Where's Philip Chen?' he said.

'I don't know,' she said.

He held her with one hand, then turned and raised the other. She heard a vehicle accelerate. Still dazed from the blow, and half drunk, she was helpless as he clamped his arm around her throat and his hand across her mouth and dragged her towards the gate.

Arms flailing, unable to breathe, she struggled to stay on her feet. Her heels barely touched the ground. He wasn't very big, but he was strong.

Gurgling and writhing, out of the corner of her eye she saw a white van pull up. The side door slid open. She struggled more determinedly, but in response, the pressure on her throat increased. She felt herself slipping.

'Stop, police!'

The command seemed to come from far away.

The man bundling her into the van loosened his grip so he could turn and face the threat.

She wrenched free, grabbed the edge of the van door and hung on. He shoved hard, trying to get her inside, but she braced herself.

'Oi!' came another shout.

The van began to move.

Her would-be abductor leapt into the back as it gathered speed, and gave her a sharp kick as a parting shot. She went down hard and rolled into the gutter.

Her head connected with the kerb.

Haileybury was seething. Perhaps it had been a mistake to involve Berlin. He made a call.

'Hello,' he said. 'It's me. Where are you?'

His hand locked around the phone, a claw over which he had no control.

'Oh yes, of course, I forgot,' he said. 'Now look, I'm sure Berlin knows where Philip is. She's asking a lot of questions, as if I'm the problem here. You know this is a difficult time, with the eighteenth birthday coming up. I'm struggling. That terrible sense of loss. It engulfs me again and . . .'

Words of reassurance were touching, but he required action.

'That's all very well,' he said. 'Call me when you know what you're going to do about it.'

He hung up and prised the phone from his stiff, unyielding fingers. This terrible malady had finally defeated him. It would be over soon. He felt it in his bones.

32

Berlin came round slowly. The first thing she saw was a familiar crack in the ceiling. She tried to sit up, but the room swam, so she gave it up as a bad job and lay down again. It was, however, enough to convince her she was in her own flat.

A face loomed over her.

'Where's Philip Chen?' said Bryant.

'Jesus Christ,' said Berlin.

He stood there glaring down at her. His suit, an old-fashioned double-breasted pinstripe that could have been a hand-me-down from his grandad, hung off him. The dark bags under his eyes were a stark contrast to his pallid complexion. It was clear things weren't going well for him, which made her feel better.

She made another attempt at rising, and this time managed to hoist herself a little further up the sofa.

Bryant put a cushion behind her back.

'How did I get here?' she said.

'I had the pool car,' said Bryant.

'What about the stairs?' said Berlin.

'I carried you,' said Bryant. 'There's nothing of you. You don't look after yourself properly.'

'You sound like my mother,' said Berlin.

'So did you just happen to be in the vicinity of Haileybury's, or have you had me under surveillance again?' she said. 'Or still?'

'I've seen that bloke with the stars on his helmet before,' said Bryant. 'He was taking photos of you going into Haileybury's. I took a closer look when I clocked him there again. Good job I did.'

'How did you get into my flat?' said Berlin.

'I went through your pockets for the keys,' said Bryant. 'As it turned out, I didn't need them.'

He pointed at the front door.

It hung limply, all the locks shattered and half the frame with them.

'Not again,' said Berlin. 'What did they take?'

'Nothing, from the look of it,' said Bryant. The cartons of Peggy's stuff were untouched. 'Not even your computer. It's still on the table.'

This was no burglary. Bryant echoed her thought.

'They weren't looking for something to flog down the market,' he said. 'They were after Chen.'

'Why would they think he was here?' said Berlin. 'And who are "they", anyway?'

'Criminal types engaged in blackmail or drug-running or something along those lines,' said Bryant. 'Haileybury's dirt is finally sticking.'

He was wandering around her flat, plucking books from the shelf and peering at them, checking out the contents of her cupboards. He frowned. She had to admit, they were bare.

She swung her legs off the sofa and managed to stand. It felt as if she was on the deck of a ship in a choppy sea.

'I appreciate your intervention,' she said. 'But don't let me keep you.'

'Don't try it on with me, Berlin,' said Bryant. 'This wasn't a mugging.'

'What happened? You called for backup and it never came?' said Berlin.

He slammed a cupboard door.

So he hadn't called it in because he was playing offside.

'Any plates on the van?' she said.

'Obscured,' said Bryant.

'Bad luck,' said Berlin. 'So thanks, Bryant. Now bugger off.'

He smiled. It was chilling.

'When I went through your coat pockets looking for the key, guess what I found?' he said.

He held up a small transparent Ziploc bag. Inside was a chunk of something sticky and dark brown. It wasn't treacle toffee.

'I'm going to ask you one more time,' he said. 'Where's Philip Chen?'

The choppy sea became a tempest.

She sat down again.

Bryant dangled the bag in front of her.

'Heroin,' he said. 'Class A. I'd say about five grams.'

She wasn't going to correct him.

'A year per gram, what do you think?' said Bryant. 'That is, if you can get out of the intent-to-supply charge.'

'I've never seen it before,' she said.

'Tell me where Chen is, keep your nose out of it, and it's all yours,' said Bryant.

Haileybury had set her up. She was holding out on him, so he'd called not for Italian, but for thugs who would persuade her to give up Philip's whereabouts. Stuffing the opium in her pocket was a nice touch if the constabulary got involved. They had.

'He's at Haileybury's,' she said.

Bryant seemed surprised.

'He must have slipped him in the back way,' he said.

'What back way?' said Berlin. The warehouse backed directly on to the river.

'He thinks he can do what he bloody well likes,' said Bryant.

'He can,' said Berlin. 'He's the eighth Earl Haileybury. You're a numpty copper.'

'We'll see,' said Bryant.

'You've got what you wanted,' said Berlin. She put her hand out for the baggie.

Bryant put it back in his pocket.

'I'm doing you a favour,' he said. 'I'm not interested in you. It's him I want, and the corrupt cronies protecting him. You're just a junkie.'

'And you're just a prick,' said Berlin. 'Shut the door on your way out.'

In the still night air, a plume of smoke hung over the Hackney Marshes. Lee dabbed at the sweat on his forehead, then held the handkerchief over his mouth and nose, protection from the acrid fumes of the burning van.

His presence was intended to humiliate his subordinates, sending a clear message that he couldn't trust them.

The same message had been delivered to him about his own performance.

He walked to the waiting car and got in the back.

'Where to?' said the driver.

'Gerrard Street,' said Lee.

In the basement of a restaurant in Chinatown he could find everything he needed: pork and pea-shoot dumplings to ease his hunger, a massage to ease his neck, and a pipe to ease his soul. So much had been stolen from him that only one thing could assuage his thirst for justice.

The investigator and the policeman were both proving greater obstacles than he had anticipated; both lacked discipline and this made them unpredictable. The British could be so stubborn when provoked.

Sterner measures were required.

'What about them?' said the driver.

He pointed at the two men still watching the fire.

'Let them walk,' said Lee.

33

Berlin took some codeine, drank some whisky and called the twenty-four-hour locksmith, with whom she was well acquainted. The mere sight of the opium had been enough to heighten a craving already threatening to careen out of control.

When Bryant had walked out with it, she had wanted to scream with frustration.

She checked her phone. There was a text message and voicemail from Haileybury wondering where she was and hoping everything was okay. It could be an attempt to deflect suspicion, but on the other hand, she might have been a bit hasty in sending Bryant to the earl's. It was a kneejerk reaction, tit for tat.

Haileybury might have slipped the opium into her pocket as a gesture of appreciation, or perhaps he thought she could get it to Philip.

Every bone in her body ached from resisting her would-be abductors. Her ears were still ringing and her head throbbed. If it wasn't Haileybury, it was the Chinese.

Bryant had confirmed that someone had her under surveillance. Lee was as anxious as the earl to get his hands on Philip, so much so that he had taken the risk of masquerading as the boy's father. Assuming, of course, that he wasn't.

Philip was the lynchpin in Lee's strategy. Although the boy hadn't given up the details of how he was to betray Haileybury, there was plenty to work with; exposing the earl as a drug-peddling paedophile would get the job done.

Betrayal was rough on the betrayer and the betrayed.

The thought sent her back to her computer, which had been of no interest to the most recent intruder. She searched again for a trace left when the CCTV video was wiped.

Experienced operatives would have no problem getting into her flat and hacking her password, but they would leave something behind. It was Locard's exchange principle: every contact leaves a trace.

She checked the Windows systems log of date and time stamps against her own movements, to try and establish exactly when the first incursion might have occurred. She had it down to someone working for Haileybury, but the Chinese would have an interest in deleting the video.

They wouldn't want Deng identified, or Philip in a juvenile facility where they couldn't get to him.

She ran through the logs again. Something niggled her about the results.

A fugue state – dissociation – is necessary before the unthinkable can be thought. The intricate defences that human beings erect against the truth are more impervious than any computer firewall.

It takes time for an unwelcome – an unbelievable – reality to sink in: your husband is gay; your son is a terrorist. Your grandfather's a killer; your daughter's a heroin addict. Your friend is a lying toerag.

It was just a shadow at first, but it soon took familiar shape. She left the computer humming and ran a very hot bath, past caring about the lack of a secure front door. When she climbed in, the steam rose around her, a cocoon that would soften the blow as she let her resistance crumble.

By the time the water was cold, the shadow had hardened into the truth.

She called Del. He didn't answer, so she left a message.

'My place as soon as you can,' she said. 'It's urgent.'

Del had to manoeuvre the door aside to get into the flat. Berlin was sitting at the table.

'What happened here?' he said. 'Are you okay?'

He was breathless. He'd run up the stairs.

'I'm fine,' she said. Her hair was still wet and she was barefoot.

'I thought it was urgent,' he said, as he re-positioned the door.

'I've got a problem with my computer,' said Berlin.

'You're kidding?' he said. 'You got me over here for that? You know I haven't a clue.'

'Yeah,' said Berlin. 'I know.'

It was as if the air around them had thickened.

'But if you've got the system administrator's password, you'd be able to use it, wouldn't you?' she said. 'Even you know how to delete a file.'

'What are you talking about?' said Del.

'Have you got my keys with you?' said Berlin.

Del nodded. He fished them out of his pocket.

'I'm getting the locks changed,' she said.

Del's eyes did that thing eyes do when someone is cornered; they looked everywhere for a way out.

'Did you do it yourself, or did you lend your keys to someone at Burghley?' said Berlin.

She saw his throat constrict. He swallowed hard.

'I would never let anyone else in here,' he said.

'So you did it yourself,' she said. 'What did it take? Threats? Promises? Or both?'

'You don't understand,' he said.

'Yeah, I do,' she said. 'Burghley gave me this computer to replace the one I had to ditch in Moscow during the last job. They would have everything on file, all the access codes. Just in case. It's routine.'

'Berlin,' he said. 'You've been under a lot of strain, with Peggy and all . . .'

'The body of Philip Chen's victim – who was, by the way, a Chinese agent – was found in the crypt at St Bride's,' she said. 'He'd also been following me.'

'What?' said Del.

'Sir Simon May is a warden at St Bride's,' she said. 'Did you know that, Del?'

He stared at her.

'Did you suggest me for this job, or did he?'

'I can't remember,' stuttered Del. 'He might have reviewed the contractor's files before we discussed it.'

They would know more about her than she knew herself. Burghley had an impeccable reputation and connections at the highest level. They'd used her because she had a dubious reputation and connections at the lowest level; as an added bonus, she could be kept at arm's length.

'So are you just a dumb pawn unwittingly doing their bidding? Or are you a disloyal fucking weasel who would betray an old friend to protect your pension?'

Her heart was pounding so hard she shook with each beat.

Del took a step towards her, his face creased with concern.

'Are you using again?' he said.

It was the final straw. She strode over, snatched the keys from his hand and shoved him in the chest. He staggered back, careening into Peggy's cartons.

'Get out,' she said. 'Get out of my fucking house and get out of my fucking life.'

Berlin called a cab and stuffed her voluminous black canvas bag with clothes, phone charger, passport and computer. They were the only things worth nicking, apart from Peggy's carnival glassware.

She doubted that collectors would be on the prowl.

34

When she unlocked the front door, there were no signs of life in the house. She checked the kitchen and front room, then, panicking slightly, took the stairs as fast as her limp would allow. Philip was asleep in her old room. The empty bottle of Scotch was on the bedside table. She supposed that was a result.

'Wake up, Philip,' she said. She shook him.

He woke, blinking and surly.

'Where were you?' he said. 'I was worried.'

'We have to talk about your mother,' she said.

He sat up, wide awake now.

'What about her?' he said.

If Del could lie to her, all bets were off. She'd been setting the benchmark too low.

'Did Lee ever give you any evidence about the existence of your mother?' she said.

'He showed me a photograph,' said Philip.

'Did you recognise her?' Berlin asked.

Philip shook his head.

'Anything else?' said Berlin.

'He gave me an address and said I should write to her.'

'I thought you didn't know where she was,' said Berlin.

'It's a mail service in Hong Kong,' he said. 'Like a private post office box.'

'Did you write?'

'Of course,' he said.

He'd been shipped off to school before he could even tie his own shoelaces. The prospect of a real mother, someone he'd dreamt of for years, would have been irresistible.

'We've been writing to each other ever since,' he said.

Berlin took a deep breath.

'Where are the letters?'

'In my room at school,' he said.

Not any more.

Philip went back to sleep, still feeling the effects of the Scotch. He needed to sleep while he could, before it became impossible to smother his anxiety with alcohol. Berlin was already on the edge.

Unable to wander the streets in her usual fashion – she didn't want Philip to wake up and find her gone – she crept about the house. Every room invoked a memory. Few were pleasant. Peggy dogged her footsteps, urging her not to move anything and not to make a mess.

Finally she lay down on the lumpy sofa.

'Leave me alone,' she mumbled.

No one was listening.

The next thing she knew, it was ten o'clock. She could hear the water running. Philip was in the bathroom. She rolled off the sofa, went to the kitchen and put the kettle on. She had to pull herself together for his sake.

The thought struck her as bizarre. She wasn't being paid as a nursemaid; in fact, after the incident at Haileybury's, she wasn't sure she was being paid at all.

She took her tea and her phone outside, to the square of concrete Peggy referred to as a courtyard, and sat on the back step. It was Saturday, but Palmerston Hall was a 24/7 institution. Someone would pick up.

In the event, it was the bursar, Mayhew.

'It's Catherine Berlin here,' she said. 'I was at the school the other day.'

'I remember,' said Mayhew.

'Is Ms Trevelyan there?'

'It's Saturday,' said Mayhew.

'You're working,' said Berlin.

'As are you.'

'No rest for the wicked,' said Berlin.

Mayhew uttered a noise that might have been a laugh.

'Perhaps I can help you?' he said.

'Philip Chen's things have been put into storage, right?' said Berlin.

'Correct,' said Mayhew.

'I wondered if I could come and take a look.'

'For what?' said Mayhew.

She hesitated.

'Some letters,' she said.

'I'm sorry,' said Mayhew. 'The school couldn't possibly allow that.'

He hung up.

'Hey,' said Philip.

She turned around. He was standing in the kitchen with a towel wrapped around him.

'I need some clean underwear,' he said.

Jesus. Now she was supposed to worry about his bloody pants.

Her phone pinged as a text arrived. She read it, then poured the rest of her tea down the sink.

'I have to go out,' she said. 'I'll drop into the pound shop on the way back.'

'I prefer Calvin Klein,' said Philip.

'Yeah,' said Berlin. 'They do those.'

Bryant had tidied himself up – run his fingers through his hair and reknotted his tie – before fronting up to DCI Tomalin's residence, but it didn't seem to be helping.

'Have you completely lost your mind, Bryant?' said Tomalin. 'Coming here, to my home, after what I said yesterday?'

Tomalin, wearing a tracksuit that didn't hide his paunch, was sitting on his sofa in his very nicely appointed Arts and Crafts drawing room. The document Bryant had prepared and printed at the station lay in his lap.

'No, sir,' said Bryant. 'You told me to treat Chen as a missing person and I have strong grounds for believing that he's ensconced at Lord Haileybury's residence.'

'*Ensconced?*' said Tomalin. 'And you expect me to sign off on this application for a warrant to search the place?'

'Yes, sir,' said Bryant. 'So I can see the magistrate on call as soon as possible . . .'

'Do you know the difference between a missing person and a wanted person, Bryant?'

'Sir, I have reason to believe the boy might have contraband at the premises,' said Bryant.

Tomalin rose. 'Contraband?' he said. 'Based on what?'

If he mentioned the business with Berlin and the drugs, it would make things worse. It would be obvious that he was alleging Haileybury was involved with narcotics, and that he was the real target of the search. At best, the heavy squad would then take over; at worst, he would be assigned to traffic and nothing else would happen.

'A well-placed source,' he said.

'Got a snout in the House of Lords, have you, Bryant?' said Tomalin.

'At the Abbey,' said Bryant. 'Chen was undergoing detox, so it's a fair bet that—'

'A fair bet?' said Tomalin. 'Is that what we rely on now? Something along the lines of women's intuition, is it?'

Bryant clamped his teeth together so he wouldn't open his mouth.

'What's the evidential connection with Haileybury? Sweet fuck-all,' said Tomalin. 'Even if the boy is at his place. And if he is, he's not missing any more, you pillock.'

He tore the document in half and let it drift to the floor.

Bryant opened his mouth, but shut it again quickly when Tomalin raised his hand in warning.

'Call the school,' said Tomalin. 'Ask them politely to confirm that Chen is at Lord Haileybury's, and if he is, take him off the misper list.'

'But, sir . . .' said Bryant.

'Do you know what it's like, Bryant, trying to rationalise the use of resources in a case like this? Have you any idea of the number of reports, memos, emails, charts, statistics and other crap I have to prepare?'

'No, sir, I—' said Bryant.

Tomalin thundered on. 'Let alone the time I've had to spend dealing with enquiries from senior officers – *very* senior officers – about why this boy, a lad with an impeccable background, is being hounded when all he did was react to some shirt-lifter's indecent suggestion by breaking his nose.'

'He didn't break it, sir,' said Bryant. 'The pathologist—'

'The pathologist says this bloke OD'd,' said Tomalin.

'What?' said Bryant. 'No one told me, sir.'

He was gutted.

'Why would they? Who the hell do you think you are?' said Tomalin.

'There you are then,' said Bryant. 'Chen's victim used drugs. That's a connection.'

'Christ Almighty,' said Tomalin.

'You don't understand,' said Bryant.

'I do,' said Tomalin. 'One more stunt like this and you're finished.'

35

The man waiting for Berlin beneath the statue of Boadicea on Westminster Bridge was, she guessed, like her, unreconstructed; he would have no truck with *Boudicca*. She was Boadicea when they were at school, and Boadicea she would remain. He squinted up at the warrior in her chariot.

'There's no mercy shown an old queen,' said Mayhew.

It wasn't the opening line she expected. She laughed.

He took a pack of cigarettes from the pocket of his belted gabardine raincoat; her guess was spot on. He offered her one, which she declined.

He was wearing a raincoat, although it was mild. As usual, she was wearing her black overcoat. They had more than a vintage in common.

On the other side of the road Big Ben chimed the hour, to the delight of the battalions of tourists jostling them.

'Let's find somewhere more congenial,' said Berlin.

Mayhew nodded and turned into the wind to light his cigarette. It gave her a moment to stare at his gaunt profile, the pink tinge to his closely shaven cheek.

He would use an old safety razor like her father's, which she had found wrapped in tissue paper in Peggy's hankie drawer. There was nothing plastic or disposable about Mayhew.

'I appreciated your text,' she said. '*Palmerston Hall couldn't possibly. I could.*'

Mayhew glanced around. He was nervous.

'Come on,' she said. 'I know a place just up the road.'

The Ship & Shovell had the distinction of being located on both sides of a lane, beneath which it was linked by a cellar. Berlin chose the snug side.

Mayhew carried their pints to a small alcove.

'Cheers,' she said.

Mayhew raised his glass. They both sipped their beer.

'You were in the services?' said Berlin.

'Is it that obvious?' said Mayhew. 'I come from a long line of infantrymen, so an infantryman I was destined to be, although I would have preferred the sappers. I joined my father's regiment. He died the year I was born. Nineteen fifty-four. Killed by the Mau Mau.'

'The independence movement in Kenya?' said Berlin.

'If that's what you want to call it,' said Mayhew. 'It was a bit more complicated than that.'

'But simple for your father, I imagine,' said Berlin. 'Kill or be killed.'

'He died and I got a scholarship to Palmerston Hall,' said Mayhew. He didn't try to disguise his bitterness.

'You think his death was a waste?' said Berlin.

'"Never think that war, no matter how necessary, nor how justified, is not a crime. Ask the infantry and ask the dead",' said Mayhew. 'Ernest Hemingway.'

'Because in the end we gave up the Empire, so it was all for nothing?' said Berlin.

'Because now the Mau Mau are suing us for human rights abuses,' said Mayhew. 'And my father is spinning in an unmarked grave in a jungle somewhere.'

Berlin wanted to understand what had brought him here, but she was no wiser.

'I gather you're not a fan of Flora Trevelyan?' she said.

'She's a fraud,' said Mayhew.

'How do you mean?' said Berlin.

He flushed slightly. 'What's your background?'

'Born in Bethnal Green, above my dad's shop. Grew up there and in Leyton, with my mum. Comprehensive school, red-brick university. All downhill since then.'

He gave her an understanding nod. She had passed muster, it seemed. Respectable working class. Clean, with neat gardens and tidy minds. Hard-working Anglo-Saxons who loved the Queen. If only he knew.

'Ms Trevelyan's only concern is to protect what she likes to call the school's brand,' he said. 'The welfare of the boys, our values – Palmerston Hall values – come a poor second.'

'And, of course, your only concern is Philip's welfare,' said Berlin. 'Purely altruistic.'

It was a pointed observation, not lost on Mayhew. He put his pint down on the table, slopping the Badger Best.

'My motivation is none of your business,' he said quietly.

It was a statement of fact, not rudeness. She watched him struggle with what he was about to say. Finally he spoke up.

'The lad's in trouble. Serious trouble. With his own people.'

'Who are?'

'Two Chinese blokes. He's been seen getting into a car with them more than once. A black Lexus. Butterworth, the gatehouse guard, told me, and I told Trevelyan. She just brushed me off. Said it was probably relatives.'

'Sounds reasonable,' said Berlin.

'He doesn't have any bloody relatives,' said Mayhew. 'These boys are cut off completely.'

'You mean the scholarship boys?' said Berlin.

Mayhew peered into his beer, as if the answer were there. 'All I know is that Philip needs protecting.'

'If you're so concerned, why don't you do something about it yourself?' said Berlin.

Mayhew drained his glass.

'It's a question of loyalty,' he said.

'When can I take a look at Philip's things?' she said.

'You can't. I can't get you in there without someone noticing.'

Berlin was about to remonstrate when he reached inside his raincoat and produced a bundle, which he put on the table in front of her.

'This is what you want,' he said. 'And I'd be grateful if you kept my name out of it.'

*

The moment she put her key in the lock, the door was flung open.

'Where have you been?' said Philip.

His hair and T-shirt were plastered to his skin with sweat. His eyes were saucers, his nose dripping.

Berlin closed the door behind her. He backed up as she walked down the hall.

'Did you hear me?' he said. 'Where have you been?'

The kitchen looked as if a whirlwind had passed through it. Philip clamped his hands to his temples. Keeping his head together.

'Okay, Philip,' said Berlin. 'Sit down for a moment, drink some water, and let's talk about what's happening to you.'

'I don't want to fucking talk,' he shouted. 'You're holding out on me, aren't you? You've got some stuff and you won't share it.'

He pushed past her, ran out of the kitchen and up the stairs.

'Come on, Philip,' she said. 'I wouldn't do that.'

She followed.

There was an almighty crash in the bathroom.

When she got there, the bathroom cabinet had been wrenched from the wall. Philip was standing amongst the remnants of the mirror. Caught in the shards, their fragmented images stared back at her.

She wasn't superstitious, but it seemed very much like a portent, which was ridiculous. She was close to losing it herself. Neither of them could go on like this much longer.

'I'm sorry,' said Philip.

'It's okay,' said Berlin.

'What are we going to do?' he said.

'How much opium does Haileybury have?' said Berlin.

Philip shrugged.

'I don't know. He keeps it locked up. I asked him once how much was down there. He said, "Enough to start a war."'

36

Haileybury answered his phone on the second ring.

'Berlin here,' she said.

'Berlin, I've been so worried,' he said. 'How are you?'

He sounded genuinely pleased to hear from her. He also sounded as if he'd been drinking. He might be a rich aristocrat, but sometimes he was just another lonely old man in pain.

'Fine, thanks,' said Berlin. 'And you?'

'I didn't want to keep calling you,' said Haileybury. 'One doesn't really know the protocol in these situations, but I was very concerned about your sudden disappearance yesterday.'

An earl, uncertain about protocol. Almost deferential.

'I'm sorry about that,' said Berlin. 'This is the first chance I've had to get in touch.'

She had to tell him what had happened; if she didn't, and he had orchestrated it, he would know she suspected him.

'I was ambushed by some thugs,' she said. 'They wanted to know about Philip.'

'Oh my God,' said Haileybury. 'That's terrible. Did they hurt you? The damn Chinese. They're incorrigible.'

'I'm okay,' she said. She was shadow-boxing, taking jabs at opponents she wasn't sure were really there. 'Have you heard from Philip?'

As if he were on holiday, and they were waiting for a postcard.

'Not a dicky bird,' said Haileybury. 'I do hope everything's all right.'

'I'm sure it is,' said Berlin. 'No news is good news.'

Silence greeted this ridiculous comment. It was appropriate.

'Anyway,' she said. 'There are some things we need to discuss, but not on the phone. It's not secure.'

'Quite,' said Haileybury.

'And I'd rather not meet at your place, given recent events.'

'I understand,' said Haileybury.

'Are you able to get out this evening?' said Berlin.

'I can call for a car. They're usually here within fifteen minutes. Is this about Philip?'

'Yes,' she said. 'Do you know the Prospect of Whitby?'

'The pub at Wapping Wall?' said Haileybury.

'That's the one,' said Berlin. 'Meet me there in half an hour.'

She hung up before he could ask any more questions.

'Was that true?' said Philip. 'About someone attacking you because of me.'

'No,' said Berlin. 'I just said it to impress him.'

Philip was jittery enough.

They were in a café in Shadwell that was only a five-minute walk from the Prospect of Whitby and a brisk ten minutes from the Haileybury residence. The earl couldn't walk it, which worked for them.

'Do you think he'll go for it?' said Philip.

'Why wouldn't he?' she said. 'I'm betting he'd do pretty much anything for you.'

He made a face.

Berlin picked up her phone and took a photo.

'Very funny,' he said. 'What are you going to say when he gets there?'

The letters purporting to be from Philip's mother were in her pocket. She knew a good hand when she saw one; the hard part was resisting the temptation to overplay it.

'I'll tell him that unless he coughs up his stash, he'll never see you again.'

'That's not funny,' said Philip. 'I feel awful, deceiving him like this.'

'You'll soon get over it,' she said.

He pouted. He resented her snapping at him. Too bad. He wasn't the only one hanging out for the dreamy embrace of opium. Even the twilight was irritating, the way it softened contours, disguising shapes without completely obscuring them. She preferred the certainty of night and day, and in particular, moonless nights that favoured the foolhardy.

She glanced at her phone.

'I'm off,' she said. 'I'll see you back at Leyton. When the car goes past, don't hang about.'

Bryant saw the car pull up at Haileybury's. It was from Prestige Cars, the local firm the earl used to ferry him to the House and his club. That was about the extent of his travels these days.

Minicab drivers were a potent source of intel and cooperated with the plod so that leniency would be shown when it came to overdue MOTs and the like.

The earl emerged from his lair on his sticks and the driver got out to give him a hand getting into the car.

Bryant put the binoculars down and checked his charts. Perfect.

When he looked again, the car was driving away.

His kit was waiting, so he grabbed it and left the flat, ready to run down the stairs if the lift wasn't working.

The gods were smiling on him.

The doors slid open and he stepped inside.

'Wish me luck, Gran,' he muttered. 'It's now or never.'

37

The pub was spacious and relatively quiet. These days it was more of a tourist trap during the day and a local at night, although the new tribe of residents in Wapping favoured Spitalfields or Clerkenwell for a night out. The Prospect still had sauce bottles on the tables.

Berlin found a discreet corner overlooking the river. In the seventeenth century it had been a favourite haunt of Hanging Judge Jeffreys. The noose that hung over the water, commemorating him, swung gently in the breeze.

She could almost feel it around her neck.

Haileybury wouldn't be far behind her, although there was a stretch of road that was one-way, which meant the car would have to take the long way round.

She settled in with a pint of London Pride.

Showing the earl the letters was a risk. The exact nature of his relationship with Philip still worried her. She imagined that, like Bryant, the Chinese thought there was a lot more to the relationship with Philip than Haileybury would care to disclose publicly.

If Philip had been used sexually by Haileybury when he was a minor, he was the victim of abuse, and as such he probably suffered from all the guilt and shame that went with it. He might not even recognise it as abuse.

Her glass was empty. The earl's trip was taking longer than she'd thought. She went to the bar and ordered another.

Bryant surveyed the warehouse. It was old, but impregnable. The buildings either side were so close that the passages were barely wide enough for a broad-shouldered man. The walls of the warehouse itself were sheer and windowless.

Both passages led to the river, one to a high embankment and the other to the remnants of the watermen's stairs, which were still just about usable at low tide. If you were prepared to make the final five-foot drop into mud.

He was as prepared as he'd ever be. The tide was out and wouldn't come rushing in and catch him unawares. The gloaming had dwindled into darkness. He hung his kit on a rusty rod above the waterline, then jumped from the last broken concrete step on to the shingle.

There was no moon, but the sulphurous yellow dome of light that always hung over the city bathed the river in molten bronze. The mud squelched as he moved along, staying close to the embankment, which was thick with rank green slime, phosphorescent in the gloom.

Far above him was Haileybury's terrace. It was an extension of the old loading platform. The chains that had once supported it were still there, as was the block and tackle above it, used to shift cargo off barges and into the warehouse.

The decadent aristocrat would sit up there taking tea and enjoying the view, and here he was, an officer sworn to uphold the good, scuttling through the mud like a river rat.

He edged along and came to a channel in the shingle. It had been carved out by the current as it surged back and forth through an arch in the embankment.

It was too high and too broad to be a storm-water drain, and was protected by a metal grille that looked for all the world like a portcullis. It *was* a portcullis.

He'd seen it through his binoculars from the other side of the river, but up close it was a solid piece of Victorian engineering. Behind it was a boathouse.

Years ago he and Gran had seen Haileybury in a sleek timber launch. This must have been where they kept it. He peered through the grille. Nothing there now, just the hollow sound of water slapping against stone.

The portcullis disappeared beneath the surface of the channel. He hoped it finished well above the bottom. He dropped into the channel, nearly losing his balance as the water swirled around his thighs. Wading close to the grille, gripped by fear, he took a deep breath and ducked.

His eyes were open but the silt billowed around him as he crawled forward. He couldn't see a thing. He would have to be careful where he came up, or get impaled on the ironwork. It wasn't far, but his lungs felt as if they were going to burst.

Without warning, the bottom fell away and he was plunged into deep water. Terrified, he struggled to the surface and gasped for air. The portcullis was behind him. He grasped it and moved along, hand over hand, until he reached the parapet that ran around the edge of the dank space.

He clambered out and lay exhausted on the rough flag-stones. He was in. Haileybury's citadel wasn't impregnable after all.

Halfway through her second pint, Berlin cursed, jumped to her feet and ran for the door. He wasn't coming. How could she have misjudged it so badly?

Her judgement had been clouded by the relentless need the earl had so artfully reignited. After decades of careful management, she was on her knees and at its mercy again.

Philip was young and had no experience in dealing with this demon, but she had no excuse.

Her damaged tendon screamed as she ran. She welcomed the pain; it served her right.

Haileybury hesitated. There was something tawdry about what he was about to do. He switched on the lamp. Philip, frozen in the soft pool of light, uttered a small cry. He looked so vulnerable. The desk drawer hung askew. The silver box glinted in his hand. Haileybury felt a surge of love and regret.

'My dear boy,' he said. 'Welcome home.'

38

Dripping wet, Bryant padded up a short flight of stairs. The door at the top opened on to a cavernous space that appeared to extend the length and breadth of the building.

As his eyes adjusted to the gloom, he could see pulleys hanging from the ceiling and a geared wheel set into the floor. Dust sheets and tarpaulins hid other monstrous objects. There was a mezzanine, and more stairs, which rose into darkness.

From the outside, the warehouse gave the impression of four floors, but the interior was a maze of false ceilings and galleries. He didn't know exactly where he was or how he'd find the front door. He was determined to leave that way, in possession of evidence that would prove that Haileybury was engaged in criminal activity.

It was up to him to find the incriminating material: drugs, pornography, or something that would expose his relationship with Chen. If Philip Chen was actually there, all well and good. He could handle the boy; he might even be able to get him to cooperate and make a statement about when it started. He was, after all, a victim himself.

Tomalin's announcement that the victim of the assault had probably died of an overdose was a setback, but Bryant hadn't entirely given up hope on that score. He would wait and see how the forensic report panned out, although he wouldn't put it past them to interfere with that too.

The old brick walls were so thick that all sound was deadened. Every so often he passed iron rings set into piers, from which hung thick cables. He shuddered.

A blue light glowed at the far end of the basement. As he moved closer, it resolved into strips of light leaking from a doorway. There was a hum, too, of a generator or an industrial fan. There was a steel door, and beside it a keypad. He reached out.

The alarm went off.

The clanging bell was so loud he plugged his ears and ran back towards the stairs he'd passed, desperate to get away from the deafening noise. He ran up them and flung open a small door at the top.

Haileybury was standing there, pointing what appeared to be a revolver. Philip Chen stood beside him, ashen.

Disoriented, Bryant raised his hands in surrender.

The room behind the pair was straight out of Sherlock Holmes. A Victorian study. He couldn't help laughing.

In the distance, sirens wailed.

Berlin could see pulsing blue lights in the distance as she ran down Wapping High Street. She prayed it was just a coincidence and nothing to do with Haileybury.

By the time she got there, it was obvious her supplications had been ignored. Police and security guards were milling around outside the warehouse, their vehicles parked haphazardly across the pavement.

Her instinct was to run back the way she'd come; this was all her fault. Philip's fingerprint was in the biometric system, and he knew the four-digit code.

Unless Haileybury had changed it. She had been so keen for Philip to get in, get what he needed and get out, it hadn't occurred to her. She had dressed up the incursion as altruism and been blinded by her own hunger.

The gate was manned by a guard clad in riot gear. The sounds of a struggle inside the warehouse were accompanied by shouts and swearing. Surely Haileybury wouldn't let them rough Philip up?

Astonished, but relieved, she watched as four coppers emerged through the front door carrying Detective Constable Bryant. Naked apart from a pair of swimming trunks, he was screaming something about perversion and corruption.

What looked like a length of plastic cable was tied around his waist; from it hung a collection of empty evidence bags of various sizes. A bit of a giveaway.

A four-wheel drive pulled up sharply and a man jumped out. A policewoman ran over to him clutching a sports bag.

'What the hell's going on?' he said.

'He managed to get in from the river, boss,' said the policewoman. She held up the bag. 'His clothes are in here. It was hanging off the watermen's stairs.'

The boss was a tubby middle-aged man with thinning hair, buzz cut so he didn't look bald.

By now, a group of bystanders had gathered to watch the show. Berlin joined them. The officers carrying Bryant paused, apparently waiting for instructions.

'You're one of them, Tomalin,' Bryant shouted at the man who had just arrived.

'Put him in the van,' said Tomalin.

Tomalin strode into Haileybury's, wringing his hands as if he'd like to put them around someone's neck and choke the life out of them. Berlin guessed it would have been Bryant.

The officers struggling with the object of his fury advanced towards the van. She took a step back, hoping to blend in with the rubberneckers, but it was too late. Bryant spotted her.

'Berlin,' he said. 'Berlin, you know, tell them. It's a cover-up.'

Some of the people turned to look, and she looked around too; he couldn't possibly be addressing her.

'Berlin!' shouted Bryant. He resisted in vain as he was shoved into the back of the van. The closing doors muffled his final plea. 'Please, Berlin, please.'

The obsessed detective had only recently rescued her from an unwanted joyride. Even though he had exploited it for his own ends, she still felt bad. More so because Bryant was right, and there was no lonelier feeling than being shut down for telling the truth.

When she looked back, Haileybury and Philip were standing side by side beneath the portico, shaking hands with Tomalin. She caught snatches of his profuse and grovelling apology.

'. . . and the Chief Commissioner . . . personally ensure that neither you nor Mr Chen are inconvenienced . . .'

A loud drubbing noise from inside the police van signalled Bryant's displeasure with incarceration. It was a desperate drumbeat.

The van moved off. Tomalin shook Haileybury's hand again, and retreated to his vehicle.

Haileybury, solicitous, ushered Philip inside.

The imposing oak door swung closed behind them.

39

Berlin was woken by her mobile. It was the middle of the night. She didn't recognise the number and she couldn't remember where she was. The taste of whisky in her mouth and a splitting headache stood between her and clarity.

In the dim light from the window she saw Led Zeppelin. Christ, she was in Leyton. How had she got here?

The phone kept buzzing. She propped herself up on one elbow and picked it up.

'Hello?' she said.

'It's me,' said Philip. He was whispering.

'Are you all right?'

'Yes,' he said. 'I'm sorry.'

She wasn't sure what he was apologising for.

'Where's Haileybury?' she said.

'Asleep,' said Philip. 'I'm downstairs. I can't talk now, but I couldn't, you know, resist.'

She knew.

'I get it, Philip,' she said. 'What did he say?'

'Nothing,' said Philip. 'Just that he was glad to have me home.'

'Are you going back to school?' said Berlin.

'I don't know. I don't think so.'

'What are you going to do about Lee?'

She could hear him breathing.

'I can't do anything until I know about my mother,' he said. 'If she's really in danger.'

The bundle of letters were lying on her bedside table.

'Write to her,' she said.

'How can I while I'm here?' he said. 'Anyway, that's no good.'

Her head was throbbing. She just wanted to go back to sleep. She rested her head on the pillow, the phone to her ear.

'I thought you could go,' said Philip.

'What?' she said.

'You could go to Hong Kong and find my mother,' he said.

'You're joking,' said Berlin.

'I'm begging you,' he said. 'I need to know if she's real.'

She wasn't sure any of it was real.

'Goodnight,' she said.

She hung up and lay down again.

Berlin was surprised to find herself in Peggy's room. Even more surprising was the fact that every drawer and door hung open: the wardrobe, the dressing table, even the bedside table.

She hadn't been in here since Peggy died. She must have been looking for something. Happy times, perhaps. There must have been some. Her childhood hadn't been marked by particular misery or violence, just the normal, unremarkable kind.

Perhaps that was what made it seem so awful. There was nothing special about her suffering, but she had failed to deal with it. Other people went through the most horrendous experiences but remained whole. She ached with anger.

Self-pity was the least attractive of her many flaws.

Her mother had died not understanding. She had never tried, had never wanted to, and worst of all, had barely realised that there was anything *to* understand.

The last time they spoke, Berlin had actually attempted to explain, to describe the source of the gulf between them. Peggy had reacted with such genuine amazement that she was forced to finally recognise the complete lack of insight she was up against.

It was pointless. Self-examination had never played a big part in Peggy's life; it wasn't suddenly going to begin now.

'Forget it, Mum,' murmured Berlin.

If only *she* could.

40

Berlin felt feverish and weak, inclined to dismiss recent events as a nightmare, except it was all confirmed by the calls logged on her mobile and the bundle of letters on the bedside table.

She wasn't the only one who was having trouble distinguishing reality from illusion; Philip couldn't have been in his right mind when he'd rung. He probably wouldn't remember, or, like her, he would think he'd dreamt it. Unlike her, right now he would be feeling no pain. Half his luck.

She picked up the empty bottles and the letters, and went downstairs.

The Good Fairy hadn't been in to clean up Philip's mess. There was something awful about such disarray in Peggy's house. She put the kettle on. When her mobile buzzed, she tried to ignore it, but the ringtone had an authority all of its own.

'Hello?' she said.

'Hello,' said a friendly voice. 'Is that Catherine Berlin?'

'Yes,' said Berlin.

'My name's Elise Henderson. I'm the director of nursing at the East London Mental Health Unit.'

'Oh?' said Berlin.

'I'm calling about your brother, Terence. Were you aware he was admitted on Saturday?'

It took a moment to register.

'Er, yes, well . . . no,' said Berlin. 'What day is it?'

'Monday,' said Elise Henderson.

Berlin wondered vaguely what had happened to Sunday.

'Are you all right?' said Elise Henderson.

'Yes thank you,' said Berlin. 'I'm just getting over the flu.'

'I see,' said Elise Henderson. 'It's going round. This strange weather doesn't help.'

'No,' said Berlin. 'It doesn't.'

'Your brother's in seclusion, but I promised him I'd call. He's very worried about his cat. Have you got a spare key to his flat?'

'No,' said Berlin. 'We're not . . . er . . .'

'You can come down and pick up his keys if you like. Just ask for me. Elise Henderson.

'I'll do that,' said Berlin. 'Thank you, Ms Henderson.'

Lee felt empty. He shuffled papers and opened and shut drawers, thoroughly demoralised. He was supposed to be clearing his desk, but retreat was unthinkable. His mobile rang. It was no doubt another harbinger of defeat.

'Madame Laurent,' he said. 'It's so nice to hear from you.'

'Monsieur Lee, I have discussed your proposition with my client,' said Laurent.

'And his response?' said Lee.

'My client finds your suggestion offensive and will consider legal action if you persist in this matter,' said Laurent.

'I doubt that very much, *madame*,' said Lee.

'Your reference to your *relationship* with Philip Chen was misleading and undermines the credibility of your threats,' said Laurent.

'Does the boy deny it?' said Lee.

'That's immaterial,' said Laurent. 'The matter is closed. There will be no negotiation. Good day.'

She hung up.

Lee put his phone down. It was as he'd expected.

Philip had slipped further from his grasp. He'd returned to Haileybury and, if questioned, would deny any contact with Lee or the embassy. But in his heart, the boy wouldn't give up on his mother so easily.

A knock at the door reminded him time was short. He'd been recalled.

The practice of criticism and self-criticism had undergone something of a renaissance. They would ask about the letters; their existence constituted a risk that he was obliged to manage.

He glanced at his watch. Time to make one last call. He picked up the phone and dialled. He was answered promptly.

'Headmistress,' he said. 'How are you?'

'Mr Lee,' she said.

If her tone had been any colder, his ear would have suffered frostbite.

'The boy's letters are still secure?' he said.

'Yes,' said Trevelyan.

'They mean so much to him. It would be upsetting if they went astray. He hasn't requested them?'

'No,' said Trevelyan.

'No one else has shown any interest in his belongings?'

'No,' said Trevelyan.

'Because if they did, and they were given access, certain other documents would fall into the hands of the board of governors of Palmerston Hall. It would be most unfortunate.'

'I'm well aware of that,' said Trevelyan. 'I've done everything you've asked, haven't I?'

'Indeed, Headmistress,' he said.

He knew she loathed that form of address.

'If the boy does at some stage want to collect his things, or he returns to school, you will let me know immediately?'

'He won't be coming back,' said Trevelyan.

'What do you suppose will happen to him?' said Lee.

'That's not my problem,' said Trevelyan.

'Quite,' said Lee.

He hung up. It was most certainly his.

41

Bryant's keys were waiting for Berlin in an envelope at reception. His address was scrawled on it. Berlin took the keys out of the envelope and tossed it.

Bryant woke parched; his tongue was a thick, dry thing that wouldn't do his bidding. His limbs felt as if they had great weights hanging off them.

'Hello, Terry,' said Tomalin. 'Feeling a bit better?'

Tomalin was sitting beside the bed, eating grapes from a brown paper bag.

'Not ill,' croaked Bryant.

'Yes you are,' said Tomalin. 'The drugs will help, but part of your recovery depends on you accepting that.'

'Not,' said Bryant.

'Do you think breaking and entering half-naked is normal behaviour?' said Tomalin.

Bryant clenched his fist.

'Grape?' said Tomalin. He offered Bryant the bag.

Bryant cleared his throat and summoned up saliva.

'They're not going to get away with it,' he said.

'Who are *they*?' said Tomalin. 'The Masons? The Druids? The Black Hand Gang?

He bent close. Bryant could smell Old Spice.

'What's the crime?' said Tomalin. 'You might not like Haileybury and his mates. I might not like them. But that doesn't make them criminals.'

'When am I getting out of here?' said Bryant.

'When you give up these delusions,' said Tomalin. 'You'll go out on medical with a full pension. Be grateful.'

'Bollocks,' said Bryant.

Tomalin sighed and stood up.

'The meek don't inherit the sodding earth, Terry,' he said. 'History is written by the winners. We're just cannon fodder in those wars.'

He glanced into the paper bag, screwed it up and shoved it in his pocket.

'By the way,' he said. 'They've got someone for that bloke in the crypt.'

'Who?' said Bryant. He tried to sit up, but only managed to raise his head off the pillow. 'Who is it? Tomalin, please.'

The lock clicked as the door closed behind the inspector.

Bryant gave up the struggle and stared at the ceiling. He was powerless. Almost powerless.

Berlin was a junkie, but she was an *old* junkie, a canny survivor, and a tough customer. He could only hope that her sceptical attitude and inbred hostility to authority would lead her to see things from his point of view. Just this once.

Halfway up the eighteen flights of stairs to Bryant's flat, Berlin needed oxygen. Pausing every few minutes, and cursing her leg, she persisted, motivated by the prospect of something other than a hungry cat at the top. Just in case, there was a tin of pet food in her bag.

When she finally got there, she went straight to the kitchen and had a long drink of water from the tap. The place was pristine and orderly. Bryant was that sort of bloke.

'Here, pussy, pussy,' she said.

The cat was a no-show. She was here for another reason.

Starting with the cupboards, she shook each tin, peered into each packet, flipped opened the fridge, the freezer, the cooker and the microwave, flipped them shut again and rattled each saucepan. Nothing.

In the living room, the view was breathtaking. She took every book off the shelf, ran her hand behind the DVDs, tossed the sofa cushions on the floor and rolled up the rugs. Nothing.

Frustrated, she paused to reconsider her approach.

Standing close to the window, she could see the length and breadth of Wapping High Street. Two pairs of binoculars rested on the sill. Bryant was a serious voyeur.

She picked up a pair and looked through them. The high street came into sharp focus; St John's churchyard, the terraced houses of Pier Head, and Haileybury's warehouse. It was as if she was standing right outside.

She put the binocs down and tried the bedrooms. One was bare, the wardrobe and chest of drawers empty. The other, which was Bryant's, was monastic. There was nothing under the pillow or the mattress, and in the wardrobe only clothes.

She returned to the living room. On a shelf above the desk, on which sat an old computer and a printer, was a pile of exercise books of the sort that were used in schools before they got laptops and tablets. There was nothing beneath the printer or tucked inside it.

She opened the desk drawer, which contained sharpened pencils all in a row and Post-it notes. She slammed it shut and took the pile of exercise books down from the shelf.

Taped to the wall behind them was the Ziploc bag he had taken from her. The opium was still in it.

Dropping the exercise books on the desk, she peeled the bag off the wall and slipped it in her pocket. It had made the trip more than worthwhile, but she couldn't believe Bryant had sent her up here as a goodwill gesture.

The exercise books had been hiding something else: Philip's Chinese passport. Flipping through it, she noticed that his eighteenth birthday was coming up. His British visa, which was linked to the scholarship, expired on the same day.

A criminal conviction might have resulted in deportation. Although Haileybury could probably take care of that.

A photo on the wall caught her eye. It was an old snap, the only decoration in the place. A woman stood outside a small terraced house, her arms folded across her chest in an uncompromising stance. She regarded Berlin sternly.

She picked up one of the exercise books and flicked through it. Narrow hand-ruled columns were headed

Date, *Time*, *Duration*, *Name* and *Position*. The entries were meticulous. She picked up another. It was just as neat, but the notes were in two different hands.

It was a surveillance log of an order she'd never seen before, going back years. Each entry was initialled: 'TB' or 'EB'. Terence Bryant and the woman in the photo.

Amongst the more generic entries, such as 'plumber', 'lift maintenance', and 'Waitrose', there were also names she recognised: Nigel Trentham, the Home Secretary during the last Labour government; Brigadier Collins, who had been embroiled in a sex scandal and had finally eaten his service pistol; and Lord Arnold Kennett, supermarket magnate and all-round right-wing rabble-rouser.

Others were unfamiliar, but were associated with vehicle registration numbers and designations: chief commissioner; judge; headmaster. Bryant had access to all the necessary databases to run down their details.

It was the comings and goings of Haileybury's visitors. No one else in Wapping High Street would be entertaining cabinet ministers and aristocrats. A beautifully detailed account of a social network, all kept as contemporaneous notes, a form of evidence with great credibility in the English legal system.

It was as good as a policeman's notebook.

Of late there was only one regular caller, apart from the tradespeople and deliveries. This person wasn't named, so Bryant and his gran hadn't been able to identify him. He appeared as 'WM#29'. White Male number twenty-nine.

The other frequent visitor was, of course, Philip, identified as 'P/H schoolboy'. The designation included a number, too. Seven.

She stuffed the books and the passport in her bag and left the tin of cat food on the table. A show of faith.

42

Berlin's locksmith always left the new keys with her neighbour, but Bella was still in rehab. The front door of the flat had been expertly repaired, so the keys had to be somewhere. She lifted Bella's worn 'Welcome' mat and there they were, indicating certain assumptions about the intelligence of Bethnal Green burglars.

The musty smell emanating from the cartons had permeated the whole flat. She had to get rid of Peggy's things, but she couldn't bring herself to do it. This was her mother's legacy, and Berlin's own history, hard won.

Perhaps she wasn't so different from Haileybury.

It was a disturbing thought. She dropped her bag. Philip's letters and Bryant's exercise books were weighing her down. She went straight to the cupboard under the sink, where she kept a bottle of Talisker for emergencies.

She poured herself a finger, slipped a smidgen of the black tar into it, as Haileybury had done, then swirled it around and drank it down. Before it kicked in, she wanted to check her email.

There was nothing from Del. The last she'd heard from Philip was when he called in the middle of the night, and she imagined that as far as the earl was concerned, the job was over.

They were all bastards, the lot of them.

She banged out a terse email to Del about getting paid, clicked send and poured another Scotch.

Someone knocked at the door. She ignored it.

They knocked again, harder.

She shuffled to the peephole, glass in hand; the good stuff was beginning to work. She was feeling more relaxed than she had for days.

There was a woman and two uniformed constables standing on the landing. She opened the door.

'Catherine Berlin?' said the woman.

'Yes,' said Berlin.

The woman took a step forward, flashed a warrant card with one hand and grabbed the glass with the other.

'I'm arresting you on suspicion of murder. You do not have to say anything. But it may harm your defence if you do not mention, when questioned, something which you later rely on in court. Anything you do say can be given in evidence. Do you understand?'

'No,' said Berlin.

43

The interview room was airless. The dough-faced officer sitting beside the woman, who had identified herself as Detective Inspector Langfield, fiddled with his uniform buttons. The chair beside Berlin was empty. She didn't want a lawyer. She wanted to sleep.

'Was the deceased known to you?' said Langfield.

'No comment,' said Berlin.

'Come on,' said Langfield. 'How did your DNA come to be on the body?'

'No comment,' said Berlin. She was getting tired of saying it.

DI Langfield groaned, tired of hearing it.

'I'm sure you could find traces of half the population of London on him,' said Berlin.

Langfield flipped open a file.

'Yeah, but you're the only one with a heroin habit who visited the crypt the day after he was found. The nice vicar thought you were a bit suspicious and gave us a call.'

'Is that a question?' said Berlin.

'And as he died of an overdose that according to the pathologist may have been administered forcibly, you fit the bill,' said Langfield.

Langfield focused on the file. 'You're local and you've been in our system since the collators used index cards in the dark ages,' she said. 'How come we've never met?'

'We don't frequent the same bars,' said Berlin.

The dough-faced officer sniggered.

'You've talked your way out of trouble before,' said Langfield. 'But not this time.'

'If you've got enough evidence, charge me,' said Berlin.

Langfield shut the file and switched off the recording device. 'You're good for this, Berlin,' she said. 'I look forward to our next chat. Soon.'

She turned to the officer. 'See her out,' she said.

On the way home, Berlin stopped in at the first pub she came to; her nerves were shot, her legs like jelly.

Langfield's case was a stretch, but she seemed determined to get a result. She would dig. She would peruse Berlin's phone records and her computer, search the flat. Examine CCTV footage and probably find her altercation with the deceased. It was an explanation for her DNA, but the nature of the contact would only serve the prosecution.

There was also the power of those who might consider her a threat, given what she now knew. It was hard to avoid the conclusion that Philip was off the hook, and she was on it. Exchange is no robbery.

She really needed to clear her head, but the publican wouldn't be impressed if she sat down without a drink. She collected half a pint of London Pride and took it to a corner to think about her next move.

Someone had left a free paper lying on the table. She moved it aside. A face gazed up at her. She recognised it, but couldn't place it. Then she did.

She stood up quickly, knocking over her drink.

London Pride washed over the corporate-style photo of a woman whose demise was 'sudden and unexpected', not least by her. Waves of shiny blonde hair framed the confident, faultlessly made-up face of a youthful Sylvie Laurent.

The beer dripped over the edge of the table, on to Berlin's boots. She stood there, frozen.

The time for thinking was over.

The Milk of Paradise

44

Berlin stood between a tiger and a dragon, both poised to devour her. Nostrils flared, eyes glared, talons extended, one crouched and one reared. She was mesmerised by their terrible gaze.

When her phone rang, the spell was broken. She glanced at the caller ID, then picked up.

'Hello, Bryant,' she said. 'They've released you?'

'Yes,' said Bryant.

'How are you feeling?' said Berlin.

His breathing was laboured.

'I'm not sure, to tell you the truth,' he said.

He spoke slowly and deliberately, as if his thoughts took time to form. He was still heavily medicated.

'I was right, Berlin,' he said. 'I knew it.' His voice broke. All of him was broken.

'Are you going back to work?' she said.

'No,' said Bryant. 'That's all over.'

'Hang in there, Bryant,' she said.

It was a stupid thing to say and he sensibly ignored it.

'You found everything?' he said.

'Yes,' said Berlin. 'Very useful.'

'That's good news.'

'Do you see anyone from your old firm?' she said.

'Tomalin visited a couple of times,' said Bryant. 'I think he feels guilty. He told me the French lawyer strung herself up. Marital problems.'

His tone betrayed his scepticism, in which she could only concur.

'He also said they wanted you for the bloke in the crypt,' he said.

'What do you make of that?' said Berlin.

Bryant's change of heart towards her might have limitations.

'It's ridiculous,' said Bryant.

'Try telling Langfield that,' said Berlin.

'I would if I had half a chance,' said Bryant. 'Look, Berlin, I know we haven't always seen eye to eye on this business, but why don't we put our heads together now? We're more or less in the same boat, aren't we?'

He was right. They were minnows darting at a whale.

Trusting her had been an act of desperation on his part, although he would have been pretty confident she wouldn't turn over the exercise books, or Philip's passport, to the law. It didn't mean she had to reciprocate.

'Our agendas are different,' said Berlin.

'I can overlook your unorthodox habits.'

'That's very generous of you, Bryant,' she said. 'But it's not a good time.'

'Well, I don't know how far you'll get on your own,' he said. 'But it's your call. I hope the logs are safe.'

'As houses,' said Berlin.

She imagined him sitting alone in his neat eyrie, gazing down on those responsible for ruining his life. The logs *had* yielded some useful information.

Philip was the most recent in a line of Palmerston Hall scholars to visit Haileybury over the years. Decades, in fact.

The earl had acknowledged it was his custom to offer the lonely Anglo-Chinese Friendship Society boys some hospitality. What else he offered them remained moot.

'Berlin?' said Bryant.

'Yes,' she said. 'I'm here.'

'I'm right about Haileybury,' he said. 'You know I'm right. There's something very wrong going on there.'

'Look after yourself, Bryant,' she said.

She hung up.

The sweet smell of incense drifted on the sultry air. People teemed around her, the traffic roared, the cries of hawkers in a nearby market summoned customers. Her linen shirt clung to her damp skin.

It was only seven a.m., but Hong Kong was a sauna.

45

Berlin sat at a quayside bar, sipping her beer and watching the rain pockmark the turbulent grey waters of the Pearl River Delta. The overwhelming impression was one of perpetual motion: a brilliant cavalcade of people, trolley buses, ferries and vendor carts. Peaks hidden in the clouds were a majestic background to bustling districts carved into steep hillsides. The energy was intoxicating.

The decision to break for the border hadn't been difficult. She hadn't been charged with any offence, so she had a window of opportunity. It would close quickly if DI Langfield had anything to do with it.

The quickest way of getting the Metropolitan Police off her back was to show them that Deng was not a Chinese junkie she had knocked off, but a Chinese agent.

Someone had killed him and dumped him in the crypt, so other plausible suspects would raise reasonable doubt. But it was going to be difficult without Philip's testimony, which couldn't be relied on. It would mean exposing Haileybury.

Even if she could get him over that hurdle, Lee still had the boy's mother in his grasp, or so he claimed.

A ferry bounced across waves wind-whipped into a foam frenzy. The moment it was within range of the dock, the crew leapt off and dragged a gangway into position.

Passengers surged back and forth. Within minutes the vessel was on its way again. A well-oiled machine.

Governments didn't like to see the intrigues of intelligence agencies, of any persuasion, rehearsed in the media. It made the public uncomfortable. Whitehall would have an interest in the CPS dropping the case.

After being caught out during a previous investigation in Russia, Berlin had put together another identity. She was ready to disappear if the going ever got that rough again. It was tempting.

Leaving London permanently was difficult to contemplate, but it was better than filling the remaining space in Peggy's plot, or serving out her days in Holloway, which was where Peggy had always predicted she'd end up.

She couldn't let her mother have the last laugh.

Philip had turned his back on her at Haileybury's when Bryant was arrested, but she couldn't blame him. She would have done the same at his age. His desperate need to know if his mother was real had stayed with her. Without certainty, it would haunt him. He'd never escape his addiction. It would consume him.

She wasn't doing it for him, though. Her own ghosts had impelled her to leave London. At home, the phantoms in her blood, newly awoken, would have driven her back to old hang-outs and long-standing connections.

So she had done a geographical. In China, chasing heroin could result in the death penalty. The 'Fragrant Harbour' would give her the time and space she needed to recall the virtues of abstinence.

At the moment, they seemed remote and unattractive.

Her other problem was proof: she didn't have any. All she had was the letters. It was a long shot, and dangerous. She slid off the bar stool and followed the lead. She had nowhere else to go.

In the chapel, Bryant listened to the rain pattering on the grimy glass panes. The clammy weather had given way to showers. The sanctuary, set in a dilapidated corner of the hospital, was nearly always deserted.

Cooperating had earned him a number of privileges: he was allowed a mobile, weather permitting he could take a turn around the garden, and he could visit the chapel alone. His medication had been reduced.

Clarity was gradually returning.

He didn't look around when he felt Gran come and sit beside him.

'I did my best,' he said.

'I know you did, Terence,' said Gran. Wind rattled the glass.

'I'm sorry I let you down.'

'You haven't,' said Gran. 'Yet.'

A draught made him shiver. It was coming from beneath a wooden door behind the altar. He went to take a closer look.

The handle rattled as he turned it, as did the lock, which was one of those old-fashioned black metal things. He found that by slipping his fingers beneath a cross-panel, he was able to lift the door away from the frame.

He heaved, pushed, and the door opened. Beyond it was a garden enclosed by a high red-brick wall.

It was after midnight and he couldn't see much, but he could hear the traffic on the other side. Life went on while he was stuck in here, doped up like a zombie. There was so much to do.

He closed the door and took a few steps across the muddy turf, nearly colliding with a wheelbarrow beside a half-turned bed. A rake and shovel lay across it.

He and Gran had lived in a flat for so long, he couldn't imagine working with the earth. It would be a good, clean job. Not like his.

Where there was a gardener, there was a shed; where there was a shed, there were tools; and where there were tools, often there was a ladder.

'What are you waiting for?' said Gran.

46

Haileybury gripped the platform handrail to steady himself as it glided down to the smoking room, where he knew he would find Philip. Since returning home, the boy had done nothing but sleep, play video games and demand pizza and another pipe.

His use was escalating, which could lead to all sorts of problems, as Haileybury knew from bitter experience. A balm when used with respect, opium could destroy the unwary.

It was a strict rule that he could only smoke down there. It had an excellent extraction system that stripped out the telltale odour and recycled fresh air.

The platform juddered to a halt.

Philip was stretched out on the cushions in a daze.

'You seem disconsolate, dear boy,' said Haileybury.

'Leave me alone,' said Philip.

'It will be your birthday soon. What would you like to do to celebrate?'

'Nothing,' said Philip. 'I'll be a year older. So what?'

'Is there something bothering you?' said Haileybury.

'No,' said Philip.

'Is there anything I can do to perk you up?' said Haileybury.

Philip looked at him steadily.

Haileybury got on to Flora Trevelyan right away, despite the late hour.

'Hello, Flora,' he said. 'Haileybury here.'

'Lord Haileybury,' said Trevelyan. 'It's so nice to hear from you. I've been meaning to call you to see how Philip is getting on.'

He could hear the television in the background.

'He's still somewhat traumatised by recent events,' said Haileybury. 'I think a change of scenery may be in order.'

'Splendid idea,' said Trevelyan. 'Will he be returning to us next term?'

'I think not,' said Haileybury. 'Actually, I'm calling to ask if you could have his things sent over.'

He could practically hear her sigh of relief.

'I'll arrange it first thing in the morning,' she said.

'I'd appreciate that,' said Haileybury.

Dreadful woman.

Lee answered his mobile. It was Flora Trevelyan.

'Headmistress,' he said.

'Lord Haileybury telephoned,' she said. 'He asked me to send Philip's belongings over.'

Lee reached for his cigarettes.

'When was this?' he said.

'About five minutes ago,' said Trevelyan.

Lee glanced at his watch. Haileybury had called Trevelyan close to midnight. It reeked of desperation.

'What do you want me to do?' said Trevelyan.

He groped for his lighter. At least here smoking hadn't been demonised. In London, to indulge was no longer a pleasure. He lit his cigarette and inhaled. It reminded him of the lawyer.

'Send Philip his things, by all means,' he said. 'But first remove the letters.'

'Supposing he makes a fuss about the fact they're not there?' said Trevelyan.

'I doubt he will,' said Lee. 'If he does, threaten to discuss it with Haileybury. That should put a stop to it.'

Philip certainly wouldn't want Haileybury to become aware of the letters.

'Very well,' said Trevelyan. 'I do hope this is the end of it.'

Lee hung up, chuckling. The British were fond of invoking the notion of fair play, but rarely abided by it.

These people never ceased to amaze him.

47

Berlin took a stool at the red laminate counter of a tiny dumpling restaurant situated on one corner of a non-descript ten-storey office building. The shopfront was open, but the cross-breeze was anything but refreshing.

Moving anywhere beyond the reach of artificially cooled air was akin to a slap in the face with a hot wet towel. But at least she understood the signposts. English was one of the official languages of the Special Administrative Region of the People's Republic of China. The upside of colonialism.

This was the third day she'd sat here, or at the bar across the street, or spent time window-shopping nearby, keeping the mailboxes lining the lobby in sight.

She ordered, then took one of Philip's letters out of her bag. The others were in the hotel room safe. All the letters from his mother bore the stamp of the Green Dragon Certified Translation Agency on the back. Their office was on the fifth floor. This was the address he used when he wrote back.

The use of a translation agency worked for Lee whatever the reality. It allowed him to control all communication, both Philip's and his mother's, whether or not she was alive, spoke English or was even aware of the operation.

Business wasn't booming at the Green Dragon Agency. No one had turned up to collect their mail while she'd been watching, unless they were coming outside business hours, which was unlikely.

She had been up to the fifth floor and knocked on their door a few times, without any response. There was no listing in the HK telephone directory, and short of camping outside their office, this was the best she could do.

In baseball cap, sunglasses and one of the white linen shirts she'd bought in a mall near the hotel, she was indistinguishable from other Anglo shoppers and sightseers. She would also be unrecognisable to anyone who knew her from London.

Her new shirts worked well with her black jeans, and she still wore her Peacekeeper boots. In a pinch, they added weight to a kick, whether it was aimed at a door or a crotch. She hoped the need wouldn't arise.

Sweat dripped from her nose into her bowl of steaming dumplings with XO sauce. It was impossible to tell if the perspiration was due to the heat, the sauce or her recent exposure to opiates.

The aches and sniffles had begun on the interminable twelve-and-a-half-hour flight from Heathrow. Business class looked appealing, but she was mindful of her credit card limit. The last of her prescription codeine, washed down with miniatures of Scotch, got her through the worst of it.

She drained her bottle of ice-cold beer.

'You really like those prawn and pork dumplings,' said the waiter. He whisked her empty bowl away.

'They're perfect,' said Berlin. 'With a chilled beverage.'

He brought her another beer and she invited him to sit down. He gave her a funny look. It was quiet, between the breakfast and lunch rushes. He shrugged, called out something in Chinese to his offsider, who was sitting in the corner reading a newspaper, and took the stool next to her.

The offsider stood, stretched and took up his position behind the counter. As far as she could tell, it was just the two of them.

Berlin took off her sunglasses.

'I'm Wang,' said the waiter. 'This is my place.'

An assertion of status.

'Congratulations,' said Berlin.

'On holiday?' said Wang.

The offsider ambled over with a pot of tea and a small cup.

'I'm looking for someone,' said Berlin.

'Official?' said Wang.

He swirled the pot a few times, then poured. The fragrance of green tea drifted from his cup.

Berlin shook her head.

'Naughty husband?' said Wang.

He spoke English with a slight American twang.

Berlin looked pained.

'Something like that,' she said. 'He uses the Green Dragon Agency on the fifth floor. Do you know them?'

'Not really,' said Wang. 'It's just a woman. She works at home, I think. I only see her occasionally.'

'I really need to speak to her,' said Berlin.

Wang hesitated. 'I have numbers of all tenants,' he said. 'In case of emergency.'

'Does a lying husband count as an emergency?' said Berlin.

Wang frowned.

'I must find my husband,' she said. 'For my son's sake.' She laid her smartphone on the counter between them.

Wang peered at the photo of Philip she'd taken in the café at Shadwell.

'Good-looking boy,' he said.

'He takes after his father,' said Berlin.

She bit her lip, slipped on her sunglasses and blew her nose. Then she put a thousand Hong Kong dollars on the table.

48

The cool, understated luxury of Berlin's four-star hotel in Tseung Kwan O, on the mainland side of Hong Kong, Kowloon, was a seductive cocoon. Expensive, but the security was good. She wanted to use the phone in her room to call the number Wang had given her, because using her UK mobile would be prohibitively expensive.

The room phone would be more secure, too. No one knew she was staying here. She dialled and waited, unable to distinguish between an engaged signal and a normal ring. It was the little things that made it difficult to conduct enquiries abroad.

A woman answered; Berlin didn't understand a word of the greeting.

'I'm sorry,' she said. 'I don't speak Chinese.'

There was a pause, then a stern voice responded.

'You mean you don't speak Cantonese.'

Berlin took a breath. 'Well spotted. I don't.' It was less than diplomatic. 'Am I speaking to the Green Dragon Certified Translation Agency?'

'You are speaking with the proprietor,' said the woman. 'How did you get this number?'

'There's something I'd like to discuss with you,' Berlin said. 'If—'

'Matters of translation are rarely so pressing,' interrupted the woman. 'I will be at our office tomorrow morning at seven if you'd like to speak in person.'

She hung up. A multilingual woman of few words.

Berlin hadn't given her name or description, but it didn't matter.

She lay down on the bed, exhausted. London was seven hours behind Hong Kong, so on top of everything else she was jet-lagged. She felt as if she was clinging to a cliff face by her fingertips.

All her senses were painfully acute; the very air pressed against her skin, a prickly, insistent force compounded by an avalanche of unfamiliar sights, smells and noises.

She'd forgotten what it was like to be cut off cold, without a soft, pharmaceutical landing. The opium had prodded all the wrong synapses, and now they were screaming for more. She had to keep going. She dragged herself off the bed. A cold shower, then she would venture out into the steaming cauldron once again.

The soaring glass tower in the Admiralty area of the central business district of Hong Kong Island was in a very different class from that of the Green Dragon Certified Translation Agency. The air in the lobby was frigid. No dumpling shop tucked in the corner here, just an espresso cart.

Berlin perused the names listed in the tenants' directory. Many were familiar: a number of major British and multinational corporations, legal firms and management consultants had their HK offices on one of the forty-two floors.

She checked the directory again, then took one of the lifts that served floors twenty to forty-one. It moved soundlessly and with such speed that when the doors opened, she was surprised to find herself on the thirty-second floor. She stepped out. The lift departed as noiselessly as it had arrived.

She was facing two frosted-glass doors. A small brass plaque on the wall beside one announced the Anglo-Chinese Friendship Society Trust and its business registration number. The plaque beside the other identified the office of the Anglo-Chinese Child Welfare Agency. Beneath its registration number were inscribed the words 'A Bridge between East and West'.

This was a result. Apart from Philip's letters, the trust was the only other lead she had. Haileybury had mentioned a trustee in Hong Kong. An online search of the GovHK business and company registration site had yielded the names and addresses of the trust and the welfare agency.

The latter was a surprise, but it made sense that if the local trustee chose orphans for scholarships, a separate arm of the business might be necessary to oversee the child's ongoing welfare.

That was the benign view.

If the process was legitimate, as Haileybury had described it, she would ask for copies of the paperwork pertaining to Philip. If they refused, she would mutter about lawyers, regulatory authorities and child protection agencies. That ought to motivate them.

They would alert the earl, but so what? If there was nothing untoward going on in Hong Kong, he shouldn't object.

On the other hand, if the trust wasn't legit, or there was something dodgy about Philip's status as an orphan, it would soon become apparent. In that case, she would need a Plan B. She'd worry about that later.

The thick carpet muffled her footsteps. She opened one of the doors and peered into an empty reception area. She walked in. The desk was unattended. She went past it and down a corridor. At the end, a door stood ajar. She knocked gently and pushed it open.

A man was sitting behind a large desk tapping away on a computer keyboard. He didn't look up.

'Wrong door,' he said. 'They're just across the corridor.'

When she didn't reply, he glanced up.

She couldn't place him, although he was vaguely familiar. But the look on his face gave away the fact that he recognised her, and it wasn't a pleasant surprise.

He was in his sixties, lined but well nourished, with lank blonde hair that fell across a forehead sprinkled with liver spots. Patrician down to the signet ring on his pinky, the chinos, blazer and striped shirt.

'My name's Catherine Berlin,' she said.

He stared at her as if she were a demon come to summon him to hell.

'What are you doing here?' he said.

'I'm sorry,' she said. 'Do I know you?'

'You work for me,' he said.

It took her a moment to make the connection.

'Sir Simon May,' she said.

He frowned and stood up slowly, as if she were an animal he didn't want to frighten away.

It was too late to run.

49

Berlin became aware of a youth slouching in a corner of the office, arms folded, staring at her.

'Would you wait in the outer office, Jian?' said Sir Simon.

Jian slunk out, closing the door behind him. Shutting her in. She had the feeling he was just on the other side.

The blinds were down, and the heavy, old-fashioned furnishings added to the oppressive atmosphere.

'Can I offer you a drink, Berlin?' said Sir Simon. 'I'm afraid I haven't got any Talisker.'

If the reference to her favourite tipple was meant to unnerve her, it did.

'No thanks,' she said.

'I think I'll have one,' he said. 'If you don't mind.'

Sir Simon was tall and moved well. Two quick strides brought him to the drinks tray. But she noticed that he needed a shave and his clothes were crumpled. There was a slight whiff of body odour in the air.

'So what brings you to Hong Kong?' he said.

He poured a double of Lagavulin. His morning tipple.

'Philip Chen,' she said.

Sir Simon ran his fingers through his hair.

'I'm assuming Lord Haileybury doesn't know you're here,' he said. 'Does the boy?'

'I'm conducting enquiries that are in his interests,' she said.

'Enquiries about what, exactly?' said Sir Simon.

She didn't want to up the ante by showing her hand, largely because she had no idea what cards she held.

'It's confidential,' she said. 'Philip is an orphan. I presume there's an orphanage. I'd like to know which one.'

'It doesn't always work like that,' said Sir Simon. 'Sometimes the boys are living with other family members when we select them for scholarships.'

'If that's the case, and he does have living relatives, I'd like to know where they are,' said Berlin.

'You're quite sure that this is going to benefit Philip?' he said.

'Yes,' said Berlin.

He sipped his Scotch. She waited.

'All information of that sort is confidential,' he said.

'Of what sort?' said Berlin. 'Was Philip plucked from an orphanage or from the arms of his poverty-stricken distant relatives?'

'I'd be very careful if I were you,' said Sir Simon. 'The boy may well end up suffering a great deal more than is necessary because of your meddling. And he won't be the only one.'

'Is that a threat?' said Berlin.

'Let's call it friendly advice,' said Sir Simon. 'I don't think you appreciate how profoundly the Chinese resent the loss of their treasures, or the lengths to which they'll go to retrieve them.'

'I've heard it all before,' she said.

'You really don't want to get caught in the crossfire,' said Sir Simon.

'Then I'll have to learn to duck,' said Berlin. 'Because I'm not leaving Hong Kong without answers.'

On her way out, Berlin passed the scowling Jian in the corridor, muttering into his mobile. The elevator doors opened; she stepped inside and it whisked her to the ground.

The confrontation with Sir Simon May had shaken her. It was like running into a brick wall. He wasn't suddenly going to be moved to explain what was going on.

She had been a pawn in this case from the beginning. It was galling, but her weakness for opiates had made her the perfect candidate for manipulation. She and Philip had a lot in common.

She crossed the lobby and walked out into a downpour. Hot rain. That was all she needed.

Admiralty station had five exits, one of which would take her close to the office of the General Registrar of Births and Deaths. Unlike the London Underground, the metro was air-conditioned and astonishingly clean. But she missed the buskers.

Stopping beneath a shop awning to check the route on her phone, she caught a reflection in the window. It was Jian.

When she turned round, he scooted through the nearest open doorway, only to emerge a moment later looking sheepish. He'd tried to hide in a women's lingerie shop.

Berlin hailed him. 'Jian, over here.'

He pretended he hadn't heard and hurried away. She ran out into the rain after him and soon caught up.

'Hey,' she said. 'Slow down.'

'Go away,' said Jian.

'There's no need to worry,' she said. 'I'm going to the births and deaths registry office. You can report back to Sir Simon. He'll never know you've spoken to me.'

He quickened his pace. Berlin limped along beside him.

'Stop following me,' he said. It was laughable. The poor kid.

'How does it feel being at the beck and call of men like him?' said Berlin.

Jian stopped dead. He looked as if he might take a swing at her. She softened her tone.

'Nothing is going to happen to you,' she said. 'I understand what you're doing, and why.'

'You understand nothing,' said Jian.

He was right. She was whistling in the dark. Her grandfather would have said, *no problem: you whistle, dog come.* He was the eternal optimist, a necessary quality for the *vory*. Thieves.

Jian was around sixteen or seventeen, with the volatility that matched his demographic. Everything he wore was branded. She suspected he was too.

He reached into his jacket pocket. At first she thought the glint was the shiny case of a mobile phone. When she realised what it was, she retreated.

He advanced, backing her into an alley. She stumbled into a gutter. Water swirled around her ankles. She was already soaked.

'And now what?' she said. 'You're going to knife me in broad daylight with all these cameras on you?' She looked up.

Like the amateur he was, he followed her gaze.

Her boot was even heavier now that it was sodden. When it connected with his crotch, even she winced.

He yowled and dropped to the ground, doubled up.

She stomped on his hand. The blade rolled from his grasp.

Berlin snatched it up, knelt beside him and put it to his throat. He was all skin and bone underneath his designer clothes.

'I don't want to hurt you, but I will,' she said.

There were no cameras. The alley was deserted. People passing by in the street had their heads down, scurrying to find shelter from the escalating torrent. The noise of the rain – a thousand hammers striking sheet metal – drowned out everything.

She had to shout.

'I'm trying to find a boy's mother, that's all. They don't own him, or you.'

It was difficult to tell if Jian's face was wet with rain or tears, or if his apparent distress was due to humiliation or fear. He blinked hard and shouted back.

'Yes they do,' he said. 'They own all of us.'

He gave her a shove. She toppled backwards and rolled into the gutter, now a burbling stream. Jian scrambled to his feet and half hobbled, half ran. She let him go.

*

Taxis were scarce, but eventually Berlin adopted London tactics and simply made for one that had been hailed by two middle-aged women loaded down with designer shopping bags. They ran towards it too, yelling what were no doubt unsavoury remarks, but stopped when they saw the knife in her hand. Needs must.

Luckily the driver didn't see it. She threw herself into the back seat.

'You tough lady,' he said. He chuckled. 'Those shopping women scary.'

The cab crept forward. Berlin wiped her face with her shirt tail and thanked God for her Peacekeepers.

'Where do you want to go?' said the driver.

'Births and Deaths,' said Berlin.

He nodded, so must have got the drift.

Apart from the drenching, she had landed hard when Jian pushed her off. Her back throbbed, as did her missing toes.

'When will the rain stop?' she said.

'September, October,' said the driver. 'Maybe.'

He grinned.

The roads were clogged with vehicles edging along because of the weather. When they finally reached the office of the General Registrar, the ground floor was crawling with workers manning enormous pumps. Water gushed out of thick hoses and joined a deluge roaring down the gutters. The building was closed. Another brick wall.

The cab driver turned round. 'Where now?'

'Kowloon,' she said.

50

The hotel was located amidst a palatial mall. Berlin ducked into the supermarket in the basement and bought a bottle of Scotch, then took the express elevator straight to her floor.

Her room had been made up by the Filipino maid. She peeled off her damp clothes and slipped into a fluffy white robe. In a country of one point three billion people, importing labour seemed counter-intuitive. The missing word was cheap.

They own all of us.

In the normal course of things, this would have been the moment when she called Del. He would listen patiently to her theories, offer advice, which she would ignore, then back up her enquiries with his own. There were leads that were difficult to follow in the field. Del would cover these and book it up to the client.

But she had no Del, no backup and no client.

It was two o'clock in the afternoon, she was half drunk and running from a host of unpalatable truths: loss, betrayal and addiction. Self-pity also belonged on the list. She was sorely tempted to give up the whole enterprise. It would mean giving up on herself.

Capitulation wasn't in her vocabulary; defiance gave her life meaning. In fact, it kept her alive.

A visit to the office of the Anglo-Chinese Child Welfare Agency was now out of the question, but the business was registered and must be regulated by the Chinese authorities.

She flipped open the computer.

Bryant enjoyed the longer days. At seven in the morning, it was well past dawn, but the thick blanket of cloud hanging over the city smudged the light. The steady drizzle didn't bother him. He opened a can of baked beans and ate them with a spoon. Gran would say he was letting himself go. She hadn't seen the half of it.

At his feet lay a stun gun, disposable restraints, a stout rope, a balaclava, and a knapsack in which to carry it all. His preparations were well advanced.

No one had come after him. He wasn't surprised. From experience he knew that coppers only bothered to pursue sectioned absconders who were very dangerous. They were difficult to find, and a right pain to deal with if you did come across them. If you were mad and harmless you were generally free to wander the streets of London, and quite right too.

But he wasn't mad. He was furious.

He finished his beans, rinsed the tin and the spoon, and set about stowing his gear in the knapsack.

He popped two packets of Fisherman's Friend in his pocket.

It was going to be a long day.

*

Berlin woke to crashing thunder and the rain beating against the windows. Visibility was nil; she couldn't see a thing through the torrent of water pounding the glass. The computer must have gone to sleep not long after she had.

Her research had yielded two versions of child protection in the PRC: the official one, and an exposé by Western investigative journalists. The words that stuck in her mind were *abduction*, *gangs* and *trafficking*.

On her way to the bathroom, she saw that a glossy brochure had been slipped under her door. It was advertising various ways of getting from the Special Administrative Region of Hong Kong to Guangdong, in China proper. She picked it up and opened it. A scrap of paper fell out. On it someone had written 'ACCWA'. Anglo-Chinese Child Welfare Agency. Beneath it, in block letters, was an address.

She opened the door and peered down the hallway. It was empty. She shut it again and put on the safety lock. The brochure and note could have been lying there for hours, while she slept. The real question was: who had put them there? No one knew where she was staying.

Who was she kidding? Her hotel registration was lodged with the authorities, her credit card charges could be tracked in real time, as could her phone and internet access. Plenty of people were authorised to access that information, and there were a lot more who could buy it.

Block letters suggested someone for whom English wasn't their first language. Jian? Someone helpful, or someone who wanted to lure her over the border?

It was too late to do anything about it now. First thing in the morning she was to meet the Green Dragon Lady.

She pushed an armchair in front of the door and went to bed.

Hours later, she was still wide awake. Lightning streaked the sky. As the erratic flashes lit up the room, she glimpsed crouching figures, ready to spring at her from every corner. Paranoia didn't come into it.

51

Lee dumped his briefcase on the bare desk in his small, cramped office. The incommodious accommodation was a sign of how far he had fallen from favour. Nevertheless, he started work immediately, before anyone else arrived. It was important to make amends and set a good example.

He adjusted the old-fashioned desk lamp, but to no avail. His sight was continuing to deteriorate, as the doctors had warned.

He lit a cigarette. When he exhaled, he imagined the burden leaving him with the smoke. The blue cloud hung over him, a wreath of regret. It was inescapable.

He opened the document that described his strategy to advance repatriation of the Haileybury Bequest. It required an update. His fingers were poised above the keyboard as he waited for inspiration. Mercifully, his mobile rang.

Unfortunately, it was the tiresome headmistress again.

'Mr Lee,' she said. 'Something's happened.'

From her tone of voice, he knew it wasn't good news. He glanced at his watch. Midnight in London. He braced himself.

'Yes?' he said.

'I don't know how,' said Trevelyan. 'But the letters are gone.'

The letters.

'Who had access to them?' said Lee.

'Only myself and the bursar,' said Trevelyan. 'The storage lockers are very secure. Keypad-controlled. I supervised the packing of Philip's belongings myself.'

A slight slurring indicated that the headmistress had fortified herself before calling.

Lee remained silent for some time. It would have the effect of further unnerving her.

'Mr Lee?' said Trevelyan. 'I can't imagine how this has happened. I hope you don't think . . .'

'What have you done with the rest of his things?' said Lee.

'I've had them sent over,' said Trevelyan. 'Lord Haileybury was very explicit.'

Stupid, stupid woman.

'Who is the bursar?' said Lee.

'Mayhew,' said Trevelyan. 'He's been with the school for years. What would he want with them? He couldn't possibly—'

'Tell me about Mayhew,' said Lee.

The Green Dragon Lady was waiting at Wang's counter when Berlin arrived at the building.

Wang didn't look at her. He was scowling. No doubt he had been rebuked for giving her the Dragon Lady's number.

Berlin offered her hand. 'Catherine Berlin,' she said.

The Dragon Lady took it in her own. Her jade mani-cured nails matched her Givenchy handbag. Despite the regular cloudbursts, she wasn't even damp. Her hair and make-up were faultless. The look she gave Berlin inti-mated that her own appearance left something to be desired.

'Emma Lau,' she said. 'How may I help you?'

Berlin sat down, took the letter from Philip's mother out of her battered canvas bag and handed it to Lau, who slipped on a pair of half-moon glasses.

'Is that you?' said Berlin, pointing to the green stamp on the back of the envelope.

'Yes,' said Lau.

'And the translation?' said Berlin.

Lau shook her head. 'No,' she said. 'The letter was given to me just like this, written in English. I simply stamped and mailed it.'

'And the replies?' said Berlin. 'What did you do with them?'

'What's this about?' said Lau.

'It's a private matter.'

Lau took off her glasses and focused on Berlin.

'In addition to translation, we provide ancillary services. Photocopying, a mailing address. That sort of thing.'

Her English was perfect.

'So someone would deliver the letters to you, you would endorse them with your business insignia, then take them to the post office and mail them to England,' said Berlin.

'That's correct,' said Lau.

'And when a reply arrived?' said Berlin.

'I called the customer and he came to collect it,' said Lau.

The obvious question hung out there. Berlin considered the likelihood of receiving an informative reply.

'My business is perfectly legitimate,' said Lau. 'I have done nothing underhand, nor have I provided services to anyone whom I would regard as undesirable.'

She snapped open her tiny handbag and withdrew a bright green mobile.

'If you wish to pursue this matter, I suggest you contact the gentleman involved,' she said.

To Berlin's utter surprise, she copied a name and number from her mobile on to the back of a business card and handed it over.

'Good day to you,' she said.

With considerable aplomb, Emma Lau rose and left the counter, perfectly balanced on high heels that would have crippled Berlin. She crossed the lobby and entered the lift.

Berlin was in no doubt that she had told the truth. Her business was legitimate, her involvement with the letters was as she had described it, and the man with whom she had dealt was a Joseph Zang.

The Green Dragon Certified Translation Agency had provided two very important elements in a trail of obfuscation: an address, and the impression that the letters had originally been dictated in Chinese, whether Cantonese or Mandarin.

That they were handwritten, rather than typed, added to their aura of authenticity.

Wang made a great show of wiping the counter, still refusing to meet her eye.

'How about some dumplings?' said Berlin.

'Sold out,' said Wang, sourly.

She needed to make a call, but she wasn't going to stand in the rain, so she walked a little further down the road to a mall.

She didn't want to jump to the conclusion that the person who had delivered and picked up the letters from Emma Lau was also the person who had written them. It was possible that this was just another layer in the smoke-screen behind which she would eventually find the elusive mother. Or not.

The enormous mall featured a marble lobby, bronze arches, wedding-cake fountains and red leather ban-quettes. Grateful for the shelter and the relief from the overpowering humidity, Berlin sat down.

Lee had spent some time making arrangements in London. It was going to be a difficult matter, and potentially very messy, but he could see no other way. Satisfied that he'd done as much as he could to manage the risks, he resumed work on his report. He swore when his mobile rang.

Flora Trevelyan had already tried his patience. If it was her again, he was going to email the images of her to her board of governors and be done with it. She was of no use to him.

It wasn't Trevelyan's number, and he didn't recognise it, so he let it go to voicemail.

'This is a message for Joseph Zang,' the message began. The voice was not familiar. There was a slight pause. He could hear muzak in the background. 'Mr Zang, my name is Catherine Berlin. I was given your number by Emma Lau of the Green Dragon Certified Translation Agency. I would appreciate it if you would call me at your earliest convenience.'

Lee called Emma Lau.

'Mrs Lau,' he said. 'It's Joseph Zang here.'

'Oh hello, Mr Zang,' said Emma Lau. 'I was just about to call you. I met this morning with an English woman called Catherine Berlin.'

'What did she want?' said Lee.

'She had one of your letters,' said Emma Lau. 'She was asking questions about it, which is why I referred her to you. I hope that was appropriate?'

'Of course, Mrs Lau,' said Lee. 'There's no need to be concerned. Thank you.'

He hung up.

This was unexpected. He couldn't imagine how Berlin had got hold of one of the letters. The woman was extraordinarily resourceful, if somewhat reckless. She might have the others. If she didn't, she almost certainly knew where they were.

It was a surprise, to say the least. But he couldn't have planned it better himself.

He realised it was too late to call off the London operation, which was unfortunate. No matter. When people interfered in the business of others, they usually got what they deserved.

He picked up the landline.

'Put me through to passport control,' he said. 'It's urgent.'

52

Berlin lingered on her hotel room balcony and gazed at the Hong Kong skyline. Night fell quickly here. There was no twilight, for which she was truly thankful, but it was still unbearably humid. She longed for a biting easterly blowing across the Essex marshes. The clouds were low and heavy, darker even than the inky sky.

Mr Zang hadn't returned her call. Speculation was pointless. She had to focus on the fact of this silence. Chinese intelligence would respond to her intervention; to ignore it was to invite further probing. The challenge would be recognising their next move.

A raindrop splattered on the tiles. Then another. She'd never seen such fat rain. There was a deafening crack and the heavens opened.

The next deafening crack was accompanied by an explosion of glass behind her. She instinctively ducked and dived back inside. Through the gaps in the balustrade she thought she saw a movement on the roof of the building opposite, but it was difficult to see through the curtain of rain.

She crawled through the broken glass further into the room and waited for her heart to stop pounding.

The wind was picking up, but it wasn't fierce enough to smash a glass door.

It was an easy move to read.

The room phone rang. Berlin inched her way to the bedside table and picked up.

'Hello?' she said.

A hollow echo punctuated by crackling static was the only response. It seemed to go on forever. Then she heard breathing, rapid and shallow. She realised it was her own.

Sheet lightning bathed the room in a garish white flash. The line went dead, but she couldn't hang up.

53

Berlin used the express service to check out and left the hotel before dawn. A short walk through the empty mall took her to the metro. Five minutes later, she boarded the first train of the day.

It was six a.m. and the passengers were mostly dozing; she changed at North Point, travelled to Central, then walked through the sparkling tiled halls to Hong Kong Station, where there was a baggage service.

Peak hour was now in full swing. After depositing her small parcel, she hurried back to Central and shouldered her way on to an Island Line train to Wan Chai.

Wan Chai had eight exits, but she finally found the one that led to a footbridge and the bus terminus. She blessed sat nav and talking phones.

The non-stop coach to Dongguan took three hours and involved crossing the border. The visa for the People's Republic had been arranged in London, in case the trail led from Hong Kong into the other China.

One country, two systems. It didn't always pan out like that. The English-language newspaper on her lap, the *South China Morning Post*, was reporting the abduction and disappearance of dissidents living abroad.

Berlin felt more than a frisson of anxiety. If she was detained by the authorities on some pretext, no one would know, much less do anything about it.

Coaches left regularly for Dongguan and she had no trouble finding the numbered boarding bay on a map of the sprawling depot. Her counter-surveillance measures were less successful. Every five minutes she was sure someone was following her, until it became obvious that she was trying to throw half of Hong Kong off her trail.

She gave up and boarded. Last night was a warning she was going to ignore, because it meant she was getting close. To what, and who it was who wanted her to back off, were details she would fill in later.

She settled back into the relative safety of her first-class seat. No one would take pot shots at her on the coach. Probably.

A charming hostess offered her a juice.

National Express could learn a thing or two.

54

Berlin joined the queue for passport inspection at the Shenzen Bay crossing. Immigration and customs clearance in both directions were in one enormous building. Passengers were obliged to get off the coach, clear immigration, and get back on again on the other side.

No welcome signs greeted her, no duty-free shops hailed her credit cards, no smiles encouraged her to stay. This was the serious face of the People's Republic of China. It wasn't pretty.

The border guard took her passport, peered at it, looked up and stared at her. She broke out in a violent sweat. Her limbs ached, her mouth was dry. It could have been the heat, nerves or withdrawal. Physical symptoms could dog her for a month. Lethargy, anxiety and insomnia could last a lot longer. How would she know the difference?

The guard disappeared beyond the partition that separated the officials from the herd. She tried not to groan.

Lee took the passport from the guard and flipped through it. He gazed at the monitor. So this was Catherine Berlin in the flesh. He signalled the console operator to zoom in. The sweat on her brow stood out. She was driven, but by what?

He handed the passport back to the guard and nodded.

The investigator was getting close. People like her never trusted information that came too easily. Using Jian had been a master stroke; the youngster had played his part well.

Berlin would expose the British as corrupt liars and demonstrate that the Chinese were honest brokers with a selfless devotion to the interests of their country. Philip couldn't fail to be won over.

Lee watched as she left border control and made her way through the crowd to resume her seat on the bus.

When the bus pulled out, he hurried to his car. The driver accelerated away smoothly as soon as he got in.

Keeping the bus in sight, Lee rubbed his temple and took his pills, ignoring the doubts that hovered at the edge of his consciousness, fleeting motes of concern glimpsed out of the corner of his eye. There were always unknowns in an operation such as this.

Men in the game are blind to the possibilities that men looking on see clearly.

Berlin was still in the game.

Berlin dozed on and off during the final two hours of the trip. There was little to see through the fogged-up, rain-spattered windows.

When she stumbled off the coach in Dongguan, almost immediately she noticed a bitter taste in her mouth. Pollution. During a brief lull in the rain, for which she was thankful, a yellow band of smog had appeared, obscuring the top floors of the multistorey buildings that lined both sides of the road. She made her way towards the taxi rank.

Lee watched Berlin limp through the crowd. Her leg must have stiffened during the journey; he knew how she had acquired that injury, and a number of others.

Most women of her age would be playing with their grandchildren. He understood: she had bypassed the predictable in favour of the daily challenge of reinvention.

Lone wolves evoked a certain sympathy in each other.

He saw his man step out of his cab and make himself available. The other drivers scowled, but sensibly gave way.

Berlin hesitated for a moment, then got in the car.

It was the sort of thing that might alert her to the involvement of others in her journey, but he doubted she had any illusions on that score.

The windows of the small blue taxi were closed, but nothing could hold back the filthy atmosphere. Berlin coughed.

Traffic roared down the broad streets of Dongguan, lined with anonymous flat-roofed buildings of grubby white concrete. Dirty Lego. The businesses on the ground floor appeared to consist entirely of garment wholesalers.

Young women leant in the doorways of these shops, listless, lacking customers to greet. The footpaths were crowded with parked cars and seas of motorbikes and scooters.

High-rise buildings sprouted amongst the flat-roofed jumble, but not the inventive architect-designed glass and chrome towers she had left behind in Hong Kong. These grey tower blocks conveyed only emptiness; blank, cheap and repetitive.

The bright, cheerful face of consumerism, the energetic buzz of trade, the optimism so apparent there was absent here. This was the dour back end of capitalism, where the real graft took place.

'Tourist?' said the taxi driver.

Berlin was surprised by the enquiry.

'What is there to see here?' she said.

'The Opium War Museum,' said the driver. 'Or the Anti-British Memorial.'

Berlin glanced at him, but he was a study in neutrality: hands lightly on the wheel, eyes on the traffic.

His comment was, nevertheless, a sharp rebuke.

She handed him the scrap of paper that had been pushed under the door of her hotel room.

'No problem,' he said.

He'd barely glanced at it.

55

Bryant stirred three sugars into his tea and yawned. It was time to swap night-vision binoculars for day. Philip Chen had gone out late last night and hadn't returned. The old earl would be beside himself, wondering what he was up to.

Bryant knew, because he had followed the boy.

A quick cuppa, then he would get into position.

There were few people about because of the weather. A bank of leaden cloud was rolling up the river, accompanied by a distant rumble. The rain was a relentless grey curtain. Foggy spring had faded into sodden summer.

Sea walls were crumbling, homes were disappearing into sinkholes, and stormwater drains were collapsing under the pressure. There was dark talk of a rising tide that could consume London from below. He could see it coming.

He finished his tea, hoisted his knapsack on to his back and grabbed the van keys. On his way out, he found himself whistling. He hadn't felt this chirpy in years.

The taxi driver directed Berlin through a revolving door and into the busy lobby of a modern medium-rise office complex. She waited until she could get into a lift alone, and took it to the fourth floor.

Seconds after she stepped out, a dapper Chinese woman in a red linen suit, lemon blouse and black high heels appeared and greeted her. She must have heard the lift arrive.

'I'm Mrs Chung,' said the woman.

'Catherine Berlin,' said Berlin.

'So pleased,' said Mrs Chung.

She led Berlin through a door and into the reception area of an air-conditioned suite. There were no signs to indicate that this was the premises of the Anglo-Chinese Child Welfare Agency. Mrs Chung appeared to regard Berlin's presence as unremarkable and part of her usual routine.

The suite was all black glass, bronze and enormous vases of flowers. Corporate chic, circa 1980. Mrs Chung showed her into a room equipped with comfortable chairs arranged around a coffee table, on which lay a pile of glossy brochures.

A spacious desk was bare apart from a sleek laptop. Framed vocational qualifications, business registrations and licences, in English and Chinese, adorned the walls. It was very reassuring.

Berlin was not at all reassured. She walked to the window and looked down on the frenzy of pedestrians and traffic in the main street. An alley ran along one side of the building, partially obscured by makeshift awnings.

Mrs Chung opened a bar fridge, took out a can of Coke, poured it into a chilled glass and handed it to Berlin. She gestured to a chair. Berlin sat.

Mrs Chung took a seat on the opposite side of the coffee table.

Berlin took a sip of the Coke to compose herself.

'I should explain why I'm here,' she said.

'No explanation needed,' said Mrs Chung. 'Welcome. All client word-of-mouth. I understand.'

Berlin nodded and smiled. If only she did.

Mrs Chung picked up one of the brochures and handed it to Berlin. 'You have one of these?' she said.

Berlin gazed at the cover. Cute Chinese babies smiled up at her. They were colour-coded. Pink headbands for girls, blue for boys. Suddenly she understood. She gulped the Coke.

'You're an adoption agency,' she said.

Mrs Chung frowned.

'I mean,' said Berlin. 'An authorised adoption agency.'

'Ah,' said Mrs Chung. 'Authorised, yes. We are a registered business. But not adoption. We work with little angels. Government authority is the China Centre for Children Welfare and Adoption. We only make the connection, you understand, with the humble home, which is government-approved.'

'You're middlemen,' said Berlin.

'If you like,' said Mrs Chung.

'And the humble home?' said Berlin. 'Where is that?'

Mrs Chung waved her hand in a number of general directions while smiling vacantly.

'Where do the little angels come from?' said Berlin.

'All belong to the state,' said Mrs Chung. 'In accordance with adoption law of the People's Republic of China, children under fourteen can be adoptees if orphaned, abandoned, or if parents unable to rear them due to unusual difficulties.'

She sat back, apparently pleased with her recitation.

'I understood . . .' said Berlin. She hesitated. If she pressed too hard, Mrs Chung would show her the door. So she conveyed confusion. It wasn't an act.

'What's your relationship with the Anglo-Chinese Friendship Society Scholarship Fund?' she asked.

Mrs Chung's brow darkened. These were not the usual questions. Or maybe she didn't understand.

'This is Anglo-Chinese Child Welfare Agency,' she said. 'Bridge between East and West.'

She took Berlin's hand and gave it a reassuring squeeze.

'Our babies are special,' she said. 'No need background checks. Read the brochure. Provenance guaranteed.'

Another rote phrase, learnt for these occasions.

Berlin flipped through the brochure to cover her shock at the use of the word 'provenance'.

'Could I see?' she said. She smiled.

Mrs Chung regarded her with a look that could only be described as inscrutable. Berlin was well beyond child-bearing age, and presumably looked as desperate as she felt.

'Appointment necessary,' she said, smiling brightly. 'And deposit.'

Bryant waited in the passage that led to the watermen's stairs. He hadn't been there five minutes when Philip Chen came slouching down Wapping High Street, right on schedule. The rain was relentless, so he had his head down and didn't notice Bryant until he stepped out in front of him.

'Hello, Philip,' he said.

The boy stopped and looked around, peering at Bryant as if he were a mirage. He was totally wasted, gaunt, unkempt, and exuding a stale smell that Bryant associated with rough sleepers, not public schoolboys.

'Over here,' said Bryant. He beckoned.

Philip walked towards him as if mesmerised.

'What?' he said.

Bryant backed up a little, to draw him further down the passage.

'I know you,' Philip said.

'Of course you do,' said Bryant. 'We're old pals.'

It was far enough. They were out of reach of the cameras.

'I'm innocent,' said Philip.

'I know,' said Bryant. 'This is for your own good.'

He pulled the trigger on the taser. The voltage was dialled down, but it was strong enough to cause Philip to stagger and fall. Bryant quickly slipped plastic cuffs around his wrists and ankles and slapped a piece of gaffer tape over his mouth. When he picked the boy up and hoisted him over his shoulder, he was astonished at how light he was.

Philip struggled in vain as Bryant carried him to the van, slid open the side door, laid him down on a blanket, then shut the door and strolled to the driver's seat.

It was all over in a minute and a half.

Philip kicked out at the door with his feet, but it was a puny effort.

'Don't you worry, lad,' Bryant called back. 'Settle down now.'

The response was muffled, but it didn't sound as if it was very complimentary.

It was Gran's belief that children needed a firm but loving hand in order to thrive. Bryant found himself relishing his new role as protector of the innocent. Well, let's say the *vulnerable*.

Gran would be proud.

56

Berlin made her excuses to Mrs Chung, took a brochure and left with a promise to return soon with a cash deposit. Instead of taking the revolving doors out of the lobby and on to the main road, where the taxi and its very knowledgeable driver were waiting, she took a side exit that led into the narrow alley. She crossed the alley, stood back and looked up.

The building extended back into the block, where it revealed its true nature: crumbling concrete streaked with rust stains, and ill-fitting windows filmed with condensation. The facade was literally just a facade.

Berlin strolled down the alley. The denizens stared at her openly, but didn't pause in their tasks. One man was repairing the spokes of battered umbrellas. A tiny, haggard woman sat behind a plank poised between two old crates. She was selling something in the jars arranged on the plank.

The jars contained yellow water in which floated pieces of something that looked like eel, but with tattooed skin.

Berlin realised it was snake. The repugnance she felt must have been plain on her face, because the haggard woman scowled at her.

A number of doorways opened on to steep, narrow stairs. Plastic bags stuffed with rubbish were piled beside the doors. One had split open and was attracting a swarm of flies. Berlin also took an interest.

She glanced to the left and right, but no one was taking any notice of her. She stepped through the doorway and into a small concrete area at the bottom of the stairs.

A youth wearing a T-shirt emblazoned with a Japanese manga schoolgirl was sitting at the top of the first flight. His eyes widened almost as much as the schoolgirl's at the sight of Berlin.

The stairwell was filthy with litter and stank of urine. Noise drifted down from above. The babble grew as she limped up each flight.

The youth followed, shouting and gesturing at her, but he didn't lay a hand on her, for which she was grateful. She smiled and shook her head. She didn't understand. For all he knew she was a lost tourist.

On the third landing, he raced past her. By the time she reached the fourth floor, the cries were cacophonous and the youth was standing in front of a door, barring the way. It was a clear signal.

Berlin chanced her arm. She shoved him aside and pushed open the door. The din and the smell smacked her in the face, but she crossed the threshold.

It was a step too far.

A dozen women stared at her, expressionless.

They were all breastfeeding, sitting on stools arranged alongside small wooden cribs fixed to the wall. The sweet-sour smell of their milk mingled with the rank odour of vomit and baby poo, the disposable nappies a feast for the flies below.

It took Berlin a moment to realise that there were only twelve women in the cramped room, six on each side, but at least three times that number of wailing infants of different ages, some 'shelved', some cradled in the women's arms. Three of the women were feeding two babies at once.

Tiny hands and feet protruded above the sides of the cribs, kicking and grasping. Their owners wailed and screamed blue murder. A woman rose from her stool, put the baby she was feeding in a crib, and picked up another.

Motherhood. On an industrial scale.

57

Berlin walked up the short flight of marble steps and into the lobby of the Grand Regency, the hotel the taxi driver had recommended. The porter hurried past to collect her suitcase from the boot. She never let the black bag out of her grasp.

The concierge came forward, bowed and escorted her to reception. The receptionist handed her a room key without asking for a credit card or a passport.

They had been expecting her.

A man in a suit stood at one end of the reception counter, watching and smoking. He smiled at her, stubbed out his cigarette and strolled over.

'Ms Berlin,' he said. 'Welcome to the real China.'

'Thank you,' said Berlin.

'I wonder if you would do me the honour of a drink in the bar,' he said. 'My name is Lee Wang Yan.'

Mr Lee. She met his eye. He held her gaze without blinking. This was the man she had glimpsed in the dark at the Abbey.

'So you're responsible for this charade?' she said.

He was small, urbane, with a grave smile and thick black hair that showed no signs of grey, although he must have been in his sixties. He spoke English with a slight French accent.

He said something to the porter, who bowed and hurried off to the lift, taking Berlin's suitcase with him.

Berlin glanced back at the taxi driver, who was still hovering on the front steps, watching through the enormous plate-glass doors. Lee dismissed him with a small gesture, then turned to her and indicated a lounge bar on the other side of the lobby.

It was furnished with deep brown leather chairs and a long mirrored bar that reflected an excellent collection of whisky.

It was a five-star set-up.

Lee waited until their drinks had been served.

'So,' he said. 'What will you tell Philip about his mother?'

He lit a cigarette. He smoked Gauloises. The same brand as Laurent. He noticed her looking at the packet.

'Did you know they were bought out by British Imperial Tobacco?' he said.

Berlin shook her head.

'Now they intend to drop Tobacco from the name, but not Imperial. Ironic, no?'

'Did you kill Sylvie Laurent?' said Berlin.

'What a question,' said Lee. 'You still believe we are the bad guys in this affair?'

'I gave up thinking in terms of good guys and bad guys when I was ten,' said Berlin.

'Yes,' said Lee. 'I'm aware of your colourful background. But I must press you, Ms Berlin. What do you intend to tell Philip about his mother?'

'I haven't found her yet,' said Berlin.

Lee inhaled deeply and flicked his ash into a marble ashtray the size of a washing-up bowl.

'But now you can at least tell him that Haileybury and the school lied,' he said. 'He wasn't an orphan, he was adopted. His mother was an unfortunate woman forced to surrender him because of poverty. One day they will be reunited.'

'An unfortunate woman. Not a brood mare?' said Berlin.

'What do you mean?' he said.

Lee knew she had seen the shiny front of the so-called adoption business, but not the back office. She leant forward to make her point as forcefully as possible without shouting.

'I've seen it,' she spat. 'If you're in charge here, why don't you close down this disgusting racket?'

He didn't blanch, just reached into his pocket, took out some pills and washed them down with the whisky.

'I may agree with you,' he said. 'But this *disgusting racket* is not my concern. It's a regional matter. I have no authority in that area, and if I acted, it would only take me further from my purpose.'

'Which is what?' said Berlin. 'To reclaim the spoils of a war you lost? Is that really more important?'

His jaw tightened, but his voice didn't waver.

'What do you think you know, Ms Berlin?' he said.

'That Philip and the other so-called Palmerston Hall scholarship boys were supplied by a baby farm that has a close association with the Anglo-Chinese Friendship Society,' said Berlin.

274

'For what purpose were these boys *supplied*, as you put it?' said Lee.

'To satisfy some perverse need of Haileybury's, I imagine.'

'And how will Philip benefit from this knowledge?' said Lee.

Berlin didn't believe the truth could set you free. It was more likely to leave you with a heavy heart and a burden you would have to carry for the rest of your life. But a lie was worse, because the truth always came out, and then the burden was doubled.

'Perhaps he won't,' she said. 'Powerful men like you and Haileybury are all the same, manipulating the weak while pretending that what you're doing is in their interests. From time to time someone has to stand up to you and let them make their own mistakes.'

Mr Lee regarded her through the pall of smoke that hung around him.

'You've come a long way for this boy,' he said finally. 'What's in it for you, Ms Berlin?'

'I'm at a loose end,' she said.

58

Bryant secured Philip to the central heating pipe. The boy was so weak, he didn't have the strength to dislodge it. Around him were arranged bottles of water, a bucket and plenty of blankets.

'Fancy a cup of tea?' said Bryant.

The way the boy looked at him, you'd think he'd gone mad.

'Why are you doing this?' said Philip.

'It's for your own good,' said Bryant. 'You're in the grip of something evil. First we have to break his hold on you. Then you'll be able to resist and tell the truth.'

'Let me go!' screamed Philip.

He tugged at his bonds, sweat already soaking his T-shirt.

He could scream as loud as he liked. No one would hear him.

'How many sugars?' said Bryant.

Haileybury shuffled through the gallery, gazing up at the Foo Dogs, who remained stoic. Every day he became a little less able; movement was a torment. His spine was brittle and on the verge of snapping. A good shove and he would go down, probably never to get up again.

He had fought a losing battle to keep everything under control, and failed dismally. He hobbled on to the platform and set off on the brief, but painful, journey to the smoking room. He desperately needed to ease his mind, and his limbs.

Philip hadn't come home. It didn't make sense. Only he could provide what the boy needed. He could be lying in a gutter somewhere, or on a trolley in an overcrowded Accident & Emergency department. He might have been picked up by the police for reasons too unpleasant to contemplate.

The smoking room was in disarray. All the glasses were dirty. The chaos was depressing. He poked with his stick at a pile of pizza boxes on the floor. He had always relied on Simon to sort things out and had never asked for details.

Least said, soonest mended, and all that.

He picked up one of the glasses and gave it a quick wipe with his handkerchief.

The Ardbeg ten-year-old was down to the dregs, thanks to Berlin.

He hadn't heard from her, which was unsurprising after her little plan to pinch his opium had gone awry.

Perhaps it was time to mend some bridges.

59

Berlin sprawled on the bed in her suite and watched the typhoon on television, although she could have just opened the curtains. The quilt was decorated with empty miniatures from the minibar in the sitting room.

She was a guest of the Chinese government.

Lee had positioned an agent on a hard chair at the end of the hallway. There was no way to leave. The weather was so foul there was really nowhere to go in any case. Her bag had been unpacked by 'housekeeping'. Her computer was connected to the internet, but like her mobile, it was now behind the great firewall of China.

She rolled off the bed and dragged back the heavy drapes. Sheets of rain lashed the windows. The panes flexed, on the point of implosion, the fluctuating air pressure tearing at the frames.

She closed the drapes again, but couldn't block out the eerie wailing of the wind. The lights flickered, the air conditioning died, then the TV.

Chimes rang out. It took a moment for her to realise it was her mobile. She picked up, reminding herself that someone was probably monitoring the call.

'Berlin,' said Haileybury. 'How are you, my dear?'

'As well as can be expected,' she said.

'Ah,' said Haileybury.

The earl might never have had to undergo the rigours of withdrawal, but she was sure he could imagine it.

'I'm so terribly sorry,' he said. 'About everything.'

He was drunk.

'What can I do for you?' she said.

'I rather wondered,' said Haileybury. 'I mean, have you spoken with Philip lately?'

'Why don't you ask him?' she said.

The line crackled. She remembered there was no line.

'I can't,' said Haileybury.

'Where is he?' he said. It was a cry of despair. 'I'll give you anything you ask, Berlin, anything. Just tell me where he is.'

This time the crackle was followed by dead air.

A moment later she heard the door to the suite open. She waited a few minutes, but when there was no further sign of activity, she opened the bedroom door.

Lee was sitting on the sofa, smoking. The aroma of French cigarettes hung in the still air. He stood and gave her a small bow. She was getting a bit sick of this show of *politesse*.

'Please forgive the intrusion,' he said.

'You're paying the bill,' said Berlin.

The lights flickered as the generator cut out and the mains cut back in.

Berlin opened the minibar. It was nearly empty.

'Could you get housekeeping up here to refill this?' she said.

She took the last tiny bottle of Chivas and slammed the door shut.

Lee smiled and sat back down again.

Philip's letters lay on the coffee table in front of him. So much for the secure baggage service at the Hong Kong MTR station.

'What do you intend to do now, Ms Berlin?' asked Lee.

'I'm going back to Hong Kong,' said Berlin. 'As soon as the weather breaks.'

'Ah yes,' said Lee. 'To attend the General Registrar's office.'

He lit another cigarette.

'Where is Philip?' he said.

'Is there any point in telling you I don't know?' she said.

'Lord Haileybury seems to think you do,' said Lee.

'Haileybury is a drunk and desperate old man,' said Berlin.

Lee gazed at her for a long moment.

'You think you're very clever, Ms Berlin,' he said. 'And I suppose you are. You are certainly extraordinarily stubborn. Have you considered that a sad accident might befall you while you are so far from home?'

Lee was not a man to make idle threats.

Philip was missing. Haileybury didn't know where he was and neither did Lee. It gave her an edge. Leverage.

She struggled to control the fear in her voice.

'I came to find Philip's mother. If something happens to me, he'll know it wasn't an accident. He'll never trust you again and he won't do anything to compromise Haileybury. You lose.'

Outside, the wind bellowed.

'Then if not an accident, perhaps . . .'

He stood and called out something in Chinese.

Two uniformed men ran into the room and grabbed her.

'Catherine Berlin,' said Lee. 'You are a British spy and an enemy of the People's Republic of China and will be detained until trial.'

So much for her edge.

60

The prison guards never spoke to her. She couldn't tell if this was a rule, or if they didn't speak English. Hand signals had been used when she arrived to indicate that she should undress, put on prison overalls, stand up, sit down, stop talking. The sign used to convey the latter was a swift slap in the face.

'I must speak to the British consulate,' she said. She said it over and over again, despite the slap, to everyone with whom she came into contact.

The gaol was straight out of a depressing dystopian film. She had visited a few prisons in her time, but never one so utterly silent. Endless corridors, electronic gates, and grim, robotic guards. Transported in a van and deposited in an inner courtyard, she had no idea of its size, let alone where it was or what it was called.

After ten days, as she sat, lay or paced in her tiny cell, she heard whispers. She strained to listen, unsure if they were real or the product of her imagination, a strange auditory hallucination to break the silence. The susurrating babble would reach a crescendo, then cut out.

The silence, momentarily shattered, was even more acute. It wasn't going to take long to break her. If the isolation didn't do it, the watery rice soup soon would.

The door of her cell opened and two guards escorted her to the interrogation room. On the way, she passed rooms packed with Chinese women sitting on the edge of a raised platform that lined three walls. Their blank, pitiless faces stared as she passed, each locked in their own silent hell.

The interrogation room was out of the same Orwellian nightmare. A uniformed man sat at a table. The guards pushed her into the chair opposite him. He thrust a piece of paper across the table and she pushed it back.

The first time she'd read it, she had laughed out loud. It was her confession to the crime of espionage, in which she admitted, in flamboyant and highly charged political rhetoric, to conspiring against the People's Republic in order to advance the heinous designs of British imperialism.

The pen stayed on the table.

The interrogator barked an order and the two guards reappeared to drag her back to her cell.

She was no longer laughing.

On the eleventh day, her cell door opened as usual. She stood, but the effort was almost too much. She felt dizzy and nauseous. She waited for the two guards to grasp her arms. When nothing happened, she looked up.

Del was standing in the doorway.

'I understand you require consular assistance,' he said.

61

A flask of tea was brought on a tray with two tiny porcelain cups. A bamboo steamer appeared. When Berlin lifted the lid, the fragrance of warm, plump pork buns filled the cell.

Del poured. The tea was green.

'I could do with a strong cup of builder's,' she said.

'Is that all you've got to say?' said Del.

She crammed a bun into her mouth.

'Did Sir Simon send you?' she said.

'Yes,' said Del. 'They've given me a temporary role at the consulate, to cover the formalities.'

'To give you diplomatic protection,' said Berlin. 'So Simon May arranged all that and flew you out here to rescue me. How chivalrous. What does he want?'

'Who said anything about rescuing you?' said Del. 'Oh, and by the way, I've just spent twelve hours in an aluminium tube, eight hours completing the paperwork for accreditation and twelve hours negotiating access with the Chinese. You're welcome.'

'Business class?' said Berlin.

Del sighed.

'What did you do to piss these people off?' he said. 'You'd only been here a week before you managed to get yourself arrested.'

'I didn't *do* anything,' said Berlin. 'I asked a few questions, that's all.'

'Well now you have to answer a few,' said Del. 'You do know the penalty for spying is death?'

'Can your boss get me out of here?' said Berlin.

Del leant forward and took a bun. As he put it in his mouth, he whispered, 'Where's Philip Chen?'

Berlin leant back against the wall.

Haileybury, Lee, Simon May. They all wanted Philip.

'Are you reporting to Sir Simon as senior partner at Burghley LLP or as a representative of Her Majesty's Government?' she said.

Del met her gaze.

There was no difference.

She poured more tea.

'The feeling is that Philip wouldn't go missing for this length of time under his own steam,' said Del.

Berlin couldn't argue with that. Every cell in his body would be screaming for the Haileybury elixir.

'I'd say try Detective Bryant,' she said. 'But he's locked up.'

'No he's not,' said Del. 'He absconded. I thought you knew.'

'How would I know?' said Berlin.

He couldn't look her in the eye. They knew Bryant had been in touch with her; they'd been checking her phone records.

Bryant had signally failed to mention to her that he was on the loose. A smart move. She had underestimated the detective.

'They've had his flat under surveillance,' said Del. 'He hasn't been there. I imagine he's too psychotic and disorganised to snatch the kid and keep him this long.'

It was always a mistake to write off the madman.

'You seem to be way ahead of me, Del,' she said. 'I don't think I can help you.'

'Come on,' said Del. 'This isn't just about Philip. There's a bigger picture here.'

She was surprised and disappointed to hear Del parrot this line. She sipped from the fragile porcelain cup. Her hands were shaking and her gall was rising, but she was too weak to give it full rein.

Del leant forward and touched her arm.

'Please,' he said. He lowered his voice. 'You'll waste away in here. I agreed to come because I want to get you out. Fuck Sir Simon's agenda. I know you're pissed off with me, but I don't want to lose you.'

'There's no incentive,' said Berlin.

'Coming home isn't enough?' said Del.

'Home is where the heart is,' said Berlin.

After Del had gone, Berlin stood beneath the light, which burned night and day. She wasn't feeling very noble.

'I want to speak to Lee,' she said.

The light didn't reply, but she had no doubt the message would get through.

'And I'd like some more pork buns.'

62

Bryant carried the tray into the bedroom and set it down on the bedside table.

'You've got to eat something,' he said. 'I've got some toast and tomato soup here.'

He was worried about the boy, who was very weak with vomiting, diarrhoea and sweats. He'd had to change the sheets three times, but daren't hang them on the line to dry in case the neighbours became suspicious.

'Sit up,' said Bryant.

He plumped the pillows, put the tray on Philip's lap and removed the cuffs and the gaffer tape.

Philip sipped some water and nibbled the toast.

'How did you know about this place?' he said.

'I knew her mum had died recently,' said Bryant. 'I put two and two together. I am a detective, you know.'

'And a housebreaker,' said Philip. 'She brought me here too. But I didn't realise she'd lost her mother.'

Bryant sat down on the end of the bed.

'This was Berlin's room,' said Philip. 'It's sort of like a museum of her life, isn't it? All those things from when she was little.'

'I expect her mum sat right here telling her stories,' said Bryant.

'They only tell you lies,' said Philip.

'That's a terrible thing to say,' said Bryant.

'Why are you doing this, really?' said Philip. 'You're going to get into a lot of trouble.'

'You're the one in trouble, lad,' said Bryant.

'How do you mean?' said Philip. 'Because of the drugs? I don't think Jack ever meant me any harm. He's very attached to me.'

Bryant grimaced.

'And to the others,' he said.

'What do you mean?' said Philip.

'You're not the only one,' said Bryant. 'Chinese schoolboys have been visiting Haileybury for years.'

'Scholarship boys,' said Philip. 'So?'

Bryant stood up. 'Are you going to eat that soup?'

'It's not my favourite,' said Philip.

Bryant sighed. 'What is?' he said.

'Mushroom,' said Philip.

'All right,' said Bryant. 'I'll pop down to the corner shop and see if they've got any.'

'Detective Bryant,' said Philip. 'What about the boys at Jack's?'

'Nothing,' said Bryant. 'I won't be long.'

He put the tape back over Philip's mouth and slipped the cuffs back on. The boy was too comfortable with captivity.

He shut the door behind him and locked it.

The sooner Philip got his strength up and realised he was free of Haileybury, and his addiction, the sooner he'd tell the truth about what had gone on in that den of iniquity. If he didn't cooperate, it would have to be Plan B.

He would soon see how long it took Haileybury to get over his 'attachment'.

It would be painful, but quick.

63

The rain was steady, but the wind had dropped. Her bag was on the back seat of the taxi. Lee was holding the door open. The driver was the same bloke who'd picked her up at the bus station when she'd arrived in Dongguan.

'Everything is for sale,' said Berlin.

'We were taught the importance of free trade at the point of a gun,' said Lee.

A three-masted clipper, complete with cannon.

'There's nothing free about it,' said Berlin.

'What did you want from Philip?' she said.

'Nothing,' said Lee.

'He said you wanted him to betray Haileybury.'

'Did it ever occur to you that Philip lied?' said Lee. 'He sought your sympathy with fairy tales: blackmail, a damsel in distress, an exploited child.'

All three. She had abandoned first principles. Believe no one.

'Then why did he react so violently when Deng approached him that morning?' said Berlin.

'Why indeed?' said Lee. 'It came as a complete surprise to us. We have only ever tried to protect him.'

'Deng must have said something to provoke him,' persisted Berlin.

'He warned him that at eighteen everything could change,' said Lee. 'He could face challenges.'

'Such as?' said Berlin.

Lee shook his head and gestured for her to get in. The conversation was over.

'Where am I going?' she said.

'We're keeping our end of the bargain,' said Lee.

She got in. Lee shut the door and the car pulled away.

Berlin glanced back at the prison, which was not the gargantuan complex of her imagination, but a small detention centre. According to Lee, the conditions there were much better than in a real prison. It was hard to imagine how much worse it could have been.

The dense traffic, milling crowds and chaotic architecture provided no clue as to the nature of the neighbourhoods they passed through.

Apartment blocks, shopping malls, office complexes, all besmirched with kitsch hoardings, strings of traditional lanterns, or lines of Chinese characters that might have been urging the population to buy cars or keep the streets clean for all she knew. They were complying with the former and ignoring the latter.

They sped south, out of Dongguan, and on to a tollway where, having paid to use it, the driver seemed to believe he could travel at whatever speed he chose.

Berlin watched the blurred images of many different Chinas race by as the car flew along the motorway: conical straw hats bobbing in rice paddies, youths in Batman T-shirts taking selfies, gleaming SUVs manoeuvring amongst bullock carts.

Did any of these people know or care about the Haileybury Bequest, or were the treasures significant only in the bigger game played between governments?

She closed her eyes.

She woke to find they were crossing into the Special Administrative Region. She must have slept for a couple of hours. A border guard waved them through and they took the exit to Hong Kong Island.

They drove for twenty minutes, then stopped beside a high wall that appeared to have been carved out of a sheer rock face. The white cliff glistened from recent rain, rivulets trickling into clumps of iridescent green vegetation that sprouted from its crevices.

The driver pointed at a pair of iron gates on broken hinges.

She got out of the car, and watched it drive off.

The street was deserted. It was an upmarket residential neighbourhood. The houses were all set well back, barely visible through the lush gardens. Only the occasional barking dog and birdsong broke the silence.

Berlin pushed open one of the gates and trekked up a steep drive, struggling with her bag. She was still weak and the heat was just as oppressive as in Dongguang, although the air was marginally fresher.

Rounding a gentle bend, she confronted a once elegant bungalow, now a decrepit shell. The house rose from amongst the lush vegetation clinging to the chalky cliff face, almost hidden beneath creepers and overhung by weeping palm fronds.

A broad veranda fringed the house and a thick vine wound through the banisters of the steps that led up to it.

A woman standing at the balustrade watched her approach. Her stance was wary as she looked past Berlin, scanning the drive as if expecting someone else. She was clutching a glass jar of steaming water in which drifted small flowers and leaves. A floating world.

'Hello,' said Berlin. 'Do you speak English?'

The woman nodded. 'Are you lost?' she said.

It was difficult to estimate the woman's age, but the ghost of the same beauty was there in the shape of the eyes, the high forehead and the sculptured cheekbones. When she smiled, the resemblance was astonishing.

Berlin could only smile back.

Berlin felt at a loss, not sure how to phrase the question now she was here.

'I believe . . .' she said. 'That is, I understand you may be Philip Chen's mother.'

There was no flicker of recognition.

Berlin took out her phone and found the photo of Philip. 'Is he your son?' she asked, holding it up.

The woman glanced at it.

'Probably,' she said.

Berlin was so taken aback by this response, the phone nearly slipped from her fingers. The woman said something in Chinese and another woman appeared at an open window. She was older, but they were very alike.

The older woman spoke rapidly in Chinese, frowning.

The younger woman didn't respond.

'Show her the picture,' she ordered Berlin.

The older woman reluctantly peered at the photo, then said something to Berlin.

'I'm sorry, I don't understand,' said Berlin.

'My mother has a question,' said the woman. She tossed the dregs of her tea over the balcony.

'Yes?' said Berlin.

'She wants to know, which one is he?'

64

Berlin sat at a table on the veranda with the younger of the two women, who introduced herself only as Pearl. The other woman, her mother, fussed about and served tea in a perfunctory manner. She wasn't happy with this intrusion.

Berlin tried to appear relaxed, but it was a struggle.

Pearl occasionally responded to her mother with a word or two, but didn't take her eyes off Berlin. There was an air of resignation, or weariness, about her, as if she'd always known this day would come. Up close, she looked to be in her late thirties. Her mother was in her fifties.

The house was very grand and very empty. The French doors and windows were wide open, their broken rattan screens propped against the wall. There was no sign of anyone except Pearl and her mother. They seemed to live principally in the kitchen, which gave on to the veranda at the back, where they were sitting.

'Are you from the British police?' said Pearl.

'Good God, no,' said Berlin.

'Why are you here?'

'I'm a friend of Philip's,' she said. 'I came to look for his mother.'

'Who brought you to this place?' said Pearl.

'Mr Lee,' said Berlin.

Pearl looked puzzled. Her mother said something, to which she replied in Chinese.

Berlin found it disconcerting.

'You know Mr Lee?' she said.

Pearl hesitated for a moment.

'There are many Lees in China,' she said.

That line of questioning was going nowhere, so Berlin tried a more direct approach.

'Did you write to Philip?' she asked.

'I don't understand,' said Pearl.

'Did you send him a letter?' said Berlin.

Pearl stared at her.

'You see, until recently he believed his mother was dead,' said Berlin.

'That's very unlucky,' said Pearl.

Berlin had the impression she was choosing her words with care. Unlucky for who? Her or Philip? Or both of them?

'But then he received a letter?' said Pearl.

'More than one,' said Berlin.

Mother and daughter exchanged a glance.

Despite the humidity, Berlin felt a chill in the air.

'How many children have you had?' asked Berlin.

'I've had three boys,' said Pearl. 'My mother had four.'

The older woman folded her arms and adopted a strangely haughty stance. Her pride was evident.

Berlin felt sweat trickle down her spine.

'Where are they?' she said.

The question was out before she realised it. It was a mistake.

Pearl's gaze dropped to the teacup in her hand. She swirled it gently, peering into the green eddies until her mother said something.

Pearl responded with obvious reluctance.

Her mother began shouting at Berlin.

'She says these are personal matters,' said Pearl. 'We are very lucky. We've been treated well.'

Berlin wasn't going to retreat now.

'What about their fathers?' she asked.

'Their fathers?' echoed Pearl.

She put her cup down.

'I'm surprised by your lack of manners,' she said. 'Their father is none of your concern. You should go now.'

'But she's only just arrived.'

The three women turned as one.

Sir Simon May was standing at the far end of the veranda.

Pearl's mother was muttering under her breath. It could have been a prayer or an incantation. Pearl had taken her arm, apparently trying to calm her.

'Well done, Berlin,' said Sir Simon. 'This is the last place I would have looked for them.'

'I didn't intend to help you out in any way, shape or form,' said Berlin.

'I got that message when you dismissed poor Delroy Jacobs,' said Sir Simon. 'That lad tries so hard. But once you had refused our generous offer . . .'

'To give you Philip,' said Berlin.

'. . . it was clear you would throw your lot in with the Chinese. Do you think he'll fare any better with them?'

'They're the lesser of two evils,' said Berlin.

'You think so?' said Sir Simon.

He seemed to contemplate this for a moment, gazing at the house.

'This is the old Haileybury place,' he said. 'Flogged off years ago. I always wondered who bought it. Now we know. How very odd. Another expression of their ridiculous repatriation agenda, I suppose.'

He was even more dishevelled than the first time she'd seen him. His hand shook as he took a pack of cigarettes and a rose-gold lighter from the pocket of his chinos.

Berlin had seen the lighter before.

'You killed Sylvie Laurent,' she said.

He lit his cigarette and returned the pack and the lighter to his pocket.

'She came into possession of some rather damning evidence,' he said. 'Of course, she didn't realise the full import of it, but I couldn't take any chances.'

'Christ,' said Berlin.

Pearl said something in Chinese.

To Berlin's surprise, Sir Simon snapped back in the same language. As their argument continued, his colour rose.

Pearl said something and gestured to Berlin.

'I tried to warn you not to get involved, Berlin,' said Sir Simon. 'The CPS would never have taken the Deng case to trial. It would have kept you out of action for a while, that's all. Instead you had to come here, blundering in without a clue. Typical Brit.'

'So why don't you fill me in?' said Berlin. 'Give me the courtesy of the briefing I should have had when I took on this job.'

Sir Simon glanced at his watch.

'It would take far too long,' he said. 'And I'm rather pushed for time. I've got to tidy up this mess, then get back to London.'

He reached inside his jacket and drew a weapon. A snub-nose revolver. A .38 Special.

She heard Pearl gasp.

Blood pounded in Berlin's ears. She gulped for air.

'No time for niceties, I'm afraid,' said Sir Simon.

'The authorities forced us to come here,' said Pearl. 'The government men.' She pointed at Berlin. 'This is nothing to do with us.'

'I have to disagree,' said Sir Simon. 'You're right in the middle of it.'

Berlin felt as if she had crashed a party where the hosts were engaged in a marital spat.

'Please, Simon, let us go,' said Pearl. 'You don't own us.'

Sir Simon laughed.

'That's rich,' he said. 'I seem to remember you were both bought and paid for.'

A brief, harsh blast faded into a scream. Pearl dropped. The next staccato blast cut off the scream and her mother fell too.

Berlin grabbed the table with both hands, upended it and ducked down. The next shot blew it apart. The splintered wood peppered her face. She closed her eyes and saw the arch of the City of London cemetery looming over her. Peggy wouldn't have been the least surprised.

Far away, bird wings beat the air.

She looked up. Sir Simon May was standing over her. He was focused, unemotional. His bright blue eyes conveyed only a determination to complete the task at hand. She imagined him efficiently slipping the noose over Laurent's head.

He put the gun to her head.

She heard a pop.

His head exploded and he toppled to the floor.

Berlin couldn't look away from the small fissure in Sir Simon's skull and the shocking crimson pulp where his face had been. Finally she looked up to see where the shot had come from.

At the other end of the veranda, the taxi driver lowered his pistol and unscrewed the silencer. Lee emerged from the dense undergrowth.

Frozen in her crouch and still gripping what was left of the table, Berlin's guts rebelled. She threw up.

'You have to agree,' said Lee. 'My man is quick on the draw.'

She had a feeling he could have been quicker, but that the outcome was exactly the way Lee wanted it. She wiped the vomit from her mouth with her sleeve. Her ears were ringing and the ground was undulating.

'Now Philip *is* an orphan,' he said. 'You will tell him the truth when you find him.'

Still on her knees, Berlin felt a hand grip her shoulder. It wasn't intended to comfort.

Hands Washed Pure

of Blood

65

The plane dipped through the clouds and a buckled steel band appeared far below. The river. Docklands shimmered; the ramparts of the Thames Barrier rose slowly, shining scales between graceful arched piers, protecting the city from storm and tide. If it failed, London would be washed away.

Berlin was no longer sure it would be a bad thing.

They taxied through drizzle to Terminal 5 as the cabin steward announced that it was five thirty-five a.m., British Summer Time. Welcome home.

It took an hour to get through Immigration and undergo a search by Customs. No one else from her flight was detained. When she emerged into the arrivals hall, her name wasn't on display at the barrier. There was no driver waiting for her. No such luck.

Instead, two tall men in dark suits and coppers' shoes approached and stood either side of her.

'Miss Berlin?' asked one.

She didn't bother to reply.

The last time Berlin had seen Detective Chief Inspector Tomalin, he had been busy apologising to Haileybury and sending Bryant off to a secure psychiatric facility.

The inspector refused to say what had precipitated this interview in an office on an upper level of the terminal.

She was 'assisting with enquiries'. It was a short step from there to being a 'person of interest', but she was getting used to that. The allegation of murder hanging over her hadn't been mentioned. Yet.

Tomalin flicked through her passport.

'Why did you go to Hong Kong?' he said.

'For a taste of the Orient,' said Berlin.

She knew that her stroppy attitude was counterproductive, but she was tired after the flight, and sitting for two hours in this small, airless room waiting to be questioned hadn't done anything for her mood.

It was a waste of time she could ill afford. Lee had been clear about what he expected of her. Her head was buzzing. All she wanted, she told herself, was a couple of codeine and a drink. That wasn't all she wanted, but it would be better than nothing.

'What happened to your face?' said Tomalin.

Fragments of the table behind which she had tried to shelter had torn into her cheeks and forehead. They'd been removed by a very efficient doctor at a state security facility. She looked as if she'd been attacked by a serial blanket-stitcher.

She chose not to reply.

'You work for Burghley,' said Tomalin.

'Sometimes,' said Berlin.

'Did you go to Hong Kong under instructions from them?'

'What's this about, Tomalin?' said Berlin.

'Why did you go Bryant's flat?' said Tomalin.

'To feed his cat,' said Berlin.

Bryant thumped the table.

'He hasn't got a fucking cat,' he said. 'I'm not here to play funny buggers.'

'Why *are* you here?' said Berlin. 'Am I suspected of something?'

'Too many things to list,' said Tomalin. 'Right now I'm interested in Philip Chen. Where is he?'

'I haven't a clue,' said Berlin.

'Kidnapping is an extremely serious offence,' said Tomalin.

'Why do you think he's been kidnapped?' said Berlin. 'Perhaps he's just run away. He's a teenager; it's the sort of thing they do.'

'You were the last person to talk to Bryant before he absconded,' said Tomalin. 'We've got his phone records. And yours.'

Tomalin put her passport in his pocket.

'Langfield still likes you for that body in the crypt,' he said. 'We can make it happen. You've been warned.'

By the time they released her, it was getting close to rush hour. The Underground platform was crowded, but someone was edging through the crowd, moving up behind her. A tail. Probably one of Tomalin's blokes.

She stepped back swiftly to cut him off.

Del registered surprise. He half smiled, rueful.

'You made me,' he said.

'You were always rubbish at surveillance,' she said.

'Yeah,' said Del. 'Welcome home.'

'Who are you taking orders from now?' she said.

'No one,' said Del. 'I just wanted to make sure you got home safely.'

'Give me a break, Del,' she said.

The crowd jostled around them. Berlin stood her ground.

'What did the police want?' said Del. 'You were in there for long enough.'

'Just a friendly catch-up,' said Berlin. 'I showed them my holiday photos, they strip-searched me, that sort of thing.'

'What happened to Sir Simon?' he said.

'He had a car accident, according to the news,' said Berlin.

'The funeral's in Hong Kong. There won't be an open casket,' said Del.

'Must have been nasty,' said Berlin.

'There's going to be a memorial service,' said Del. 'At St Bride's.'

He gave her a look that said he knew more than he was letting on.

He put a hand on her arm.

'Be careful, Berlin,' he said. 'There's no cavalry.'

The train pulled in, the doors slid open and people spilt out. It was already packed.

'Wait for the next one,' said Del.

'Fuck you,' said Berlin.

She squeezed into the carriage, pushing and heaving. She could win this struggle. It was probably the only one. She tugged her bag through the doors as they closed and left Del standing on the platform.

66

Nose to nose with the other passengers, Berlin was grateful for the fact that they didn't stare, even though her battered face was only inches away from theirs. British manners. Tomalin could do with some.

Taking on the Metropolitan Police, the peerage and the Chinese government would require more energy than she could muster. Added to which she was about to break the heart of a desperate, drug-addicted teenager. If she could find him.

Seeing Del had rattled her. She had wanted to hang on to him for dear life and tell him everything: about the horrors she'd seen in Hong Kong and the web of exploitation and deceit in which she was ensnared.

She couldn't trust him. He had betrayed her, although now at least she understood why. The people controlling both of them engaged in the sort of heedless cruelty that was usually the province of psychopaths.

The body count was rising: Sylvie Laurent, Deng, Pearl and her mother, and Simon May, who had murdered or arranged the deaths of all of them. What had precipitated this lethal spree still wasn't clear. What was clear was that she had survived at Lee's behest. As long as she remained useful, she would draw breath.

The train screeched to a halt at another busy station. She marked out her territory as passengers got off, not giving an inch to those boarding.

Lee wanted her to believe that May had been killed to protect her, but she wasn't buying it. Should the British government persist with awkward questions about the untimely death of a knight of the realm, he would be able quite truthfully to say that May had just shot two women; Lee's subordinate had prevented him from murdering a third.

Forensics, and Berlin's statement, backed him up.

The story about the car accident had been quietly agreed at a diplomatic level as *best for all concerned*.

All her grand intentions – to break Haileybury's hold on the boy and save him from a lifetime of dependency – had evaporated in the face of one overriding imperative: to make sure she and Philip survived.

If she didn't do as Lee asked, she had no doubt she would end up with a nine-millimetre shoved down her throat, or, more likely, a hot shot administered in her own bed. No better way to off a junkie.

The train pulled into Bethnal Green, the doors slid open and she stumbled out, limping along the platform.

She could never climb the last flight of steps to street level without thinking of the one hundred and seventy-three men, women and children crushed to death on them in 1943 as hundreds poured into what was then an air-raid shelter.

Reports of the disaster were censored on the grounds of avoiding propaganda for the enemy and loss of morale for the country. The truth was always an early casualty.

Priceless Chinese treasures, an emperor's ransom in opium and a seventeen-year-old boy. The spoils of war.

67

Berlin trudged up the last few stairs to her flat. She could hear someone crashing about in Bella's place across the landing; Bella was back. Her heart lifted.

It sank again when she saw the state of her front door: boarded up and secured with a padlock. She dropped her bag and read the 'Notice to the Occupier' nailed to it.

A search warrant had been executed. A copy was attached. Both the notice and the warrant were endorsed by the officer in charge of the search: Tomalin.

She crossed the landing and knocked on Bella's front door. No reply. She knocked louder.

The door was opened by a barrel-chested bearded man in a grubby T-shirt. 'What?' he said.

Berlin stared at him. He was clutching one of Bella's treasured dancing trophies. A robbery in progress. She took a step back.

'What are you doing in there?' she said.

'What's it to you?' said the beard.

'Where's Bella?' said Berlin.

'Dead,' said the beard.

She hadn't heard right. 'What do you mean?' she said.

'Gone. Had a stroke in the clinic,' he said.

So much for rehab.

'Oh Christ,' said Berlin. 'Who are you?'

'I'm her stepson,' he said. 'Who are you?'

Berlin indicated her front door.

'Oh yeah,' he said. 'The junkie.'

'When did it happen?' said Berlin.

The beard just glared at her.

She glanced at the trophy in his hand.

'Plate, innit?' he said. 'Not worth much.'

He tossed it over his shoulder.

Berlin heard it strike the floor with a clunk.

'Learn a bit of respect,' she muttered.

Her Peacekeeper boot seemed to have a life of its own as it connected. The beard doubled up, gasping. She picked up her bag and limped back down the stairs as fast as she could.

The beard wasn't the only thing motivating her to get moving; Tomalin had found the exercise books and the opium at the flat, and she was in the frame not only for murder, but for possession of Class A. Perverting the course of justice and kidnapping were possibilities, too.

The future was bleak.

The minicab office on Bethnal Green Road was busier than she'd ever seen it; the constant rain and the disruption to public transport caused by the flooding had created a bonanza for them.

Through the throng of damp patrons waiting impatiently for a car, Berlin recognised an old driver she knew on the other side of the thick safety glass. She raised two fingers, as if bidding in an auction. Twice the fare.

Harold nodded and slipped out the back door.

Berlin left the office, complaining loudly about the delay, hurried down the road and turned the corner. Harold was standing beside his car.

'Get in quick,' he said. 'If anyone sees you, there'll be a bloody riot.'

Queue-jumping was the least of the risks she was about to take.

'Someone's following me,' she said. 'Can you lose him?'

'It's not the old bill, is it, love?' he said.

'No,' she said. 'It's the bloke who did this.' She gestured to her face.

'Don't worry,' said Harold. 'You know I used to be a wheelman.'

'Before you reformed, of course,' said Berlin.

Harold winked.

Berlin glanced over her shoulder. The vehicle following them soon became apparent, a five-door black BMW 1 Series hatchback that was a lot bigger, and a lot faster, than the banged-up three-door Ford Fiesta hatchback, which wheezed almost as much as Harold.

This was London. Speed was not of the essence. Size mattered, and knowledge. Harold had both on his side.

'I drove a black cab for thirty-five years,' he said. 'Until fuckin' Uber.'

'You could get into that,' said Berlin.

'Can't deal with the phones, love,' said Harold. 'I'm all fingers and thumbs.'

'Let's lose them,' said Berlin.

'You're the boss,' said Harold.

He was a genius. He managed to find more narrow roads, impossibly tight roundabouts and unforgiving lanes than she'd ever seen. His wipers had a problem with the steady downpour, but the Ford was nippy.

Finally Harold got what he wanted: a lorry coming towards him on a road where only one vehicle could pass at a time. The lorry driver was relying on the might-is-right principle.

The former wheelman, using skills honed driving a getaway car, gunned the motor and shot forward, forcing the lorry driver to slam on his brakes and veer to one side. As they passed, with barely an inch to spare, abuse rained down on them.

Berlin turned to watch as the lorry drove on, forcing the two cars behind them, including the BMW, to pull over.

'Worth every penny,' said Berlin.

'About that,' said Harold. 'Was that three fingers you were holding up?'

Her phone rang.

'You can't avoid us, Berlin,' said Lee. 'Attempting to do so simply makes us less forgiving.'

'I thought you were the police,' said Berlin.

There was silence for a moment.

'I see,' said Lee. 'I'll overlook it this time.'

'How very bloody generous of you,' said Berlin.

Lee chuckled.

'Berlin, I must remind you that the only reason you are in London at this moment is because you were right about Detective Constable Bryant,' he said.

'Why would I lie?' said Berlin.

'In any event, the items we found at his premises confirmed your powers of deduction. He was preparing to kidnap Philip. Now you must deliver as agreed.'

'I'm working on it,' said Berlin.

'You are fully aware of the consequences if anything happens to the boy,' said Lee.

'You made your point loud and clear in Hong Kong,' said Berlin. 'Just after you used me as bait to flush out Simon May.'

'He was a very bad man,' said Lee.

'What about Pearl and her mother? You timed that well,' said Berlin. 'They were innocent.'

'Of what?' said Lee. 'Don't forget you are accountable for any harm that befalls the boy.'

She hung up. Everyone wanted to protect Philip.

No one was too bothered about protecting her.

68

It was nearly eleven by the time Harold drew up at the gates of Palmerston Hall. The barrier was down and there was no one in the guardhouse.

'I'll walk up,' said Berlin. 'Will you wait for me?'

Harold held up three fingers.

Berlin rang the night bell, expecting Mayhew to respond. The school was very quiet, so perhaps they'd already broken up for the summer. To her surprise, Flora Trevelyan opened the door.

'I saw you on the monitors,' she said.

She looked over Berlin's shoulder, glancing left and right, then unhooked the chain and ushered her inside.

'Where is everyone?' said Berlin.

'Half term,' said Trevelyan.

The dark rings under eyes, which were bloodshot, were evidence of sleepless nights. Trevelyan's former arrogance had been supplanted by a tremulous timidity.

The woman was frightened half to death.

Berlin didn't think she'd ever seen quite so many empty Chardonnay bottles in one kitchen. Trevelyan's flat was a shambles.

'Drink?' said Trevelyan.

'Have you got any Scotch?' said Berlin.

Trevelyan opened a cupboard to reveal a hoard of spirits. She took out a bottle of Macallan twenty-five-year-old.

'Will this do?' she said.

Not a whisky fan, then.

'I'll manage,' said Berlin. 'Is Mayhew about?'

'He had an accident,' whispered Trevelyan.

An old episode of some trash chat show was frozen on the screen. Crisp packets littered the floor. All was not well.

'What happened?' said Berlin.

Trevelyan hesitated.

'I don't know where to begin,' she said.

'With Philip Chen's letters,' said Berlin.

Trevelyan stared at her.

'How did you know?' she said.

'Because Mayhew gave them to me,' said Berlin.

'Jesus Christ,' said Trevelyan. 'Do you realise who's behind this?'

'A charmer by the name of Lee,' said Berlin. 'Who told him that Mayhew had access to the letters?'

'I did,' said Trevelyan.

'Well done,' said Berlin.

Trevelyan winced.

'They broke his fingers,' she said 'One by one. He's still in hospital.' She shuddered.

Berlin was touched that Mayhew hadn't betrayed her. He was old school. But it had been for nothing.

'How did you get involved?' she said.

Trevelyan's lip quivered. A tear ran down her cheek. No one had broken her bloody fingers, but her trepidation conveyed that she was more involved than Berlin had realised.

'You're the third trustee,' said Berlin.

Trevelyan nodded.

'It's always the head of Palmerston Hall,' she said.

Always. The perfect triumvirate, controlling an end-to-end process: production, processing and logistics. A vertically integrated operation keeping everything in-house. No weak links in the chain. Until now.

It took a while to calm Trevelyan down.

Berlin hoped Harold was a patient man.

Finally the Palmerston Hall spirit kicked in. Trevelyan blew her nose and pulled herself together.

'I did a very stupid thing,' she said. 'I allowed myself to be drawn into a compromising situation with a senior pupil. Just once, but that's all it took.'

Berlin was warming to her.

'He was nearly nineteen, but . . . anyway, later I realised it was a scam. He'd been bribed or blackmailed, or thought it would be amusing to inveigle me into committing an indiscretion.'

It was banal, but that was because it happened so often. Careers were trashed every day in the same fashion, by lust or love. The outcome was the same. Ruin.

'Then Lee blackmailed you in turn,' said Berlin.

'Yes,' said Trevelyan.

'What did he want?' said Berlin.

'He wanted me to turn a blind eye when Philip went off with them, to make sure the letters got through and to let them know when he was with Haileybury. That sort of thing,' said Trevelyan.

'Did you know who the letters were from?' said Berlin.

'Sort of,' said Trevelyan. She was slurring her words.

'Sort of?' said Berlin. 'Either you knew or you didn't.'

'I more or less guessed,' said Trevelyan.

Berlin had the feeling Trevelyan had taken a close look at the letters before they were distributed with the scholars' mail. Probably steamed open one or two.

'You knew,' said Berlin. 'You were a trustee of the scholarship fund and his legal guardian. Where the fuck did you think the trust had got him from if he wasn't an orphan?'

'I thought the letters were a scam Lee was running,' said Trevelyan. 'To get at Haileybury.'

It was a pathetic attempt at rationalisation.

'But what about the boy?' said Berlin. 'Did you think about him?'

'I . . . I thought . . . I didn't think . . .' said Trevelyan.

She'd run out of excuses.

'You betrayed the boy and gave Lee what he wanted,' said Berlin. 'To save your own arse.'

'And now I suppose you want something,' said Trevelyan.

Berlin nodded.

'Information,' she said.

'We mainly use this database for fund-raising,' said Trevelyan. 'Mayhew would be more familiar with it.'

She tapped 'Anglo-Chinese Friendship Society' into the search box. When the next screen appeared, displaying details of the scholarship boys, she turned to Berlin, confused.

'I don't understand,' she said. 'It's wrong. It must be a mistake.'

'It's wrong,' said Berlin. 'But it's not a mistake. Print it out.'

Trevelyan did as asked. Berlin plucked it from the printer as it emerged.

'What does it mean?' said Trevelyan.

'How long have you worked here?' said Berlin.

'Three years.'

'What about the head before you?'

'He died with his boots on,' said Trevelyan. 'He was a scholar in the sixties, then a master, and finally the head.'

'How did you think Lee was going to use Philip to get at Haileybury?' said Berlin.

'They were having a relationship, I suppose. He spent an awful lot of time there. I imagine Lee wanted Philip to threaten to expose him.'

'He'd spent an awful lot of time there for years, hadn't he?' said Berlin. 'It didn't occur to you to enquire how long it had been going on?'

'Well, now you put it like that,' said Trevelyan, 'I suppose I should have been more engaged. But since he turned sixteen, it wasn't an issue.'

'You didn't ever wonder what hold Haileybury had over him?' said Berlin.

She either didn't know or didn't want to know about Philip's addiction.

'I'd been caught up in a similar situation,' said Trevelyan. 'I didn't regard that as exploitative. Philip never complained and Lord Haileybury is, well, a lord. The school would have suffered incalculable damage if there was a scandal.'

'Do you think Lee would have bothered to set this whole business up if Haileybury had nothing to hide?'

Trevelyan stared at her.

'I can't imagine,' she said.

Berlin waved the printout at her.

'What do you imagine now?' she said.

Trevelyan shook her head and raised a hand, as if she could push those thoughts away. A very common reaction.

'There has to be more than just a list in a computer,' said Berlin. 'The school would have original documents, medical records, that sort of thing. Where would they be?'

'In the archives,' said Trevelyan.

'Let's go,' said Berlin.

Lee couldn't sleep, despite administering twice as much medication as usual. He preferred to think of it as analgesia, a balm that mercifully addressed more than just his physical pain. He was almost relieved when the phone on his bedside table burbled.

'Headmistress,' he said. 'You're up very late.'

He reached for his cigarettes. He listened. She had been drinking, but that didn't diminish the import of what she was saying.

'Thank you,' he said.

He hung up, swung his legs out of bed and went to the attic window. Rain had left pale trails in the grime.

The view was limited, but a partial impression was better than none. Perhaps he would sleep easier now.

Flora put her phone down on the coffee table.

'Satisfied?' she said.

Berlin nodded.

Flora poured herself more Chardonnay. 'You're a fool, Berlin,' she said. 'You can't win against these people. Look what they've done to Mayhew.'

'There aren't going to be any winners,' said Berlin. 'We're all losers. You, me, them. It's just a question of who's going to lose the most.'

Harold was sound asleep by the time she got back to the car. She knocked on his window and he released the locks.

'I nearly went home,' he said. 'But I didn't want to leave you stuck out here in the wilds with all my money.'

Spoken like a true Londoner. They were a forty-minute drive from Trafalgar Square. She handed him the bottle of Macallan.

'What's this?' he said.

'A bonus,' she said. 'Liberated from the ruling class.'

'Cheers,' said Harold. 'Up the workers.'

At least she had brought joy to someone.

Lee wouldn't be overjoyed, but he would be placated by hearing from a third party that she was on the case. It might deter him from taking more extreme measures, temporarily. She just needed some breathing space.

69

Berlin prevailed on Harold to go up with her to the flat and help prise open the front door. He brought a tyre lever. Good. It would also come in handy if the bearded stepson was still awake.

There was no sign of life at Bella's, which was a win, if an unfortunate way of thinking about it.

Harold slipped the tyre lever under the edge of the plywood and it gave easily. Nails popped out one after the other as she pulled and Harold pushed. The police weren't carpenters.

Harold gave a final heave and the padlock fell without a fight.

'Here,' he said. 'This might come in useful.'

He handed her the tyre lever and set off down the stairs. She was touched. It was the first kindness anyone had done her in a long time.

Once inside the flat, she propped the plywood back in the hole and pushed the table up against it. The state of the place was a surprise; she'd expected Tomalin's men to have trashed it, but everything was in reasonable order.

A few books had been moved and cupboards opened, but the cartons of Peggy's stuff appeared to be untouched.

The exercise books and the opium weren't under the sink, which wasn't a surprise.

Tomalin had also taken her emergency bottle of Talisker, which was a blow. She had been hasty in handing over the Macallan to Harold, but she didn't have time to go out again now.

She sat down at the table and fired up the computer. It didn't take long to find what she wanted. She surrendered her card details, hoping she wasn't going to suddenly hit her credit limit, and entered details of her request, paying extra for an express service.

That done, she retrieved two cans of London Pride from the cupboard, took some codeine, and lay down on the sofa.

She'd won her get-out-of-China card from Lee by convincing him that although she didn't know where Philip was, she was the best person to find him. She was of no use to Lee in gaol. The deal had been brokered on the basis that he would come clean about the boy's mother. That had not played out as she'd expected, to say the least.

Lee had been two steps ahead of her; locking her up had presented Simon May with a dilemma. If she cooperated with the Chinese, she knew enough to make life very difficult for him and Haileybury. May had sent Del on a so-called rescue mission, but when she refused his help, something had to be done to shut her down.

Sir Simon had calculated that she would persist with her mission to find Philip's mother. She'd explicitly told him that she wasn't going home without answers. Either way, all he had to do was keep track of her, as Lee had known he would.

She checked the computer; it was too soon to expect a response from Hong Kong, but she was anxious for a result. She was relying on one thing the Chinese and the British had in common. Bureaucracy.

In the middle of the night, Berlin encountered Peggy on the landing at home in Leyton. Philip was downstairs. She could hear eggs and bacon sputtering in the pan, the boy humming, the shipping forecast on Radio Four. The opium was on the table between the brown sauce and the teapot.

Sweet domesticity.

'Getting in touch with your maternal side?' said Peggy.

Berlin knew she was arguing with a phantom. 'I never managed to get in touch with yours,' she said.

Tears welled up in Peggy's eyes. 'Be careful, Catherine,' she said. 'You'll catch your death.'

'What do you mean?' said Berlin. 'He's just a boy.'

'It can be fatal,' said Peggy.

The tears ran down her cheeks and washed her away.

Berlin didn't have time to say goodbye.

70

Berlin woke early and left the flat before the bearded stepson was awake. There wasn't much she could do about the front door, so she just propped the plywood back in the gap and hurried downstairs.

On her way across the yard, she passed the dustbins.

Rubbish was spilling out, as usual. The recycling bin was full, and empty bottles were piling up beside it. One caught her eye.

The Central Line going east was still quiet because everyone going to work was heading west. The shopping centre at Stratford didn't get going until ten, when a surge of shop assistants – or, as they were now called, customer service teams – would head in that direction.

There was no sign of a tail. Lee would have a fix on her mobile, but after Trevelyan's call last night, he would also believe he knew exactly what she was doing. He was right. Trevelyan had told the truth. Whether Berlin could actually pull it off was another matter.

The house smelt different when she opened the front door. Cooking smells overwhelmed the usual scent of lavender polish and Brasso. She nudged the front door shut behind her and went to the kitchen. It was pristine, which was not how she'd left it.

She ran upstairs and flung open her bedroom door.

Philip lay on her bed, shaking his head. His mouth was sealed with gaffer tape, but his intent was clear.

She whirled around. Too late.

The blow caught her cheekbone.

She put her hand to her face. It came away bloody.

'Sit down,' said Bryant. 'That was just a taste of what you'll get if you don't do as you're told.'

She sat down on the bed next to Philip.

'Are you okay?' she said.

'He's fine,' said Bryant. 'He's had me running around, waiting on him hand and foot.'

Philip raised an eyebrow, but he didn't seem scared. In fact he looked quite healthy.

'What's this?' said Berlin. 'The Wapping cure?'

'It's a lot more effective and a bloody sight cheaper than the Abbey,' said Bryant.

She was inclined to agree.

'Can I get a towel?' she said. 'You've burst my stitches.'

'Stay there,' said Bryant.

He left the bedroom for a moment and returned with a wet flannel.

'Here,' he said.

He tossed it over and she held it to her cheek.

'What happened to you?' said Bryant.

'I walked into a door. What on earth are you playing at, Bryant? Half the Met are out looking for you.'

'No they're not,' said Bryant. 'Tomalin hasn't got the manpower. When did you get back from Hong Kong?'

'How did you know?' said Berlin.

'Philip told me,' said Bryant. 'Now you're here, you can make yourself useful.'

'How's that?' said Berlin.

'You can deliver a message for me.' He looked her up and down. 'Have you got any other clothes with you?'

Bryant locked her in with Philip. They were both bound, feet and ankles, but he'd taken the tape off Philip's mouth.

You'd have to scream the house down before anyone would do anything about it. People minded their own business in Leyton. An Englishman's home was his castle. Women and children died in their homes all the time and nobody heard a thing.

'Are you really okay, Philip?' said Berlin.

'Fine,' said Philip. 'You?'

Well mannered and well bred. He was a different person when he wasn't hanging out for opium.

'What's going on?' she said.

'I don't know,' said Philip. 'It's weird, it's as if he's fattening me up.'

'He hasn't hurt you?' said Berlin.

'Quite the opposite,' said Philip. 'Except for keeping me tied up.'

'What does he want?' said Berlin.

'No idea,' said Philip. 'He hasn't mentioned money or anything like that. He keeps on about how evil Jack is and how all the Haileyburys are tainted. So I suppose it's to make Jack sweat.'

More people than Jack were sweating.

She was lying at one end of the bed and Philip was at the other, top and tail, as Peggy would have had it.

'How did you know I was in Hong Kong?' she said.

'I heard Jack on the phone,' he said. 'He didn't say your name but I guessed it was you he was talking about. He mentioned the registrar. I thought you must be making enquiries. Well, I hoped you were.'

He looked expectant, but she couldn't think of what to say.

Downstairs, Bryant was listening to Radio Four.

'Someone stole my mother's letters,' said Philip finally. 'They weren't with my things when they arrived from school.'

'Oh?' said Berlin.

It was pathetic, but it was all she could manage. If she hadn't been tied up, she would have run away. He wasn't her responsibility, for Christ's sake. Peggy's ghost had been right. Getting involved like this could be fatal.

She heard him take a deep breath.

'Did you have any luck in Hong Kong?' he said.

His tone was determinedly light, devoid of expectation.

Her heart was breaking.

'No,' she said. 'No luck. Only dead ends.'

Philip had turned to the wall so Berlin couldn't see his face. She guessed he was crying. He'd taken the news, or lack thereof, badly.

He didn't seem to fear Bryant, or to care much about his situation. It was a kind of surrender and grew from the same root as his addiction. Submission wasn't in her nature, and she wouldn't recommend it to Philip.

If they ever got out of this mess.

The bedroom door opened and Bryant appeared, carrying one of her old black coats. She'd left it with Peggy for the charity shop years ago. Why had she hung on to it?

'Right,' said Bryant. 'You're on.'

71

Haileybury had drunk a little more than he ought, but it was after lunch, and under the circumstances people would be forgiving. The taxi sloshed through the rain-drenched streets. Gutters were overflowing, forcing the driver to crawl at times, the water up to the cab's axles.

The vile weather suited his mood. The last time such ghastly misfortune had befallen him, he was fourteen.

He peered through the window. What had happened to the little terraced houses? He fished his wallet out of his suit pocket and opened it to gaze at the photo, a reminder of happier days.

Time was playing tricks on him; how long had Philip been out of short trousers? All the boys were required to wear them, surely. Why should this one be any different?

Two ushers rushed forward to help him out of the car when he arrived. They escorted him through the silent crowd and into the church. St Bride's looked splendid, as always. Shown to his seat in the front pew, he arranged his sticks ready for the moment when he would be required to rise again, at a sign from the vicar.

He bowed his head and prayed for Philip's safe return.

*

Berlin was surprised by the number of people queuing to get into St Bride's, and disconcerted by the fact that they all appeared to have invitations.

Given the status of many of the mourners, she realised security would have insisted on it. Former prime ministers, members of the Cabinet, even minor royalty. She looked up. There were snipers on the surrounding rooftops.

Haileybury was probably already in the church. She wouldn't be able to get near him on his way out, so she had to find a way in.

Circling the churchyard, looking for a weakness in the cordon, she spotted Del. He was wearing a very smart suit and tie and stood out as one of only a couple of black faces in the crowd. He was standing with a group of men and women who had that pink, beefy look peculiar to the hunting set.

Burghley's partners.

They were close to the church door and brandishing their invites. She pushed through the throng, caught up with Del as he reached the steps and took his arm.

'What the fuck?' said Del, under his breath.

He tried to tug free, but she hung on, smiling at the people around them.

'I've come to pay my respects,' she said. 'So unless you want a scene, get me inside.'

They had reached the usher checking the invitations.

Berlin wasn't sure if a memorial service would invite 'plus one', but she was confident that Del wouldn't have been invited without his other half. Nearly every man there was accompanied by a woman in a discreet hat.

The usher glanced at the invitation, then scowled at Berlin. Her outfit, the old black coat, wasn't quite the thing. She winked at him, and he gave Del a pitying look.

They passed under the portico.

Once inside, Berlin slipped away from Del, no doubt to his great relief, and positioned herself at the back of the church behind a marble plinth. The vicar took his place at the lectern, the organist struck up 'Jerusalem' and the congregation rose. So predictable.

Someone tapped her on the shoulder. Hard.

She turned around. Tomalin was right in her face.

'How did you get in?' he said.

The hymn drowned out her protests as he took her elbow and steered her, smiling and nodding at anyone who noticed, towards the crypt. He shoved her through the door and shut it behind them.

'Do you go around looking for trouble, Berlin?' he said. 'What the hell are you doing here?'

'Believe me, it's not by choice,' she said. 'I wasn't a fan of Sir Simon May.'

'Who happened to die when you were in Hong Kong,' said Tomalin. 'Another coincidence, I suppose. People seem to drop like flies around you.'

'Let me go, Tomalin,' said Berlin. She tried to wrench herself free of his grip. 'I'm not going to cause any trouble, but I must talk to Haileybury.'

'Lord Haileybury to you,' said Tomalin. 'And what's wrong with the telephone?'

'I don't know who might be bloody listening,' said Berlin.

Tomalin gave her a strange look.

'What's that supposed to mean?' he said. 'What's so important that you had the cheek to crash his brother's memorial service?'

Berlin stopped struggling.

It went quiet in the church. 'Jerusalem' had come to an end. Bryant opened the door a crack. The vicar's voice carried to them over the click of Haileybury's sticks as he manoeuvred himself down the aisle.

'And now Valerian Tremayne May, the eighth Earl Haileybury, will read the lesson he has chosen in memory of his younger brother, Sir Simon Maxwell May. Romans 14, verse 13: "Let us not therefore judge one another any more: but judge this rather, that no man put a stumbling block or an occasion to fail in his brother's way."'

Sir Simon May had killed to protect his brother.

Berlin sat at the top of the crypt stairs, gazing into the pitch dark.

Simon May hadn't just feared the exposure of his baby-farming operation. He was responding to a more profound threat to his brother and the family legacy.

Tomalin sat down beside her.

'What's going on, Berlin?' he said.

She was still struggling with the fraternal bond and had almost forgotten why she was at St Bride's.

'You have to let me speak to Haileybury,' she said.

'Not unless you tell me what the hell's going on,' said Tomalin. 'You're a loose cannon, and a dangerous one at that.'

If she didn't deliver Bryant's message, Philip was at risk. But if she sold Bryant out, Philip would be returned to Haileybury, a prospect that was equally fraught. An impossible situation, made worse by her deal with Lee, that she would find Philip and tell him the truth about his mother.

'If Philip Chen has been kidnapped, why isn't it all over the news?'

Tomalin hesitated.

'Whitehall,' he said.

'You're kidding me,' said Berlin. 'National security?'

Tomalin nodded.

'So is your inquiry official or what?' said Berlin.

'I do as I'm told, and they don't tell me much, so you tell me,' said Tomalin.

'This is how the shit gets covered up, Tomalin,' said Berlin. 'On a nod and a wink from up high. Everyone follows orders and covers their own arse.'

'Who the fuck do you think you are, Berlin? The caped fucking crusader?'

The opening bars of 'Abide with Me' drifted to them.

'If I told you that Simon May killed the bloke in the crypt and Philip Chen's lawyer, what would you say?'

'I'd say you were as deluded about that family as Bryant,' said Tomalin.

'Why is Bryant so obsessed with Haileybury?' said Berlin.

'He blames him for the death of his grandmother,' said Tomalin. 'After they were rehoused, she wasn't a happy camper, by all accounts.'

Bryant was driven by revenge. He wanted Haileybury to suffer as he had, by depriving him of someone he loved.

Tomalin gave her a hard look.

'What's your excuse?' he said.

'I don't need a bloody excuse, Tomalin,' said Berlin. 'I've been up close and personal with them. Have you? Why didn't you arrest me at the airport?'

'What for?' said Tomalin.

'After you searched my flat,' she said.

'We were looking for Chen,' said Tomalin.

If Tomalin hadn't found the exercise books and the opium, someone had got there before him.

'If you've got anything on Haileybury, you should hand it over to the proper authorities,' said Tomalin.

'Meaning you?' said Berlin. 'Why should I trust you?'

'Because there's no one else,' said Tomalin.

He'd read her mind.

The third verse of 'Abide with Me', one of Peggy's favourites, swelled in the silence: 'Where is death's sting? Where, grave, thy victory? I triumph still, if Thou abide with me.'

'Bryant's got Philip,' said Berlin. 'He sent me to set up a meeting with Haileybury. If the earl doesn't cooperate with his demands, it will be the worse for the boy.'

Tomalin reached for his mobile.

'Where?' he said.

Berlin grabbed his arm.

'Philip mustn't go back to Haileybury under any circumstances,' she said. 'Please, Tomalin. Give me your word he'll be protected.'

'Where?' said Tomalin.

72

Tomalin had directed a constable to detain Berlin in the crypt until the mourners had all departed. Presumably he didn't want her getting in the way. By the time he let her go, the place was completely empty.

She strode across the churchyard, desperate to get to Leyton. Del stepped into her path.

'What do you want?' said Berlin.

'You strongarm your way inside, then disappear,' said Del.

'I haven't got time for this,' said Berlin.

'Please,' said Del. 'You haven't give me a chance to explain.'

'You mean I haven't given you a chance to wheedle your way out of what you've done,' said Berlin.

They were standing close together and she could smell his breath; he'd been drinking, which was completely out of character.

'This is no good, Del,' she said. 'Stay away from me.'

A flock of pigeons, disturbed by the crowd attending the service, had returned to their regular pecking ground. They strutted across the flagstones, burbling, hunting for crumbs at Del and Berlin's feet.

There was a ping. One of the birds suddenly rose three feet in the air, then dropped to the ground again, dead.

The corner of the flagstone it had occupied was now crazy paving.

'Jesus Christ,' said Del.

'Stay away from me,' yelled Berlin.

She ran out of the churchyard and into Fleet Street, waving her arms. A cab drew up almost immediately and she jumped in the back.

'Leyton,' she said. 'As fast as you can.'

They'd only got as far as Gray's Inn Road when the cab pulled over again.

'What's going on?' said Berlin. 'I'm in a hurry.'

The back door opened.

'This cab's taken, mate,' said Berlin.

Lee sat down beside her. She lunged for the other door, but heard the *thunk* of central locking. Lee's hand was in his raincoat pocket. It held a gun.

Her breathing space had just run out.

'If you continue to ignore my instructions, the next time the pigeon will be spared. It will be your friend,' he said.

The cab took off again, cutting into the traffic. Horns blared.

'You're too late,' said Berlin. 'The police are on their way to collect Philip.'

She was panting, due to fear or exertion she couldn't tell.

Lee's fury was in his cold eyes and the set of his jaw.

'You have no idea what you've done,' he said.

'I didn't do anything,' said Berlin. 'They were going to find him eventually. They're rather better resourced than I am.'

The cab pulled up fifty yards down the road from Peggy's, where Tomalin was ushering Philip into an unmarked car. There were no uniforms in attendance, just two heavies in suits.

'Who's that?' said Lee.

'Detective Chief Inspector Tomalin,' said Berlin.

'Find out what he intends,' said Lee. He put a hand on her arm. 'Don't forget, we know where your friend Delroy lives.'

She got out of the cab and hurried up the road towards Tomalin. He quickly closed the car door when he saw her coming and stood in front of it, arms folded.

'What are you going to do with him?' she said.

'Protective custody,' said Tomalin.

Berlin bent down to try and signal to Philip through the window, but Tomalin blocked her. He lowered his voice.

'I appreciated the heads-up, Berlin, but now stay out of it.'

'Where's Bryant?' she said.

'God only knows,' said Tomalin. 'He went out the back way and I didn't have the bodies to send after him.'

Tomalin got in the car beside the driver and the two heavies got in the back, either side of Philip.

Berlin watched them drive off. Philip didn't look like someone who had been rescued. She walked back to the cab.

Lee rolled down the window.

'They're going to keep him in protective custody,' she said.

'Who are they protecting him from?' said Lee.

'You, I suppose,' said Berlin.

'Ah yes,' said Lee. 'The godless Celestials. But how does the inspector know of my interest?'

'Perhaps Haileybury told him,' said Berlin.

'Who was holding Philip?' said Lee.

'A man called Bryant,' said Berlin.

'The policeman who arrested him for the assault on Deng?' said Lee.

'Yes,' said Berlin. 'He's not a fan of Haileybury.'

Lee frowned.

She knew he was stymied, because her explanation was entirely plausible.

He tapped the glass to alert the driver, who started the motor.

'Stay as close as you can to the boy, Berlin,' he said. 'You have my number. Let me know immediately if they move or release him. Don't disappoint me. You don't want to be a sitting duck – or pigeon.' He smiled.

You survived around Lee only as long as you were useful.

Berlin went back to the house once Lee and Tomalin had gone. No one had asked who lived in the house where Bryant had kept Philip, although Tomalin could quickly establish it belonged to her mother. Then things would get awkward.

The front door had been opened with a battering ram. She would have to call her regular locksmith and persuade him to travel all of four miles to the far-flung territory of Leyton.

They hadn't treated the house as a crime scene. It was a small blessing; she could imagine Peggy's despair if they had. Barely cold and already Berlin had managed to desecrate her home.

There wasn't much of a mess, probably because Bryant hadn't stayed to put up a fight. For a brief moment she missed them, the mad copper and the opium-addicted public schoolboy.

Her missing toes cramped as she limped through the empty house. Absence can be painful. She was sure Lee would eliminate her if he thought it necessary. He was a cold, calculating bastard.

He could have prevented the slaughter of Philip's mother and grandmother, but their deaths at May's hands, in front of a witness that Philip trusted, furthered his cause: to turn the boy against the British in general and the Haileyburys in particular.

She called the locksmith, who grudgingly agreed to trek out to Leyton if she paid for his travelling time. There was no point waiting. He would come via the Khyber Pass.

73

Bella's front door flew open. The bearded stepson had been waiting for this moment. Berlin had tried to knock politely, but the sneer on his face indicated that he wasn't going to respond in kind.

'I know what you want,' he said.

At least he hadn't taken a swing at her.

'Let's do this inside,' said Berlin.

Bella had been a fall-down drunk, but her housekeeping standards were straight out of Mrs Beeton. This quality hadn't been passed on to the next generation, but the spare key to Berlin's flat had.

'What's your name?' said Berlin.

'You're lucky I don't tear your fucking head off after what you did to me.' He paused. 'Albert. My name's Albert.'

'Did Bella bring you up?' said Berlin.

'My old man married her after my real mum died.'

Bella would have made a wicked stepmother.

'Let's get down to business,' said Berlin. 'Give me back my stuff and we'll say no more about it. You've already drunk the Talisker.'

'Or what? You'll go to the filth?'

'Are you a user, Albert?' said Berlin.

'Recreational. I'm no junkie.'

'Well, as you know, I am,' she said. 'And the people I deal with are very powerful and very nasty. Do you know where I'm going with this?'

Albert showed signs of consternation as this penetrated his thick skull.

She took a punt.

'Ever heard of the Triads?'

The colour left Albert's face.

'Those Chinese blokes . . .' he said.

Like Bella, her new neighbour didn't miss a thing. He'd seen Lee, or one of his henchmen, paying a visit.

'I haven't got time to muck about,' said Berlin. 'Give me my stuff and I'll persuade them not to beat you to a pulp.'

'I've smoked it,' said Albert.

'You'll have to pay for it, then,' said Berlin.

'I'm skint,' said Albert.

'Bad news for you then,' said Berlin.

Ten minutes after she'd walked in, Berlin left Bella's flat with what she wanted. She legged it up to the high road and hailed a cab.

'Limehouse police station,' she said.

'Grove Road's flooded,' said the cabbie. 'I'll have to go the long way round.'

She was going broke fast, but at least she'd have Peggy's house to fall back on. Money was the least of her problems right now. If she didn't come out of this alive, little

Molly, Del's daughter, would get the lot. She should probably change her will.

The cab crawled down Bethnal Green Road and passed the shop once occupied by Lenny, her dad, and Jacob Berlinsky, her grandad. Her *zayde*. Peggy had always said she was her father's daughter, and blamed Zayde for both their bolshie attitudes. Zayde had taught her to never look back.

'*Vpered*,' she muttered.

'What's that, love?' said the cabbie.

'Forward,' said Berlin.

74

The moment the constable behind the front desk pressed the button to release the inner door, Berlin elbowed aside the poor sod who was next in line and barged through.

A cry of disbelief went up, but the door snapped shut behind her. She heard banging on the safety glass.

'I need to see Tomalin,' she said to the constable. 'It's urgent.'

'Get back in the queue,' said the constable.

'This is very important,' said Berlin. 'Chief Inspector Tomalin will want to see me.'

'It's after six on a Saturday. He'll be long gone.'

The constable glanced past her at the irate crowd in the waiting room.

'Please,' said Berlin.

He sighed

'They don't pay me enough for this,' he said.

He disappeared out the back.

Berlin ignored the fists beating on the glass, and the muffled curses. They were a dangerous mob, and these were the victims of crime, not even the criminals.

The constable returned.

'He'll be down in a minute,' he said.

Fifteen minutes later, Tomalin appeared behind the counter and beckoned her to follow him. The door to the inner sanctum clicked open.

Berlin tried to compose herself. She had to tell a coherent story in a measured fashion or he wouldn't give her the time of day. She followed him into an interview room.

Detective Inspector Langfield was sitting there.

'Hang on,' said Berlin. 'Tomalin, what's going on?'

Tomalin closed the door behind them.

'DI Langfield would like to put some more questions to you concerning the death of Mr Deng,' he said.

Langfield switched on the recording device.

'I must remind you, Catherine Berlin,' she said, 'that you do not have to say anything. But it may harm your defence if you do not mention when questioned something which you later rely on in court. Anything you do say may be given in evidence. Do you understand?'

She understood. Tomalin had done the dirty on her. Bryant had been right. They were all in it together. The detective inspector was in Haileybury's pocket. The dependable British bobby.

'Where's Philip?' she said. 'Do you know what you've done, Tomalin?'

'I'll leave you to it, Langfield,' said Tomalin. 'I'll send one of the constables in.'

He left the room, and a moment later a burly PCSO appeared.

'Sit down, Berlin,' said Langfield.

She sat.

'Further to your last interview,' said Langfield. 'In relation to the death due to a fatal opiate overdose of the male identified as an illegal alien and known only as Deng—'

'I'd like to confess,' said Berlin.

'What?' said Langfield.

She exchanged a look with the PCSO.

'I wish to go on the record and make a statement,' said Berlin. 'I also wish to produce the following documents.'

She reached into her bag and began to unpack it.

She dropped the pile of exercise books in front of Langfield.

'Contemporaneous notes logging visitors to the premises of Lord Haileybury, kept by Detective Constable Bryant and his grandmother over a period of roughly twenty-five years.'

'I don't understand what this has got to do with . . .' said Langfield.

'Documents from the Hong Kong registrar containing details of Philip Chen's parentage,' said Berlin.

Langfield peered at the birth and marriage certificates spread out on the desk. She looked up at Berlin in surprise.

Berlin saw an opening – the DI was no fool – and quickly produced the next item. She handed it to Langfield.

'This is a list of the seven recipients of Anglo-Chinese Friendship Society scholarships,' she said. 'And these are the Chinese passports of six of them, kept at Palmerston Hall, where the head was their legal guardian.'

'I'm not sure . . .' said Langfield.

'How did they leave the country without their passports, Langfield?' said Berlin.

Langfield shook her head and frowned.

'Look at them,' said Berlin.

One by one Langfield opened the passports and laid them on the table, gazing at them in disbelief.

From the bottom of her bag Berlin produced her ace.

'This is the passport of the seventh boy on the list. He's supposed to be in the protective custody of the Metropolitan Police as we speak. Is he?'

She slapped Philip's passport down on the table.

Langfield and the PCSO both jumped.

It took a moment, then Langfield murmured to the PCSO.

'Would you find DCI Tomalin and ask him to step back in for a moment?'

Tomalin couldn't be found. Berlin was left alone in the interview room while Langfield also went to search for him.

When she came back, she didn't look very happy.

'Who told you that Philip Chen was in protective custody?' she said.

'Inspector Tomalin,' said Berlin. 'Earlier today when he rescued Chen from the clutches of Detective Constable Bryant.'

'Bryant?' said Langfield. 'What the hell is this?'

'Did Tomalin tell you to re-interview me?'

Langfield nodded.

'For no good reason,' said Berlin, 'except to get me out of the way. Now he's gone, and so has Philip.'

She could see the wheels turning.

'Fuck Tomalin,' said Langfield. 'He knew I was supposed to be going out tonight.'

75

Berlin walked out of the station.

The entrance and exit were separate, so she didn't have to confront the people in the vestibule. She set off, half jogging, half running, cursing her leg and hailing every cab that passed her. None deigned to stop. The rain whipped her and mingled with the sweat dribbling into her eyes. All her options were unpalatable, to say the least.

She made the call, but it went straight to voicemail.

'Tomalin lied,' she said. 'Philip isn't at the station. Do something, for Christ's sake.'

It was a good forty-minute walk from Limehouse police station to Haileybury's in Wapping High Street. Fear drove her on, a bulwark against pain and exhaustion. Narrow Street was the quickest route, which meant crossing the Limehouse Basin.

Her panic grew as she reached the gentle rise in the road that signalled the cut beneath, a finger of the river that filled her with dread. She had never seen the water so high. She put her head down and hurried across.

Bryant appeared, as if by magic.

'The flood,' he said, squinting at the sky. 'Wapping has been inundated more than once over the centuries.'

Berlin kept walking. Bryant was unpredictable and wouldn't be too impressed with her recent treachery. But he just fell into step beside her, as if they were on a pre-arranged date.

'In the disaster of 1841, Wapping High Street was described as having the appearance of a canal,' he said. 'Furniture floated out of the houses and down the road. They even found an infant drifting in a cradle. You'd be amazed at what came up from some of those warehouse cellars.'

Berlin glanced down the road, praying for a taxi.

'You were there, of course,' she said.

'My great-great-grandfather was,' said Bryant.

Berlin picked up her pace, anxious to leave him behind.

'You did what you had to do, Berlin,' he said. 'I don't blame you. But the price is going to be high. Very high.'

The sound of his footsteps died away.

Berlin willed herself not to turn around, but couldn't resist.

Bryant had gone.

Haileybury was so happy to see Philip, he nearly forgot his manners.

'Forgive me, Chief Inspector Tomalin,' he said. 'May I offer you a drink?'

'Thank you, sir,' said Tomalin. 'Just a small one.'

'Philip, will you make the chief inspector a drink?' said Haileybury.

It was impossible to read the boy's mood. According to Tomalin, he had been kept a prisoner, but he looked none the worse for his ordeal. In fact, he looked quite well. He hadn't said a word since he'd arrived.

'This fellow Bryant never asked for money,' said Haileybury.

'No, sir,' said Tomalin. 'He had other concerns. What you might call *issues*. He sent Catherine Berlin to the church with a message.'

'Berlin was in on it, was she?' said Haileybury.

'Oh yes,' said Tomalin. 'Mr Chen was being held at her deceased mother's premises.'

'But what did Bryant want?' said Haileybury.

'A confession,' said Tomalin. 'He threatened to harm Mr Chen if you didn't comply.'

'To what did he want me to confess, exactly?' said Haileybury.

'He had a bee in his bonnet about his grandmother,' said Tomalin. 'I believe one of your family's business concerns was involved in developing the area in which she lived.'

'They were slum-cleared?' said Haileybury.

'Yes,' said Tomalin. 'In the eighties, I believe.'

'Good God,' said Haileybury. 'There's no pleasing these people. You move them from damp, dark terraces into homes with proper bathrooms and central heating, and they still complain.'

Philip handed Tomalin his drink and he knocked it back.

'I should be off,' he said. 'I'll make sure you're not bothered again, sir.'

'This won't be forgotten, Tomalin,' said Haileybury. 'I'll be having a word with the Chief Commissioner.'

'Just doing my job,' said Tomalin.

76

The warehouse was silent, cloaked in a shroud of misty rain. Breathless, Berlin made sure she stayed out of range of the portico camera. She wouldn't be welcome.

The place was a fortress, but Bryant had somehow managed to get inside. The officer who had discovered his clothes near the watermen's stairs said he'd found a way in at the back.

She hurried down the narrow passage, but the stairs were completely submerged. Hanging out over the parapet, she could see a dark shadow in the embankment immediately below the warehouse, beneath the waterline.

Even if she managed to swim to it against the powerful Thames currents, she would never be able to hold her breath long enough. There was no way of knowing how far the water had risen. Short of storming the place, she was running out of options. She limped back to Wapping High Street.

A delivery van pulled up outside Haileybury's. The driver jumped out, strode to the back, opened the double doors and lifted out two large crates packed with bags of food and bottles of champagne.

Someone was having a party.

The driver lugged the crates to the portico, pressed the entry phone buzzer and waited.

She knew the routine. In a moment, the door would click open. He'd carry the crates to the platform and the heavy oak door would swing slowly closed behind him. She could make a quick dash and catch it before it shut, but the reality was that there would be no time for her to slip in without him seeing her. Unless he was distracted.

She kicked at the cobblestones until she found a loose one. By this time, the delivery bloke had disappeared inside. The door was beginning to close. She threw the stone with all her might. *Bang*.

The bloke came running out, glanced up and down the street, and then took off around the van to see if there was any damage. He didn't notice Berlin sprinting across the portico and slipping inside just before the door closed.

The crates were still on the platform. Keeping close to the wall, she made her way around the vestibule, fearful of triggering the lights.

The platform whirred into action, rising slowly, but she daren't go with it. Instead, she tried a door to one side of it. It opened on to stone steps, but they led in only one direction. Down.

Cursing, she began the descent, hoping that on the next level there would be another set of stairs that led up. The steps were steep and precipitous.

Keeping one hand braced on the wall, she slowly made her way down. When she stepped into calf-deep water, she knew she'd made it to the bottom.

Total darkness gave way to gloom. She sloshed across a cavernous basement towards a blue glow in the corner, scanning either side for a door or stairs. The water was still rising.

The blue glow flickered. There was a snap, crackle and hiss, and it died. Water had got into the system and shorted it out. The hiss was followed by a sound like a sigh, then a rush of air, as if a seal had been broken.

A moment later, a generator kicked in and the blue light came on again. Berlin held her breath, waiting for an alarm, but nothing happened. The door of a small room, illuminated by blue fluorescent tubes, stood open.

She stepped inside. One wall was fitted with racks similar to those in a wine cellar. The spheres the size of cannonballs arranged on them didn't contain burgundy. This was the vault that Philip had mentioned.

When she turned, her heart slammed against her chest.

Empty eyes gazed back at her.

In a bid to elicit some sort of response from the sullen boy, Haileybury offered him the filigreed box of opium.

'Happy birthday,' he said. 'Something to stimulate your appetite.'

Philip took the box and put it in his pocket.

'I've told you, Jack, I'm leaving,' he said.

'But where will you go, dear boy?'

'To Hong Kong,' said Philip. 'To look for my mother.'

'Then let's drink a toast to your eighteenth before you run off,' said Haileybury. 'Would you do the honours?'

A magnum of Veuve Clicquot, already open, rested in a bucket of ice.

The sun broke through the clouds.

'Splendid,' said Haileybury. 'Let's step out on to the terrace.'

77

Berlin's hand was shaking so much, she could barely grasp the handle of the door at the very back of the vault. She used both hands and managed to get it open. In front of her was a narrow flight of stairs. She strode up them, putting as much distance between herself and the vault as possible.

The stairs were dry, but thick with dust and cobwebs. The doors she passed on each floor were bricked up. Finally she reached the top. There was no door here, only a gap in the wall. She edged through it, her heart pounding from the climb, her legs aching, and found herself behind a granite plinth.

The guardian lion squatting on it stared down at her, appalled. The long gallery had a festive air. Bright red and gold lanterns hung between the stanchions. The smell of joss and the oily smoke of opium hung in the air.

Under the watchful eyes of the lions she inched forward, staying well hidden. She thanked God for the riches crammed into Haileybury's loft.

A silk canopy fluttered beneath the high roof. Chairs were arranged round the ornate lacquered tables, as if to accommodate guests who had failed to attend.

Haileybury and Philip were on the terrace. The earl was resplendent in a red cloak with ermine collar. Philip stood awkwardly beside an enormous birthday cake ablaze with candles.

Berlin expected to see Tomalin, but there was no sign of him. He was just another delivery boy.

Bryant stood behind the old horse chestnut tree. The rotten limb still hadn't fallen.

He left the church garden and crossed the road, peering over the iron railings as he passed. The biometric pad glowed beside the entry phone. He kept walking towards the narrow passage, but as he turned into it, a black four-wheel-drive squealed to a halt just down the road.

Bryant was astonished to see a Chinese man jump out of the car, run towards Haileybury's building and spray the lens of the security camera with black paint.

For one stupid moment Bryant thought of calling the police. He edged out to take a closer look. The vandal had tossed the spray can and was hooking something up to the biometric reader.

A couple of minutes later, the front door opened.

A taller man in a smart mackintosh, also Chinese, then got out of the car and walked into the building as if he owned the place. The door closed behind him. His friend lounged against the portico and lit a cigarette.

Bryant recognised him. He usually wore a crash helmet.

Berlin watched from behind a pillar as Haileybury raised his glass in a toast. Philip raised his too, but hesitantly. When she heard the familiar whir of the platform rising at the other end of the gallery, she took a step back and remained hidden.

Lee stepped off the platform and strode through the gallery. He had eyes only for the pair on the terrace.

Berlin followed him.

Haileybury always found this moment of the birthday ritual very affecting: the champagne, the candles reflected in the boy's eyes, the sheen on his skin as the tincture took effect. He held his breath as Philip put the glass to his lips.

'Hello, Jack,' said Lee.

Haileybury turned. There was a man standing in the doorway.

'Who are you?' he said. 'What do you want?'

Philip put down his glass.

The man approached and pushed back his thick mop of hair. A deep, irregular cavity marked by twisted ribbons of scar tissue, followed the curve of his skull.

Haileybury felt faint. He dropped his glass on the table. The pink champagne dribbled down the cloth.

'No,' he said. 'It can't be.'

Berlin had to step out on to the terrace to hear them.

Haileybury was mumbling.

Philip was edging away from Lee.

'Don't be alarmed,' said Lee. 'I'm here to protect you.'

'From what?' said Philip.

'From Jack,' said Lee. He moved closer, pointing to the ugly scarred indentation.

'Stay away from me,' said Philip.

'Leave him alone, Lee,' said Berlin.

Neither he nor Philip took any notice of her.

'The seventh earl did this,' said Lee. 'Jack's grandfather. He found us together when we were fourteen years old. The other servants saved me and the earl shipped me to France.'

'Philip,' moaned Haileybury.

He was addressing Lee.

Philip looked as confused as Berlin felt.

Haileybury began weeping.

'My Chinese name is Wang Yan,' said Lee. 'They couldn't have that, so they called me Philip.'

'All these years I thought you were dead,' whispered Haileybury. 'I couldn't live without you.'

Lee stood very still.

'I want Philip to know the truth,' he said.

'What about?' said Philip.

'Your mother,' said Lee.

Berlin saw Haileybury's distress evaporate, replaced with a cold anger.

'Don't believe a word he says, my boy,' he said. 'His government sent him. He's not interested in you; he wants the Bequest.'

'You don't have to believe me, Philip,' said Lee. 'Berlin will tell you what she's seen with her own eyes.'

They all looked at her. She'd called Lee for help, but now she had no idea which way this was going to go.

'Philip, listen to me,' she said. He blinked as if she were an apparition. She held his gaze. 'Sir Simon May was your father.'

Philip swayed, as if struck by some unseen force.

'Uncle Simon?' he said.

'You need to get out of here,' she said. 'Come with me, now.'

She edged along the terrace, keeping one hand on the parapet and reaching out to Philip with the other. She could see he was reeling.

'Let's go,' she said. 'The others weren't so lucky.'

'What others?' said Philip.

'The scholarship boys,' said Berlin.

'I don't understand,' said Philip.

Berlin couldn't bring herself to tell him. She took his arm.

'You can't leave, dear boy,' said Haileybury. 'I can't let you leave.'

Philip shook Berlin off. 'Tell me about my mother,' he said. 'Or I'm not going anywhere.'

Berlin glanced at Lee. The challenge was in his eyes.

'Simon May fathered seven boys,' she said. 'To feed his brother's sick compulsion.'

'What happened to my mother?' demanded Philip.

'He killed her,' said Berlin. 'And your grandmother.'

'No,' said Haileybury.

'I was there,' said Berlin.

'They were fine women,' said Lee.

'They were whores,' said Haileybury.

Lee couldn't take his eyes off Philip. This was his greatest gamble.

The boy's attack on Deng, which had seemed such a disaster at the time, had proved a valuable lesson.

If this failed, it would be up to him.

He slipped his hand into his pocket.

Berlin moved quickly to get between Philip and Haileybury. The boy's chest was heaving and his eyes were blazing.

'Philip,' she said. 'No.'

Deaf to her, he snatched up Haileybury's walking stick and raised it high above his head.

Haileybury reached inside his cloak and drew a gun.

Berlin hurled herself forward. Somewhere a balloon burst. It punched the breath out of her and sent her flying back into the parapet.

The stick roared through the air.

Bryant heard the shot and ran down the passage. He reached the watermen's stairs as Berlin struck the water, arms and legs splayed, and disappeared.

The scarlet streamers that drifted from Berlin hung about her, strands of a bright garland that twirled through her fingers as she reached out to grasp them.

Bryant stood poised on the top step, watching the red bloom spread across the surface of the river.

He glanced up at the tower block and saw his grand-mother step from their window, fleeing her prison, glad of the air and the peace that was waiting. Leaving the flat for the first, and last, time.

'I can't swim,' he said.

'What are you waiting for?' said Gran.

The ripples were dying away.

Berlin felt she would go on sinking forever. It was impossible to resist. A grey shape above her obscured the light.

In the darkness, she closed her eyes and let the current take her. Her mouth and ears and nose filled with bubbles. She was amused to discover that death had a noise.

The current seized her.

78

Berlin squirmed, resisting sheets tucked in too tight. Pain was lurking behind a barrage of analgesia, shots they'd been giving her every six hours. With luck it would soon be time for another.

She opened her eyes, aware of someone standing at the end of the bed. It was Lee.

'You knew,' she said.

'Not that they were dead,' said Lee quickly.

'Bullshit,' said Berlin. 'Eighteen was their use-by date. Everything expired: the visa, the scholarship, the fantasy of adolescent love.'

'There was a possibility they had been given new identities and paid off,' said Lee. 'It happens.'

'You played politics with human lives,' said Berlin. 'You must have realised Haileybury couldn't simply cut loose his drug-addicted discards.'

Lee gave her such a look that she felt a pang of guilt. It was an irrational response; she wasn't complicit in this wickedness.

'Why didn't you expose Haileybury?' she said.

'Why didn't you?' said Lee. 'Because you wanted the opium. We tend to put our own needs first. I don't condemn you for that. Thanks to Jack's grandfather, like you

'I'm at the mercy of a craving I struggle to control. We all are.'

'But at least we can struggle,' said Berlin. 'Those boys didn't have a chance.'

'Our civilisations have different views concerning the importance of the individual,' said Lee.

'So the six individuals whose remains rotted in Haileybury's vault didn't matter?' said Berlin.

'You must understand,' said Lee. 'Exposing the Haileyburys wouldn't have taken us one step closer to retrieving the Bequest; it would have just made the task more difficult.'

'That's your excuse?' said Berlin.

'I'm not apologising,' said Lee. 'Philip wanted me to come. The earl was protected at the highest levels. Even if he were to be disgraced or imprisoned, the government would have found a way to prevent repatriation of the collection. The route we chose was certain.'

'As long as you were able to persuade Philip that his allegiance lay with you,' said Berlin.

'And you persuaded him,' said Lee. 'For which we are both grateful.'

'The Haileyburys were sick,' said Berlin.

Lee shrugged. 'Dynastic decay.'

'Philip is one of them,' said Berlin.

'No,' said Lee. 'He's one of us.'

In the end, it came down to that: you're one of them or one of us.

'Six boys, created to service Haileybury's obsession, then destroyed because of yours,' said Berlin. 'You could have stopped it before it began.'

'That is my burden,' said Lee.

For a fleeting moment she felt sorry for him.

'Fuck off,' she said.

79

British Summer Time was over. As far as Berlin was concerned, it had never started. She sat in a corner of Pellicci's waiting for her full English.

Someone had left a newspaper on another table. It was the *Times*, so she nearly didn't bother. Pellicci's clientele had certainly changed over the years. But she needed something to browse. She reached out and winced.

Her shattered shoulder had taken months to heal and still punished her when she overdid it. She grabbed the paper. A banner above the august title reminded readers to turn their clocks back an hour before they went to bed.

Autumn was the season of mellow something, but she couldn't remember what.

Leafing through the paper, she came to the social pages and caught her breath. A grand party had been held to celebrate the assumption of Mr Philip Chen May to the title of the 9th Earl Haileybury.

The article breathlessly explained that he was the heir presumptive; the letters patent that had created the title allowed a nephew to succeed. Sir Simon May had married Pearl Chen to ensure custodial rights over her sons.

The ninth earl. The seventh Philip.

Berlin wondered how they would manage to get the blood out of the cloak with the ermine collar.

There was a photo of the beaming guests. The great and the good stood around Philip, including Flora Trevelyan in a god-awful hat.

The new earl had recently signed an agreement with the government of the People's Republic of China that would see the repatriation of the greater part of the Haileybury Bequest. From the glazed look on Philip's face, she guessed which part he was hanging on to.

The magnanimous gesture was warmly welcomed by Ambassador Lee Wang Yan, who said it would open a new chapter in the relationship between the two countries. Both economies would benefit. Whitehall had made no comment.

Berlin got up and walked out.

'Oi!' shouted the waiter. 'What about your breakfast?'

She couldn't eat a thing.

The noise and dust from the builders working in Bella's flat was relentless. It was on the market. At least the bearded stepson wouldn't be living there, although new neighbours could be a problem, especially if they were the sort of people who could afford the outrageous price he was asking.

A letter from the solicitors in Leyton was waiting for her on the doormat. At last. It was time to move on.

She slit open the envelope, read the short missive inside and walked out again.

80

Berlin stood beside Peggy's grave clutching the letter.

'Well done,' she said. 'You managed to have the last word.'

Peggy had left everything, including the house, to the Battersea Dogs Home.

She hadn't even liked dogs.

Berlin gave the tombstone a small kick.

'Not that I blame you,' she said.

Her phone rang. She checked the ID and answered.

'So they made you a partner,' she said.

'They even signed Sir Simon May's capital over to me,' said Del.

'You've really joined the dark side now,' said Berlin.

'Ten per cent is yours, if you want it.'

'The wages of sin is death, Del,' she said. 'Not ten per cent.'

She hung up. Her bonus was in the bathroom cupboard.

For medicinal purposes only.

On her way out of the City of London Cemetery and Crematorium, Berlin paused beneath the grand arch. She looked up and raised her middle finger.

Not dead yet.

ACKNOWLEDGEMENTS

Special thanks to my editor, Tom Avery.

Robert Jeffries, retired serving officer and honorary curator of the Thames River Police Museum, was a very helpful and entertaining source of information about the river and Wapping.

The titles of the four parts are taken from the following works that deal, amongst other things, with the use of opium:

The Gate of a Hundred Sorrows, Rudyard Kipling, 1884.
Strange Heavens and Dull Hells, Oscar Wilde, 1890.
The Milk of Paradise, Samuel Taylor Coleridge, 1798.
Hands Washed Pure of Blood, Thomas De Quincy, 1821.

In Her Blood

The first instalment in the Catherine Berlin series

'A stylishly written and assuredly paced debut that heralds a
promising new series.'
Financial Times

When heroin addict and investigator Catherine Berlin finds the
almost-headless body of her informant, 'Juliet Bravo', she is
unsurprised to discover the death is linked to a local loan shark.
But when Berlin's own unorthodox methods are blamed for the
murder, she realises bigger predators are circling.

Then, after stumbling upon the body of her GP (an unconventional
doctor who would still supply prescription heroin), Berlin begins
to fear for more than her job...

Suspended, incriminated, and then blackmailed into cooperation
by the detective leading the investigation, Catherine Berlin has
seven stolen days of clarity in which to solve the crime – and find
a new supplier.

'I'm hooked on Annie Hauxwell and hanging out for my next fix.'
Radio National Books and Arts Daily

arrow books

ALSO BY ANNIE HAUXWELL

A Bitter Taste

The eagerly awaited second instalment in the
Catherine Berlin series

*She was ten years old, but knew enough to wipe clean the handle
of the bloody kitchen knife. The night was stifling; the windows
were closed, sealing in the chaos. A table upturned, shattered
crockery. Her distraught mother, bare shoulders raw with welts,
knelt beside her motionless father. The child snatched up her
backpack, and ran...*

London sweats in the height of midsummer, and Catherine Berlin
hides her scars from prying eyes. At the methadone clinic, she
meets an old friend, Sonja Kvist, who begs her to help find her
missing daughter. But the case is not as straightforward as it first
appears, and Catherine soon realises that in order to find the girl,
she must tackle a far greater threat...

arrow books

ALSO BY ANNIE HAUXWELL

A Morbid Habit

The third instalment in the Catherine Berlin series

The hands were warm. Soft fingers, but flesh inflected with iron. Squeezing. The tongue lolled and protruded from the mouth. Vertebrae fragmented, one, two, three, until finally the hands relaxed and the limp body slid from their embrace.

Blood turned to ice and sealed the nostrils.

It's the week before Christmas. Catherine Berlin's scars have faded, but she still walks with a limp. Broke, she's working nights as a relief CCTV operator, and looking for something more substantial. Her heroin habit is under control – only just.

The night shifts end, but now Berlin herself is being watched. When an old friend offers her a job in Russia, she quickly agrees. The details are vague: an oligarch with a shady past, a UK company offering a high fee for Berlin to investigate. Easy enough.

But Berlin arrives in Moscow to find that her problems are only just beginning. A body is found at the airport: a man clutching a sign reading 'Catherine Berlin'. There are figures following her, and her guide, a Brit named Charlie, has secrets to hide. When Berlin's oligarch goes missing, she finds that she cannot trust anyone or anything, even her past, if she is to survive.

arrow books